Gotou Mitsuya

Izumikawa Yuujirou

Teia Eiichi

Kasugano Asuka

Kaihouin Hotaru

Tachibana Ryuuji

Ichijou Susumu

Keikain Runa

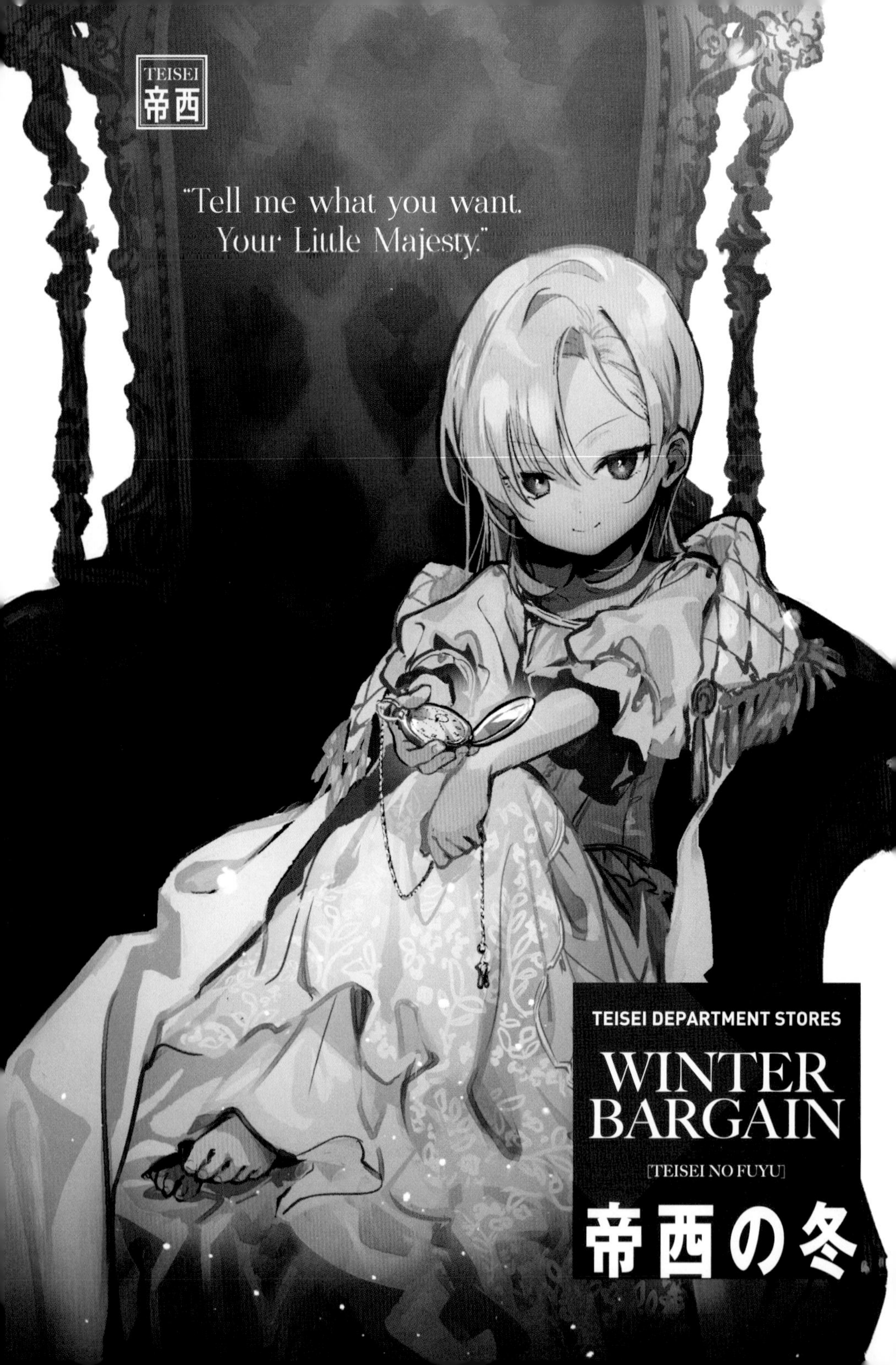
TEISEI
帝西
"Tell me what you want.
Your Little Majesty."
TEISEI DEPARTMENT STORES
WINTER
BARGAIN
[TEISEI NO FUYU]
帝西の冬

MODERN *Villainess*

IT'S NOT EASY BUILDING A CORPORATE EMPIRE BEFORE THE CRASH

**NOVEL
1**

WRITTEN BY
Tofuro Futsukaichi

ILLUSTRATED BY
Kei

Airship

Seven Seas Entertainment

MODERN VILLAINESS: IT'S NOT EASY BUILDING
A CORPORATE EMPIRE BEFORE THE CRASH
VOL. 1

Gendai Shakai de Otome Game no Akuyaku Reijou
wo Suru no wa Chotto Taihen Vol. 1
©2020 Tofuro Futsukaichi

First published in Japan in 2020 by
OVERLAP Inc., Ltd., Tokyo.
English translation rights arranged with
OVERLAP Inc., Ltd., Tokyo.

TRANSLATION: Alexandra Owen-Burns
COVER DESIGN: H. Qi.
INTERIOR LAYOUT: Clay Gardner
COPY EDITOR: Meg van Huygen
LIGHT NOVEL EDITOR: Mercedez Clewis
PREPRESS TECHNICIAN: Melanie Ujimori
PRINT MANAGER: Rhiannon Rasmussen-Silversteinrstein
PRODUCTION MANAGER: Lissa Pattillo
EDITOR-IN-CHIEF: Julie Davis
ASSOCIATE PUBLISHER: Adam Arnold
PUBLISHER: Jason DeAngelis

ISBN: 978-1-63858-209-0
Printed in Canada
First Printing: June 2022
10 9 8 7 6 5 4 3 2 1

MODERN
Villainess

IT'S NOT EASY BUILDING
A CORPORATE EMPIRE
BEFORE THE CRASH

CONTENTS

Advisor to Keika Corp.'s former head of resources supply at the Iwazaki Corporation.

TOUDOU NAGAYOSHI

Runa's friend. Comes from a noble religious family. She's unfindable in hide-and-seek.

KAIHOUIN IOTARU

A politician in the House of Representatives for the Fellowship of Constitutional Government. Former Minister of Health, Labor, and Welfare.

KOIZUMI SOUICHIROU

A dietman in the House of Representatives and a member of the Fellowship of Constitutional Government. Current Minister of Finance.

IZUMIKAWA TATSUNOSUKE

A maid of the Keikain household. Likes cameras.

TOKITOU AKI

A maid of the Keikain household. Formerly revered for her night business in Ginza.

SAITOU KEIKO

TAKANASHI MIZUHO
The main heroine of the otome game, "Love Where the Cherry Blossom Falls."

TEIA SHUUICHI
Head of the Teia Group and Eiichi's father.

KATSURA NAOYUKI
Works in the Hokkaido Kaitaku Bank's integrated development department.

TAKAMIYA HARUKA
Manager of the Imperial Gakushuukan Academy's communal library.

MAEFUJI SHOUICHI
An inspector who works in Foreign Affairs for the National Police Agency's Public Safety Bureau.

KATSURA NAOMI
A descendant of the Keikain bloodline. Has a son named Naoyuki.

A villainess reincarnated into an otome video game world set in modern society.

KEIKAIN RUNA

MODERN
Villainess
IT'S NOT EASY BUILDING A CORPORATE EMPIRE BEFORE THE CRASH

CAST OF CHARACTERS

Youngest son to Dietman Izumikawa Tatsunosuke. A potential love interest.

IZUMIKAWA YUUJIROU

Son to the family that owns Teia Motor Co., Japan's top automobile enterprise. A potential love interest.

TEIA EIICHI

Keikain Runa's personal butler. Supports Runa in both public and private affairs.

TACHIBANA RYUUJI

The only son to Gotou Mitsutoshi and a budget analyst in the Ministry of Finance's budget division. A potential love interest.

GOTOU MITSUYA

Runa's friend. Her father is a dietman in the House of Representatives. Calls mandarins "oranges."

KASUGANO ASUKA

Branch manager at Far Eastern Bank's Tokyo branch. Set up the Moonlight Fund alongside Tachibana.

ICHIJOU SUSUMU

Keikain Family Tree

Keikain Ruriko
From a Branch Family in the Iwazaki Group. Deceased.

Woman from Local Pharmaceutical Industry
Legal Wife. Later "Keika Pharmaceuticals." Deceased.

Keikain Nakamaro
Next in line to the Keikain Dukedom. Works at Keika Pharmaceuticals.

Keikain Kyomaro
Current Head of the Keikain Dukedom. Head of the Keika Group. CEO of Keika Pharmaceuticals.

Keikain Hikomaro
Predecessor of the Keikain Dukedom. Deceased.

Natasha Alexandrovna Romanova
Great granddaughter to Alexander III.

Keikain Runa
Main Protagonist.

Keikain Otsumaro
Founder of the Far Eastern Group. Deceased. Personal History Erased.

Defected Russian Daughter to a Grand Dukedom
Mistress. Deceased.

Tokitou Aki
Secret Illegitimate Child. Keikain Maid.

Saitou Keiko
Mistress. Keikain Maid.

Younger Brother
Illegitimate Child.

Katsura Naomi
Illegitimate Child. Keikain Maid.

Katsura Naoyuki
Works at Hokkaido Kaitaku Bank.

Other Relatives

I STOOD ON THE TOP FLOOR of the Teia Tower in Daiba, Tokyo.

There in the tower's lounge, one of Japan's most distinguished zaibatsu, the Teia Group, was holding a party to unveil the completion of its latest project. I, meanwhile, was gazing at the skyscrapers out the window. This was supposed to be where my engagement would be canceled, leading to the ruin of my family and myself—if events unfolded just like the game I knew.

Especially since this was the setting for the final scene of *"Love Where the Cherry Blossom Falls,"* an otome game I played, once upon a time.

My reflection in the window's glass still confused me. I wasn't supposed to have such beautiful blonde hair. I wasn't supposed to have such pale skin. I wasn't supposed to be so...bewitching. Then again, I also wasn't supposed to be so *wicked*.

"I've been looking for you, Runa."

I wasn't supposed to be called Keikain Runa either.

Hearing that name, I turned around and found my fiancé

standing there: one Teia Eiichi. He was the next successor to the Teia Group and, while young, showed incredible resourcefulness when it came to business. Right now, his gaze was cold as he looked at me.

"Oh, Eiichi-san. Why not go and see Mizuho-san instead of me?"

I feigned disinterest and tried to brush him off, but Eiichi-san continued to stare at me with clear distrust in his eyes.

"What exactly are you up to?" Far from a soft, loving whisper, his tone was full of accusation. Granted, he had every reason to be suspicious of me.

This was a party, and yet the conversation was proving to be anything but frivolous.

"*Wall Street is in an uproar right now. I wonder what the problem is.*"

"*I heard some of the top dogs have been called to Washington because of you-know-what...*"

"*Oh, is that why we're missing some of our bankers here tonight?*"

"*Looks like the main players are finally starting to feel the heat from those subprime loans...*"

"*We can't talk as if this won't affect us. We don't know how widely the damage is going to spread.*"

In the game, this was where I was supposed to be denounced and meet my downfall.

"I intend to take appropriate measures so as not to cause trouble to the Teia Group," I said.

"That is *not* what I'm talking about!" Eiichi-san's voice was pleasant even when he was angry.

His good looks and his attractive voice were supposed to act as a reward for the player. Though it was a little different when I was the one he was shouting at.

"Why didn't you come and speak to me?! Mitsuya and Yuujirou have been keeping an eye on you too! And Mizuho, she..." Eiichi-san trailed off after I turned away to look at the night view outside again.

I could hardly have been more obvious in my rejection of him.

Gotou Mitsuya's father was Japan's administrative vice minister of finance—a talented bureaucrat. Izumikawa Yuujirou was the son to a politician—a member of the House of Representatives who was affiliated with the ruling party.

The three of them were supposed to condemn me tonight, thus leading to my downfall. According to the game, that was.

This was your common reincarnation narrative. Armed with memories of my previous life, I'd worked hard to avoid my ruin, and now...here I was.

Despite that, I still ended up at odds with these handsome men.

"I suppose I was never going to be able to hide it from all three of you," I said lightly.

I hadn't done anything too egregious. I'd simply created a shell company in a tax haven and raked together some capital to finance independent fund traders. It was all about knowing the right people.

"Runa-san! Why didn't you ask for my help? I thought we were *friends*!"

Takanashi Mizuho, the protagonist, ran out of patience and came out of her hiding spot. I couldn't help but be a bit tickled by the situation; her entrance was identical to the game. It seemed I couldn't fulfill the role of a villain in the end.

"Runa-san! What's so funny?!"

Mizuho-san was cute even when mad. That was why I decided to take my leave with an obvious lie for her, just like a true villainess.

"Mizuho-san. Did you know that I *hated* you?" The two of them stared at me, but I continued smiling as I wrapped things up. I would draw the curtain on this tale and take my loss with grace. "May you find happiness. Farewell."

I gave them a backward glance before leaving the lounge behind. When I did, I was greeted by a quiet Tachibana Yuka, my personal maid.

"My lady." She looked worried, as though what she had just witnessed was something to be concerned about, but I urged her to continue with her duties.

I had half-expected her to turn up here.

I suppose you would call it my former life. It was that event that had made my life take a turn for the worse. I believed it would happen here too; this world may have been part of a video game, but it was set in modern Japan. Unfortunately, I was right on the money.

"Lehthan Sisters, that investment bank, has just filed for Chapter 11. The New York Stock Exchange is in chaos."

My downfall had begun.

My former life was worthless. The cutthroat, immoral company I worked myself to the bone for, with very little reward, had collapsed and let me go with a snap of their fingers. Left with nothing, I ended up dying an unceremonious, unremarkable death. It was a time period that treated its contemporaries like toys.

Yet this isn't a story of my conviction. This is a story of my— no, *our*—revenge on the age in which we were born.

It was time to open the curtain on my final chapter. Me, whose life was taken by that age. I was going to face my loss with all the boldness and elegance of a villainess. My usual smile never faltered as I uttered the words to open the scene.

"Very well. Now let the game begin."

GLOSSARY

TAX HAVEN: A territory used and operated in order to avoid paying higher taxes. A source of money for less scrupulous funds.

SHELL COMPANY: A bogus or fake corporation that exists solely on paper, with no employees or locations. A company created solely for enjoying the assets afforded to companies.

CHAPTER 11: Chapter 11, Title 11, United States Code. Similar to Japan's Civil Rehabilitation Act. Filing for Chapter 11 won't leave the creditor in a very good spot, but it's still preferable to not filing.

SEPTEMBER 15TH, 2008: The date that the Lehman Brothers go bankrupt in the real world.

THE LADY'S FLIGHT

ONE OF MY EARLIEST MEMORIES was of the unfamiliar words spoken by my wet nurse.

"You have the blood of the Keikain Dukedom running through your veins."

What was nobility doing in modern *Japan*? And wait, the Keikain Dukedom...? I'd heard that name *a lot*. I wanted to say something, but I hadn't yet mastered articulation so all I could say was "goo goo ga ga." That also meant I didn't have time to wonder why I wasn't dead anymore, or why I was suddenly a toddler. There was something else I needed to confirm as soon as possible.

"Una?"

"Yes. Good girl!" My wet nurse rocked me gently in her arms.

She didn't get it! I need to try again!

"Eiain Una?"

"Yes, yes! *Very* good girl."

She still didn't get it! Here I go again!

"Eikain Runa?"

17

"Oh my! That's right, Runa-sama! Your name is Runa. Keikain Runa-sama!"

"*Una!*"

"Runa! That's right! *Ru-na!*"

Keikain Runa. The villainess in that otome game I used to love. The same one who, on September 15th, at the age of eighteen, was brought down by the game's heroine and its handsome love interests.

I had the same name as the villainess whose fate was to be ruined. *Ruined.* Could I have been any more unfortunate than that?

It was fair to say that after said realization, I spent a fair portion of my life trying to work out if I *really* had been reborn into a game as the villainess Keikain Runa.

The first thing I thought to investigate was whether my inevitable ruin was truly set in stone. I didn't know whether that much would hold true for me the way it did for the Runa in the game—in any case, I didn't have a way to check. At the very least, I wouldn't know whether I had the ability to avoid that fate until the promised day, so this was something to leave until later.

The next thing to test was whether I really was Keikain Runa, born into the Keikain Dukedom. This took a little bit of time to confirm. It wasn't difficult to work out that my name was Keikain Runa and that I was born into a dukedom, but maybe I just happened to share a name with the villainess. To know for sure, I needed to remember the names and positions of the villainess's closer relatives and check them all one by one. The names all ended up being a one-to-one match, meaning I couldn't deny the possibility that I was the very same Keikain Runa.

The third test was to find out whether I'd been reborn into the game or not. Evidence pointing toward the contrary came relatively quickly. Aside from the fact that there were no jingles indicating my relationship status with people I was meeting for the first time, or any choices presented to me in a UI window (though that may have been because I wasn't the protagonist), there was something a lot more obvious telling me I wasn't in a video game: the scenery.

The sky wasn't a flat blue surface with white and black lines, and the clouds weren't completely identical when the weather was clear enough to tell. They had lighting, shading, and details: their shape would change from moment to moment. In fact, the clouds were overwhelming real. The trees in the garden were just as realistic too. The responses I got from other people were varied and unique to the situation; they weren't just stock phrases.

This definitely wasn't a game.

There was always a chance this was like that one movie where I was inside a simulation of some world that was inside another simulation that was a perfect replica of the real world. Realistically, it would take some highly advanced technology to create such a thing. Even if it were true, it would still be no different than reality to me, and so I should treat it as such.

Did that mean this was one of those parallel worlds then? A world right next to the one I knew, where most things were the same, but a few were different. In that case, I'd want to find out how different this world was to the one I was born, raised, and died pitifully in, and therefore, what I should do.

I wasn't in a game, but if this was a parallel world, it was one that resembled the game's setting very closely. Assuming my fate was sealed to follow the events of the game too, then what awaited me was utter ruin.

I wanted to do whatever I could to avoid it.

When I was two or maybe three years old, I pretended I was starting to read and sought out illustrated reference books in the study.

The history depicted in those books was very different to the history I knew.

"Oh. The Pacific War ended in surrender. The Allies lost at Normandy, and Germany kept on fighting until the very end. I wonder how that happened."

Skipping over the finer details, the history of postwar Japan was slightly different in this world, but the overall trend was the same.

Japan allied with the west during the Cold War and sent troops to fight in the Manchurian War (probably equivalent to the Korean War in our world) and in the Vietnam War. It even sent troops to the more recent Gulf War to form a core part of the multinational forces.

Interestingly enough, despite all of that, the Allied Forces had still intervened with Japanese policy after the country's surrender, and the Japanese Self-Defense Forces still existed. The House of

Peers became the House of Councilors, and after several reforms, it was decided that members of House of Representatives were to be elected by public vote and would have authority over the House of Councilors.

These game designers sure put a lot of effort into making sure their villainess could hold a noble rank. And there was one more thing they'd put work into: the zaibatsu. After losing the Pacific War, Japan's zaibatsu were dissolved and changed into business groups that were more like inter-business alliances.

In this world, Japan's surrender was not unconditional, meaning the zaibatsu had *survived*. Their survival meant their weaknesses had time to come to light; now that the economic bubble had burst, the weaker zaibatsu had been crushed and effectively dissolved themselves.

Teia Eiichi, one of the love interests of the game, was born into the family in charge of the Teia Group, which had taken advantage of this reshuffling to swallow up one of the smaller zaibatsu and make theirs bigger. They were now one of Japan's leading zaibatsu—but they were also moving ahead with a ton of bad debts to their name.

I pondered over my surprise at their ability to survive as I recalled the game's relationship map.

Izumikawa Yuujirou came from a family of politicians who held power over the Ministry of Finance, while Gotou Mitsuya's dad was going to end up as the administrative vice minister of finance. What if it was decided that the Teia Group was too big to fail, and thus, was bailed out by the government?

The Teia Group owned banks too, so they would qualify for a special bailout loan from the Bank of Japan after making themselves bigger via a merger.

Back to the topic at hand: I'm getting completely off track.

Apparently, the Keikains were a noble family, founded by a member of the Imperial Family who stepped down as a vassal. The family bloodline came to an end during the Great War before my grandfather, Keikain Hikomaro, was adopted into it. While his name might have sounded grand, he was born an illegitimate child, and went to work for the Ministry of Home Affairs. He worked for the police force and made it to superintendent of the Special Higher Police when the wartime political upheaval happened. He took charge of the investigation into the assassination of Japan's prime minister at the time but was unable to find the culprit. In true Japanese style, he ended up taking responsibility for the lack of results and ultimately resigned from his post.

My grandfather was then gifted a dukedom for the Keikain family, despite them having no blood heirs. I was almost as though his failure to find a perpetrator was being rewarded. The way the family gained its position earned the Keikains a lot of enemies, but my grandfather held a lot of information over his political opponents from his time managing the police, which would end up being the cornerstone of the family's growth.

Japan's production facilities survived the lost war, and by selling military supplies during the Manchurian War, the Chinese Civil War, and the Vietnam War, the country got back on its feet—something the Keikain family also benefited from.

The family's main business was Keika Pharmaceuticals. It worked with the overseas portion of the JDSF post-war to manage the distribution of medicine and built its fortune that way. They then went on to become a mid-range zaibatsu incorporating Keika Chemicals, Keika Shipping, Keika Corp, Keika Maritime Insurance, Far Eastern Bank, Far Eastern Life Insurance, Far Eastern Hotels, and Far Eastern Developments, riding the tide of the economic bubble before working hard to deal with the fallout afterward.

At the center of this story was the engagement between me and Teia Eiichi: an engagement that was supposed to rescue the Keika zaibatsu. A zaibatsu that profited from war with its pharmaceuticals and used its founder's privileged position in the Special Higher Police to gain knowledge about Japan's underbelly...

It was probably best to pretend I didn't know anything about those aspects.

I was still too young to know about a lot of things. I snapped the reference book shut and left the study. Facing myself in the hallway mirror, I began to fiddle with my blonde hair. Initially, I wondered about a Japanese native having hair and skin as fair as this, but that was, again, down to the hard work of the game's design team.

My wealthy and powerful grandfather had an unabashed habit of chasing after women, to the point where he found himself at the center of *several* scandals. One of those women had noble Russian ancestry who had sought asylum in Japan. There were no records to be found, so the details surrounding said tryst must have been pretty bad.

That was how my father was born, but as an illegitimate child, he wasn't recognized as a true heir and was frequently overlooked when it came to family matters. He was, instead, approached by a group with a business proposal. This was the Far Eastern Group, a group created primarily by defected Russians. It seemed as though my father used the Keikain name and fortune without telling my grandfather anything, married one of their women, expanded the Far Eastern Group, and made a name for himself.

It turned out that the group was backed by an eastern spy organization and created for the purposes of stealing western technology. Nobody won when that fact was uncovered.

My Russian mother died just after I was born, and since my father was a Keikain, he was protected from arrest. Soon after the investigation was wrapped up, it was said he died by suicide, so I never met my parents.

My grandfather, a man capable of sorting out this mess, was already on the road to Hades, and the state involved in setting up the Far Eastern Group no longer existed. In order to quietly tidy up the scandal, the Keikain zaibatsu absorbed the Far Eastern Group with the help of national policy. That was when the economic bubble burst and likely when the Teia Group absorbed the Keika Group and its bad debts.

I had no allies left at this point. I lived in a residence away from the main Keikain household with my attendants. It was messed up—every effort I made was futile. From their point of view, there wasn't any reason for the Teia Group to want me marrying into their family.

Was the annulment of our engagement perhaps planned from the very start?

I had my good looks, with which I could be mistaken for European, as well as my beautiful blonde hair. I also had a little knowledge from my previous life.

But that was it.

I guess my looks were supposed to be some sort of compensation for me getting my engagement broken off.

There were no photos of my parents at my house. The scandal with the East meant their existences had been completely wiped out.

My father's name was Keikain Otsumaro. The distinct lack of "*ichi*" (or "one") in his name was a clear sign that he wasn't meant to succeed the zaibatsu. He must have been treated with some favor though, as he was able to make use of his heritage. My grandfather aside, the fact that all traces of my grandmother were also erased must have meant that her lineage was a big deal too—for better or worse. It might have been those gloomy feelings locked up inside him that pushed him toward becoming a businessman. He ended up getting involved in the Far Eastern Group's management.

"He got caught up in the times. That was what made it so tragic when the times abandoned him," my butler, Tachibana, told me sadly. He knew my father quite well.

The "times" Tachibana spoke of were just before the economic bubble. The Far Eastern Bank, the top regional bank in

Yamagata Prefecture, created its connection with my father when it financed his Far Eastern Developments company. Far Eastern Bank was nothing but a bank: it didn't want to be swallowed up by a competitor, so it was working to expand itself. This piqued my father's ambitions, and since the Keikain Group paid no attention to northern Japan, he used his name to try and gather capital.

Incidentally, Keika Pharmaceuticals were produced in a factory in Kyushu linked with the Shounou Group, and Keika Chemicals had factories in Mizushima in Okayama prefecture, and Yokkaichi in Mie prefecture.

After that, the Far Eastern Group rode the bubble and expanded, establishing their central business, Far Eastern Hotels, with locations all over the country.

They were thinking of expanding out into resorts when the scandal with the East erupted.

"What did they do?"

"They violated CoCom."

The reality was worse than I'd expected. My expression automatically turned grave.

The Port of Sakata had a ferry link with the East, and there had been talk of the creation of a petrochemical combine there before the bubble. The general plan was for Far Eastern Developments to prepare land for Keika Chemicals to build a factory for the combine. Then, they would then import oil and natural gases from the east to create products to sell in Japan.

However, at the time of construction, it was discovered that the majority of the machine tools and construction machinery had been sent to The People's Democratic Republic of Northern Japan, which was part of the East. That was investigated, which was when it was discovered that the Far Eastern Group was housing spies from the East in various companies, leading to the scandal.

Because of his bloodline, it looked like my father got away with his crimes, but he ended up killing himself, and the Far Eastern Group was swallowed up by the Keika Group without any traces. Eventually, all that was left was the bubble's burst and the Group's enormously bad debts.

After all of that, I should have no business being in high society—under normal circumstances, at least.

And yet in the game, the villainess flaunted her power without hesitation. The question was less about what my father did exactly, and more about how he'd messed it up.

"Tachibana. Could you tell me about Mother now?"

We were currently in a taxi, heading for a cemetery in Sakata that looked out over the Sea of Japan. It was where my parents' graves were. My mother requested a place where she could see her homeland across the ocean shortly before she died, and my father was adamant that he would not share a grave with the rest of the Keikain family, who abandoned and betrayed him.

Thus, the two of them ended up here.

"According to your father, your mother was like the season of spring."

Her name was Natasha Alexandrovna Romanova.

The honeytrap was apparently set up by the Ministry of National Security, an intelligence agency of The People's

Democratic Republic of Northern Japan, which owned Sakhalin. After the recent unification led to freedom of information, the purpose had been to deal a blow to my grandfather, Duke Keikain Hikomaro, a powerful right-wing figure.

It may very well have been true. The government of Northern Japan wasn't just after superiority over our country and its maintained imperial family: it apparently wanted to keep the Romanov bloodline alive as a trump card to use against its ally, the Soviet Union.

However, when the Berlin Wall fell, internal rifts and conflict broke out between the Communist Party, the Ministry of National Security, and the army, leading to the nation's collapse. For some baffling reason, it was our country that intervened to unify them again.

I lost the thread there, but the point is: my mother came from the House of Romanov, so loosely speaking, I could also claim Romanov heritage as well.

Her great-grandfather was apparently Alexander III of Russia. While the Emperor considered marriage with a woman he loved, he instead ended up marrying someone else out of duty. However, when he had resigned himself to the marriage, he found his wife to be already pregnant—a tale as old as time.

Along came the Russian Revolution and the Second World War, which pushed the Russian imperial family into ruin—the East then used my mother in order to ensnare my father.

Which was why my hair was this beautiful blonde color.

"We've arrived, my lady."

"It's *freezing*!"

My body and blood may have been three-fourths Russian, but my soul and lifestyle were wholly Japanese, and Yamagata at this time of year was incredibly cold.

I'd brought a bouquet of white lilies—my mother's favorite flowers. My mother's grave was in the shape of a crucifix, while my father's was an ordinary tombstone. As a pair, they were a little mismatched, but it didn't matter to me as long as they were happy in the next life.

I placed the lilies on my mother's grave while Tachibana placed a bouquet of chrysanthemums on my father's, and the two of us put our hands together. Despite my appearance, I still considered myself Japanese, and so I started to recite a sutra.

"Lord, have mercy on their souls. How are you both, Mother, Father? I am living a good life thanks to Tachibana, Keiko-san, Aki-san, and Naomi-san. I'm in kindergarten now." I never knew my parents and yet, strangely, my voice was quivering and my cheeks were wet with tears. "I want to come back for a more formal visit and clean up your graves when I get the chance. Goodbye for now."

I stood up and Tachibana passed me a handkerchief, which I used to wipe my tears. Were these really my tears, I wondered, or was it the weeping of the real Keikain Runa's heart?

I was nearly five years old, so I took the opportunity to get up to mischief, such as exploring the house and playing hide-and-seek. It helped me to gradually learn more about the people around me. I'll now introduce the people who were a part of my day-to-day.

"Would you like to play after breakfast, my lady?"

"Yes!"

That was Tokitou Aki-san, a maid who was sent over from the main Keikain Estate. She spent a lot of time interacting with me. She was an orphan and worked as a maid while continuing her studies.

"Please excuse the wait. I've prepared your favorite: salmon filet."

"Yay! Salmon!"

Saitou Keiko-san acted as my wet nurse, did the cooking, and was the head maid. Though she was unmarried, she looked just like she could be Aki-san's mother when the two of them stood together. I pretended not to notice. There was a lot of depth to those associated with high society who weren't nobility themselves.

Katsura Naomi-san would fill in for the other two's shifts when they were off. Naomi-san wasn't working today, but she'd spend time with me when Aki-san had school.

"Let's eat!"

Everyone put their hands together with me and then started to eat. Though I was still young, I was the mistress of the house, and so I sat at the table's head. The house had male workers as well as female, and they all supported its running together.

"When you've finished studying, my lady, why not take a nap?"

Tachibana Ryuuji was one of said male workers—in fact, he was my butler. A near-elderly gentleman, Tachibana helped to solve many problems on my behalf. Sometimes, he would look at me as though he were trying to figure me out, which was a little unnerving; I was still trying to act like an unassuming, innocent child.

I didn't have that many helpers for the daughter to a dukedom, but this was my life now. I found it funny that none of the staff ever appeared in the game.

"Where are you, my lady?"

"Not telling!"

I explored the house while playing hide-and-seek with Aki-san. It was a western-style, two-story house built fifty years ago with a garden. It was the villainess's home in the game too: I remembered recognizing it as a real version of the same location in-game. It was located in Den-en-choufu, a prosperous neighborhood in Ota, Tokyo. Originally used as a secondary residence for the Keikain family, it was passed down to me by my father, and now, nobody came here; it was just the house where I lived. The main Keikain residence was in Shirokane, located in Minato, Tokyo.

I hid myself in the shadow of a tree, where I heard a voice coming from over the wall.

"Doesn't this place belong to the Keikains? The gate never seems to be open though."

"Yes, it's their secondary residence. I believe their main residence is in Shirokane. There is a young lady living here by herself."

"Oh, poor girl. Though the Keikain family themselves are struggling now, with all their fortune and influence coming from the previous generation."

"Well, that's true for everybody, isn't it? Oh, how I miss the days of the bubble..."

The bubble had burst.

Whether one or two, the Lost Decades left this country in a long, stable economic slump. We were smack dab in the middle of it at the moment. The woman on the other side of the wall sounded a little concerned, even for a family of total strangers. The situation was only set to get even more dire from now on, but I was the only one who knew that, for now.

"Ah!"

"I found you! My lady, I have told you that you mustn't hide inside this tree!" Aki-san picked me up from out of the tree.

"Sorry!" I giggled, before suddenly thinking of something else. "You go to school, don't you, Aki-san? Is it fun?"

"It is! I'm currently in senior high school, and I am thinking of going to university if my scholarship application is accepted. But I'm not going to be leaving you alone even if that happens, of course."

I understood immediately what she was saying. Whether nobility or simple upper class, high society operated on appearances. Any family who wouldn't do as much as pay for its maid's school fees was inevitably going to be looked down upon, both from within and without. People would think they were going through financial difficulties.

Despite that, Aki-san had mentioned a "scholarship." That meant the main Keikain family didn't have money to spare on her. I realized that my current lifestyle had an expiration date attached to it.

"Whoa! They're spending *that* much?!"

I picked a time I knew Tachibana would be absent to check the account books in secret. There, I saw there how much this lifestyle cost. Because I was alone, they seemed to be economizing: four members of staff cost two million yen. Energy, heating, and other utilities came to around a million yen, meaning they were paying three million yen a month. Their income, on the other hand, or to be exact, the money coming in from the main Keikain family, was clearly dwindling. Where this place once received five million yen, it was now down to three million a month—and Tachibana was managing the surplus to fill any holes where the current income didn't quite cover our expenses. That income would likely go down, what with the final crushing nail in the economic coffin that I knew was coming.

"I don't want to lose them. Tachibana, Keiko-san, Aki-san, Naomi-san..."

I wanted to do everything I could for those who stood by me, villainess or not. In fact, that was just what a good villainess should do.

I didn't want to say goodbye. So I decided it was time to stop being a good little girl.

As with everything in life, I couldn't do anything without first having some money. I'd determined my place in this world, so now, it was time to start struggling.

"I'd like to go out. Please get ready."

My order was clear, but still Tachibana leaned down to me

and asked for confirmation. The gray-haired butler had worked under my grandfather, and he never outwardly treated me like a child when we were in public. I'd rather he treated me like a child than see me as a kid trying my best to act grown-up to him though.

"Of course, my lady. Where would you like to go?"

"The Tokyo branch of the Far Eastern Bank."

Part of the Keika Group, the regional Far Eastern Bank had its headquarters in a provincial town along the western coast of Japan. The Far Eastern Group won the bid for their main branch there because of its ties with the East, but it too had its fair share of troubles thanks to the bursting of the bubble. To make matters worse, the Far Eastern Bank was now internally treated as a side interest of the Keika Group, so it was constantly at risk of being shut down.

"Welcome, Miss Runa. What may I help you with today?"

The branch manager came to see me in the room for esteemed guests. One look at him told you he was a banker, down to his suit, his hairstyle, and his glasses. He placed a glass of orange juice atop the extravagant table in front of me. I was impressed with the professional smile he'd greeted a small child with, especially in such a fancy room like this. My request, however, was anything but childlike. I decided to see what would happen if I spoke with the heavy lisp of someone my physical age.

"It's nothing big! I just wanna see this bank's balance sheet!"

"...Huh?"

"Huh...?"

I eyed the two men in the room as I glugged down my orange juice. I decided to keep up the blatant childlike act.

"I like grape juice better than orange. Make sure you get some for the next time I'm here."

"Forgive me for that. As for the balance sheet, I'm afraid I cannot—"

"Because I'm a child? You should understand that I know a lot more about this place than you might expect."

I changed my tone. It was vital to keep hold of the initiative in conversations like these. My real objective here was to get Tachibana on my side rather than this branch manager in any case. I was a kid; if I wanted to start making money now, I'd need an adult's help.

"I've come before this place's bad debts stop being something you can just shrug off. The main house is thinking of washing their hands of you. These excessive mortgage loans are starting to cause trouble, and I think you know who'll be first in line to lose their job." I folded my arms as I explained in an unaffected tone.

An overinflated trust in real estate-related loans had left everyone with bad debts. The Jusen problem of excessive mortgage loans was making things worse now in the Diet, which would be the final nail in the coffin that led to the 1997 financial crisis.

"Excuse me, madam. If what you say is true, then what exactly can you do about it?" The branch manager tried a counterattack.

I retaliated immediately. "Well. I'm female. What is the one thing *women* can do?"

I wonder who it was that said, while women were born female, they still had to perform their femininity. Even young girls had picked up the tricks to deceiving men while in their mothers' wombs.

"A political marriage. I'll marry into a zaibatsu in order to help save the Keikain Group."

The two men kept silent at my declaration. There was nothing they could say: marriage was the only reason I was still here.

"So please, show me the balance sheet. Ah, and the ones for your secret accounts too. Otherwise, how should I know which zaibatsu I should accept a proposal from?"

When several ledgers were lined up on the table in front of me, I realized I might have been a bit in over my head. This branch manager was no fool; in fact, he'd just served me another glass of juice without a word, making sure it was grape this time. But then, fools didn't score jobs as branch managers in Tokyo.

"This is a real mess..."

I suppose this was what I'd expected. Far Eastern Bank's bad debts were already nothing to laugh at. The investment Far Eastern Developments had made for its real-estate project, the regional resorts, was nothing short of insane, and it was Far Eastern Hotels that was managing the project. The best thing for them now was to cut their losses as soon as possible.

Keika Maritime Insurance and Far Eastern Life Insurance were also suffering from bad debts before the bubble burst. Thanks to the strong yen, Keika Chemicals and Keika Shipping were just about staying out of the red, and the composition of these companies meant any in a slump would be supplemented by Keika Pharmaceuticals.

"Say, how much of a loan could we get if we mortgaged the estate I live in?"

I'd already presented them with the truth, so I might as well let them see my forked tongue and devilish tail. At this point, the branch manager was well beyond treating me like a mere child.

"As it is a Keikain residence in Tokyo, the land and building together should assure you around a billion yen."

Even if this place was decaying, it was still part of a zaibatsu. If I waited until the center collapsed, I'd no longer be able to fool them.

"Mortgage it for 500 million. We can always remortgage in a few years." I looked at Tachibana. The main family didn't want anything to do with me, so he was essentially my guardian. "I'm going to be doing some conspiring that no one will believe a child to be capable of. For that, I need an adult I can trust. Do you know of anyone?" I asked sweetly.

Tachibana let out a deep sigh. "...You are much like your father in that regard. Just tell me what I must do."

Nice. I've got my trusty ally.

And since he was here already, I might as well get the branch manager on side too. The Tokyo branch manager of the Far Eastern Bank: Ichijou Susumu. I remembered his name.

"Say, do you know what the internet is? And have you heard of a browser?"

The business world would refer to it as Far Eastern Bank's clutch home run, hit in the last half of the ninth innings with two out and two strikes. The bank's investment in the high-tech sector made unbelievable returns, and for a time, grew to make up 80 percent of the Keika Group's overall earnings. The Far Eastern Bank was at the heart of a financial big bang—and Ichijou Susumu was its unsuspecting hero. Whenever the topic of an important investment came up, he would always go and see Keikain Runa at her estate first.

I was visiting the branch manager's office at Far Eastern Bank's Tokyo branch. I had expected the earnings report from the bank's boarding of the dot-com bubble to be huge, but seeing it still made my head spin. Despite all my expectations, I could barely believe that the figure I was hearing was actually a real number.

"This US browser company listing has amassed a one-hundred-million profit for the Moonlight Fund. With the investments and shares we purchased in those IT companies at the same time, we have another return close to a one-hundred million. And here are our profits from our foreign exchange dealings."

I tried to keep my expression calm as Ichijou-san explained things to me, but my body was trembling. Right now, we had two-hundred-million dollars lying in America. These were the profits this time period was capable of producing.

We'd exchanged at 80 yen to a dollar, made several hundred times our investments in the IT companies, and now that the exchange rate had recovered to a hundred yen to a dollar, our profits had swelled up to 50 *billion* yen.

"The profits this branch made, with your assistance, total 50 billion yen."

As collateral for buying the IT company shares, we put up Far Eastern Life Insurance and borrowed insane amounts of money with a Japan premium—the extra interest charged for offshore loans to Japanese banks—all as part of our gamble on the foreign exchange market.

The magnificent jackpot that had paid out earned Ichijou the nicknames of "Far Eastern's Hedge Fund Manager" and "the man who saved the Bank of Japan," from various related parties.

With the entire banking sector in dire straits after the bursting of the bubble, his was the only example of massive profits in some time.

That was when I learned how much taking advantage of the times could earn you.

"I have a feeling you're really going to be making important moves, Ichijou. Largely because I intend to involve you in several more conspiracies to come."

"I'm not sure whether I should be happy or scared..." Ichijou responded, his gaze sharpening.

That gesture reminded me that he was a banker, not a trader.

"We can start dealing with our bad debts now, correct?" he asked.

"Of course! You saw how easy it was to get this money. We might as well make use of it," I replied cheerfully.

The Far Eastern Group, now a part of the Keika Group, was made up of four companies: Far Eastern Bank, Far Eastern Developments, Far Eastern Hotels, and Far Eastern Life Insurance. Far Eastern Developments paid the construction costs for Far Eastern Hotels, and the Far Eastern Bank gave loans to Far Eastern Developments to secure plots of land. These exchanges led to huge amounts of bad debts that straddled the three companies when the bubble burst.

Then there was Far Eastern Bank's child company—Far Eastern Life Insurance. The bank was responsible for Far Eastern Life Insurance's asset management and stock holdings, and took the full brunt of the bank's paper losses from bad debts, leading to a deterioration in its management.

When the Far Eastern Group was taken over by the Keika Group, the Keika Group promised to take over the debt from these dealings should the Far Eastern companies' default.

The source of the group's bad debts was essentially Far Eastern Developments.

"We should request corporate rehabilitation proceedings for Far Eastern Developments. Correct?"

"In return, I'll purchase Far Eastern Hotels. At a high price, of course."

This was how we were going to deal with the bad debts.

Firstly, the Moonlight Fund would buy Far Eastern Hotels from Far Eastern Developments for 30 billion yen. This would allow Far Eastern Developments, which was already under the management of Far Eastern Bank, to repay its debts and apply for corporate rehabilitation to be liquified.

The aggregate debt would reduce to around 15 billion yen, which the bank would take on and write off with its recent earnings from the Tokyo branch. The Moonlight Fund would then take its remaining twenty billion to invest in Far Eastern Bank and buy up the stocks in the bank owned by Far Eastern Life Insurance, at which point I would support Ichijou as a shareholder.

"Tachibana."

My butler dipped his head quietly when I called for him. Officially, I couldn't do anything. Tachibana and Ichijou were the ones who moved publicly.

"I have finished laying the groundwork in the relevant places. As this is a matter of dealing with bad debts, there is no blame to be laid. Other than on you, that is, my lady."

This was just a butler cleaning up the mess his mistress's parents had left in their wake. It wasn't something anyone would argue against. I was still safe hiding in the shadows behind Tachibana and Ichijou.

"Today, Far Eastern Developments, who have their headquarters in Sakata, Yamagata Prefecture, have applied for corporate rehabilitation to the Yamagata District Court, effectively declaring bankruptcy. Their debt totals 15 billion yen. Far Eastern Developments, which owns Far Eastern Hotels, expanded its business during the bubble, but struggled with mountains of bad debts when the bubble burst and the price of land fell. Before the application, Far Eastern Hotels was bought up by an American fund called the Moonlight Fund for 30 billion yen. Its remaining debts are to be financed by the Far Eastern Bank. Far Eastern Bank is to suffer a tremendous 15-billion-yen loss, so why is there no change in its profit forecasts?"

"Far Eastern Bank, headquartered in Sakata, is set to receive a contribution from the Keikain family. They are not just buying out the shares in Far Eastern Bank owned by Far Eastern Life Insurance, but are also getting a third-party allocation of shares, setting their stake in the company at 33 percent. Far Eastern Bank, a member of the Second Association of Regional Banks, has struggled with its bad loans, but by the corporate rehabilitation of its biggest headache, Far Eastern Developments, it has now settled all their bad debt. The Keikain house, which owns the Keika Group, has taken responsibility for and paid off its affiliates' bad debts, and economics circles in Far Eastern Bank's home base have welcomed the move."

I stared at what was placed before me on the table in my home living room. I'd asked Ichijou-san to send this along with a security officer. Keiko-san's tone was exasperated as she brought me some cake and grape juice.

"Are you still looking at that, my lady?"

"I'm learning about the magic of money. Want to look at it with me?"

"No thank you."

One hundred million yen, neatly wrapped in plastic. The Tokyo branch of the Far Eastern Bank had it brought by the Bank of Japan, and it was then withdrawn from my account and brought here to me.

That was why I'd asked for a security guard just in case. There he was now, standing in the corner of the room and staring at the little girl who was staring at 100 million yen—an incredibly surreal sight indeed. But I'd already stopped acting like a little girl though.

"This is enough to buy some unfortunate soul's entire life. I'm in the middle of processing the profoundness of it all."

"I've been lucky to have a small taste of luxury in my life. But now this modest life of taking care of you is enough for me."

The luxury she spoke of likely coincided with the time my grandfather held a deep affection for her. Keiko-san was famous in Ginza at the time, and my grandfather helped her to open her own store. I'd call that more than a "small" taste of luxury myself.

Plus, the first use for my fast-earned fortune was to pay for Tokitou Aki-san's university fees—and it was then that I was fairly sure that she was Keiko-san's daughter. I didn't miss the tears sparkling in Keiko-san's eyes as she witnessed Aki-san's joy.

I now had the financial foundation built that I needed. This shabby second home-slash-doll house could continue to function until I grew up.

"You don't need to force yourself to mature, my lady," Keiko-san admonished me as she put down my grape juice and cake.

She'd taken the one-eighty-degree change in personality completely in her stride. Her mental fortitude impressed me.

"Tachibana-san, the others, and I will work for you until you're bigger, so take your time growing up into a beautiful woman."

"Mm..." I responded with a casual nod.

Keiko-san broke into a smile at my reaction. Maybe it would have been better to end things here. But I knew history liked to lift its victors to more incredible heights than they could achieve on their own—right up until they crashed and burned.

"My lady. Branch Manager Ichijou from Far Eastern Bank is here to see you," Naomi-san called for me.

I blinked in confusion. Was he here to collect the money? I looked to the security guard, who shook his head. He didn't seem to know why Ichijou was here either.

"Very well. Send him in. Could you ask Naomi-san to serve us some cake and tea?" I asked Keiko-san.

When Ichijou came in, he ignored the money on the table, and instead looked directly at me.

"Our MOF clerk gave me an urgent message. They are apparently keeping an eye on the elimination of our bad debts. Depending on how things proceed, we might be faced with their intervention."

What? Why was the Ministry of Finance interested in *us*?

What had the Far Eastern Bank done to draw their attention?

The reason lay in different areas of control. The Ministry of Finance was an enormous government office, and it was divided into various governing sections. The financial section was split into banks, insurance, and securities, each having their own regulated spheres that mustn't cross.

"It is apparently the use of the American Moonlight Fund which has caught their attention..." Ichijou muttered.

The fund did more than collect the returns from our investments in IT; the Moonlight Fund traded stocks in IT companies to increase its profits.

"It's an American fund. Surely, Japanese regulations can't touch it?" I asked.

"That doesn't mean they're necessarily *happy* about it. They must have traced back the clearing of Far Eastern Bank's debt to the Moonlight Fund."

Japanese bureaucrats did outstanding work, especially when it came to those who threatened the peace in their own sphere: they were quick to launch a sophisticated counterattack. By clearing its bad debts, Far Eastern Bank had created a hole in the Ministry's systematic operations, which was exactly why they were now trying to seal it back up.

"Does it look like the Ministry is planning to do anything?"

"It seems they're just keeping an eye for now. If we do anything else to catch their attention though, we'll likely get in trouble. Our current bank president is a retired Ministry official, you see."

Suddenly it all made sense. Ichijou was my sole pawn in Far Eastern Bank, but if the Ministry of Finance felt like it, they merely needed to leverage their power and give the word to the president and they could have Ichijou removed. Anything more we did, now that they were "keeping an eye," was destined to end in absolute failure.

"Very well. Let us lay low for now. But I'd also like to invest in domestic IT companies."

A certain American operating system sold in 1995 made such a huge splash that it became the de facto standard and caused the IT industry to explode and spread worldwide. Its next iteration, sold in 1998, only cemented its staying power. I knew the dot-com bubble would expand practically overnight in this country as well, so I wanted to get on board in time.

"Tachibana. As a shareholder of Far Eastern Bank, might I suggest you buy yourself a brokerage firm? And make sure the bank president hears about it."

"Yes, my lady. I believe there are several midsize domestic firms we can choose from."

"Many of those firms are in possession of huge amounts of unfortunate bad debts. It would be no good if we were to buy the wrong one, only to have that debt wipe away our profits."

Tachibana nodded, but Ichijou raised an objection. If all we cared about was making money, he said, then it would be safer to start a new company and avoid any paper loss at all.

"Hmm. I'd like some time to think about that, if you wouldn't mind. Please continue investing in IT companies unless you hear otherwise."

I ended up deferring the decision until later.

"Far Eastern Bank is rapidly accelerating its aggressive business practices. Now that its prior debts are paid off, it is using the Moonlight Fund to continue its investments primarily into IT corporations. Its current business model is to ride the trend of computers spreading through industrial and home environments to increase its profits. While it would do the company good for its model to succeed and leave its previously unfortunate debts behind, the Ministry of Finance is concerned about a loans company acting in such a manner and is currently seeking a solution. As part of our coverage of the

Far Eastern Bank, the bank has informed us that it understands the concerns and is now examining whether it should create a new brokerage firm, or whether it should buy out a domestic mid-sized firm already in existence."

I may have been done with acting like a kid, but that was how the maids of the house still saw me. It seemed that for as long as I was physically a child, anything I did would be interpreted as childish.

"I have a snack for you, my lady. It's your favorite: pudding!"

"Yay!"

That wasn't a problem for me. I was thinking so hard a lot of the time that I ended up craving sweet things. So there I was, heartily enjoying my pudding topped with whipped cream, as its creator, Naomi-san, smiled fondly at me.

"Making these treats is so worth it to see you enjoy them so much, my lady."

Naomi-san was related to the Keikain family, and while not directly part of the household or its close branches, her blood connection allowed her to be considered such partly because she was a woman. Apparently an illegitimate child of my grandfather's younger brother, the emerging Keikain family had taken her in when she had nowhere else to go. She was someone on the very edge of the family; she accepted that there was a distinct difference in the way they treated her and ended up marrying a partner of their choosing. Her son was currently working at the head office of a bank.

"Your son works at a bank, doesn't he? Does he work for Far Eastern?"

"Unfortunately not, my lady. He's not one to use familial connections, so he studied hard to end up at a bank a little more prominent than yours. I may introduce him to you one day, so I hope you'll be nice to him."

If he was in a "more prominent" bank, that meant one either belonging to the Regional Banks Association of Japan or a metropolitan bank. Considering its dealings of the Keika Group, I wondered whether it might be Iwazaki Bank, owned by the Iwazaki zaibatsu.

"I'll look forward to it. What bank does he work for then?"

Naomi-san was able to give the name with pride; she didn't know what the future held.

"It's Hokkaido Kaitaku Bank. He works in the integrated development department."

A low-level metropolitan bank. Its failure came down to massive bad debts accrued primarily by one *particular* department: integrated development.

"Looking at the stock prices alone, it has essentially collapsed."
March 1997.

A commentator on the news program, *Nichiyou Project*, continued the countdown to Hokkaido Kaitaku Bank's collapse. Meanwhile, my fortune was expanding so fast I could practically hear it whirring in my ears. When the yen passed 120 yen to the American dollar, I temporarily canceled my positions to work on steadying my profit, and even after settling Far Eastern

Bank's bad debts, I still had the same amount of Japanese yen to hand. I hadn't done anything with the money amassed by the Moonlight Fund either.

"I suppose there's nothing left to do but to buy a brokerage firm now. I just don't want to end up with a mountain of new bad debts..."

I gave new instructions to Tachibana and Ichijou—I now had my intentions set on buying a brokerage firm, but for that, I needed a watertight set of rules.

My target was Sankai Securities, a second-tier domestic brokerage firm struggling with loads of bad debts. It was being battered in the market, and the Ministry of Finance was desperately trying to rescue it.

"Dismiss all the executives. Make sure anyone involved in malpractice takes suitable responsibility. Take all the bad loans, hidden or otherwise, separate them, and pass them to the Resolution and Collection Corporation. We'll be allowed a special loan from the Bank of Japan to protect us in case of financial crisis or if Sankai is bought out or gets involved in a merger. Tell the Ministry of Finance that we'll buy Sankai Securities if they agree to these conditions."

Sankai Securities was small, but the Ministry of Finance needed to rescue it if they wanted to save face. The firm started falling into the red in 1992, and in 1994, the Ministry of Finance's securities division merged it with a more successful firm in an attempt to revitalize it. That said, it was still in the red now, its situation not having improved one bit.

I was confident the Ministry would agree to my terms to protect its reputation, and I was right. I also presented them with my Keika Rules: a set of principles with the purpose of disposing of Sankai Securities' prior bad debts, all of which promised a rescue of the firm, further sweetening the pot for them.

It was June when the securities division at the Ministry of Finance accepted my rules.

"Breaking news! Far Eastern Bank has bought out Sankai Securities! The Yamagata-based bank has announced its acquisition of Tokyo-based second-tier brokerage firm, Sankai Securities. The buyout price is estimated to be 40 billion yen, and Sankai's executives have taken responsibility and resigned across the board. Sankai Securities, which held numerous bad debts, previously applied for corporate rehabilitation for its similarly indebted child company, Sankai Finance. The rest of its bad debts have been sold at current market value to the Resolution and Collection Corporation, a loss that has been factored into the estimated buyout price. Far Eastern Bank will reduce its capital to hold Sankai Securities' shareholders responsible, and use investments to make up for the losses from the acquisition's insolvency. Even with these measures, due to the firm's low equity ratio, it has taken out a special loan from the Bank of Japan to ensure financial stability."

We'd saved Sankai Securities before it found itself at an impasse, thus eliminating the trigger that would lead to a series of nightmarish failures for Sankai Securities, Hokkaido Kaitaku Bank, and Ichiyama Securities. Without that chain reaction, none of those individual companies would implode.

At least, that was what I believed at the time.

"Please, help me, my lady!"

July.

The previous day, it had been reported that negotiations regarding a merger between Hokkaido Kaitaku Bank and another large regional bank in Hokkaido had broken down.

He was here now, kneeling down and pressing his forehead to the ground in front of me: Katsura Naoyuki. Son to my maid, Katsura Naomi-san.

Naomi-san was standing next to me in a panic, totally unsure of the situation.

"You come here, out of the blue, and ask for my help. You know I cannot just say yes, can I? At least give me a clear explanation of the situation, please."

Katsura Naoyuki was still in his thirties, and his face was wan and haggard. There were deep, dark circles under his eyes. Naoyuki-san must have been sleep-deprived. I could only imagine that he was both physically and mentally exhausted from pushing himself hard at work.

"You may know a little of this already from the news, but the Hokkaido Kaitaku Bank where I work is bleeding money right now. Please, my lady, could you lend some of your fortune to our bank?"

Every since spring when Hokkaido Kaitaku Bank had been declared "essentially collapsed" by the media, its clerks had been using any connections they could in an effort to secure deposits.

Here before me was a man who joined his bank because he *hated* using connections. Now here he was begging for help at the feet of one of those connections. It only went to show the injustice in society.

"My lady..." There were tears in Naomi-san's eyes as she looked at me, her mistress, her son on the floor in front of me.

He was so desperate to gather funds that he was making his mother cry. I was reminded of my former life.

A long, unending recession: moral obligation, money, and self-responsibility were the words that dragged my frail self along their unforgiving current, until in the end, I was left without anyone or anything to rely on and departed from that world completely alone.

Anger was the first emotion sparked by those memories. I wasn't angry at society for pushing me to such a dismal dead end; instead, I was angry at such an era that created a society that wouldn't reward even the hardest of efforts.

I was a villainess.

Or at least, that was who I was in *this* life. That was who I was destined to become as I carried on living my life here.

I now understood just what my role meant. Eventually, I would lose to the protagonist and fall into ruin. In some ways, it was like a natural promise: a striking end to my story. I was happy to take on my role, even if it meant accepting my loss gracefully and dramatically.

But what was happening in front of me right now?

There were these countless people being swept away by the current of the times. There was me from my previous life.

If being a villainess meant I was supposed to sit back and idly watch, then I wasn't prepared to just go along with simply living anymore. I'd lose to the protagonist, and only the protagonist— not to anyone else. Especially not to the hopelessness of the times!

"Call Tachibana and Ichijou. One hundred million will be enough to start with, won't it?"

"Thank you so much! Oh, thank you, my lady!"

Both Katsuras took my hands and thanked me profusely, tears streaming down their faces. With my funds, I could save these two. I could make more money because I knew the nature of the waves that loomed on the horizon.

I could save them.

I could save Hokkaido Kaitaku Bank, and I could save Ichiyama Securities.

I could save Japan's economy.

I could save all of us: all who suffered during my previous lifetime.

I sighed and shook my head lightly. Suppose I didn't bother saving anyone: I could live a lavish life as a villainess, right until my downfall. I'd already laid down the foundation to be able to do so. But suppose I gambled all of that away, for the chance to save Japan's *entire* economy?

"You called, my lady?"

Ichijou arrived just under an hour after the Katsuras asked for my help, and came to me with Tachibana. They didn't ask any questions; Naomi-san must have filled them in already.

"We're going to buy out Hokkaido Kaitaku Bank," I simply explained.

"Pardon me, my lady, but have you gone *insane*?!" Ichijou cried.

I shrugged, keeping my tone light. "Perhaps. But since we have the opportunity...please do explain why you consider buying out Hokkaido Kaitaku Bank to be an act of insanity, Ichijou. In simplistic terms so that I can understand."

Tachibana had yet to utter a word.

Having calmed down a little, Ichijou stared at me evenly. "Where would you like me to start, my lady?"

"From the beginning, of course. I'm not certain this is the correct course of action myself. If I hear your explanation and it turns out I'm wrong, I won't speak any more of it."

Ichijou sighed, not keeping his eyes off me. He pulled out a 100-yen coin and a 10,000-yen note from his wallet and placed them both in front of me.

"Allow me to ask you a question, my lady. You know that with this money here, you are able to buy things. Why is that, exactly?"

"Hmm, a difficult question indeed. Is it perhaps because money has *value*?"

"Ah, I was hoping you might say that! However, the correct answer is because money is generally *perceived* to have value."

"Generally perceived..." I murmured.

Ichijou pulled out five 1000-yen notes from his wallet along with some change, but then turned to Tachibana; apparently, he didn't have enough on hand.

"Tachibana-san. Have you any 500-yen coins?"

"I have one, if that will suffice."

On the table were a single 10,000-yen note, five 1000-yen notes, one 500-yen coin, and five 100-yen coins.

"We understand this money here to have the same value. But what about an alien who knows nothing about Japan and its currency? Would it place the same value on these notes and coins? *That* is what I mean by the shared perception of value."

I nodded profoundly to let him know I was still with him. Ichijou returned Tachibana's 500-yen coin and put his own money back into his wallet.

"Now that you understand that value is the essence of money, I shall now move on to how that value is assigned. There are several rules to the concept of value. The first, and most absolute rule, is that there is no value in money if you have nobody to trade with."

I inclined my head. Ichijou took a 100-yen coin back out of his wallet and placed it in front of me again.

"If I were alone, there would be no problem in me claiming

that this one-hundred-yen coin has the same value as a 10,000-yen note, yes?"

"Ah, yes." I clapped my fist down onto my hand.

So, value only came into play when there was another party involved.

"Now let's bring you into this scenario, my lady. Should I insist that this coin is worth a 10,000 yen, you would say instead that it is simply a 100-yen coin. Which of us is correct?" Ichijou smiled at me: it was clear he was waiting for a particular answer.

I was more than willing to give it to him; after all, I was the one who asked him to explain.

"It would be *me*, wouldn't it? It even says '100' on the coin itself."

Ichijou's smile widened, and he followed up on the trap I'd just walked into. I knew something was lacking in my answer.

"The correct answer is that *neither* of us is correct."

"Hm? But a hundred yen is a hundred yen."

"Is *this* hundred yen *really* a hundred yen though?"

I stared blankly at him, at which point he pulled the 10,000-yen note from his wallet again and placed it beside the coin.

It might be easier if he just keeps the money out this time...

"Think it through carefully, my lady. Do you truly believe that *this single scrap of paper* has the same value as a *hundred* of these coins?"

I fell silent. This was the grand, revolutionary manner of thinking at the center of modern economics—it was all about building beliefs.

"We are already speaking under the preconception that this coin is worth a hundred yen," I said.

"To be more precise, we have faith in the guarantee of a third party that this coin is worth a hundred yen. That third party being the Bank of Japan, or the state. That is the true essence of money in our modern economy. You can think of it as a credit system." Ichijou averted his gaze. He still had a long way to go in his explanation. "I'm a little thirsty. Shall we take a coffee break?"

"I'll have grape juice!"

"Very well. Please wait while I prepare your beverages." Tachibana left.

I realized then how much Ichijou's lesson was engrossing me. Part of me felt that I wouldn't have met such a dire end if I knew about this sort of thing in my previous life, but when Tachibana and Aki-san came back with the drinks and snacks, my grumbling stomach overrode the thought. No matter how grown-up I tried to act, my body still had its childlike desire for snacks.

"Here you are. It's pudding: your *favorite*."

"Yay! Pudding!"

It was when the pudding arrived that Ichijou, who was sipping at a cup of coffee, resumed the lesson.

"My lady, that looks like a *very* delicious pudding. Would you sell it to me for a hundred yen?"

"Only a hundred yen? No way! This pudding's *lots* more valuable than that!" I gave a harsh reprimand, even though I knew it was just pudding. This pudding was handmade by my staff, making it both delicious *and* valuable.

Seeing my reaction, Ichijou held out the 10,000 yen note to me. "Would you sell it for this much then?"

I nearly choked. As the lady of a noble house, it shouldn't have been a big deal, but I was a commoner in my previous life. Something deep within my soul reacted to that 10,000 yen note. All three adults in the room smiled at my reaction.

"Thank you for valuing our puddings so highly, my lady. But please try not to tease her, Ichijou-sama," Aki-san said.

Ichijou raised his hands to feign innocence, and I laughed.

"May I borrow that pudding for a moment?" he asked. "I don't mean to eat it, of course."

"...You'd better not," I said after a pause.

Ichijou placed the 10,000 yen note in front of me, while placing the pudding in front of himself, making it as though I had sold it to him for the money.

"I have bought your pudding for 10,000 yen. However, I do not intend to eat it. Instead, I intend to sell it on to someone else in order to turn a profit. So, Tachibana-san. Would you like to buy this young lady's pudding for *20,000* yen?"

Tachibana glanced at the pudding over his black coffee. "Hmm, I'm not particularly fond of sweet things..."

Tachibana had performed his part perfectly, and now Ichijou was looking around the room with an anxious furrow in his brow. I realized now the significance of the pudding in this skit. Aki-san's homemade pudding was playing the part of Japan's land and shares.

"Oh, dear. I don't really want to eat the pudding myself, and simply leaving it will cause it to expire, and then *nobody* can eat it—and they certainly won't want to buy it then. I'm left with no other choice. My lady, would you like to buy this pudding?"

"Yes! I'll buy it for one hundred yen!" I took the coin that was still on the table and handed it over to him. Then, Ichijou took it and returned the pudding to me. The whole act was very obvious at this point, but Ichijou seemed intent on continuing the lesson.

"I managed to deal with the pudding, but I have lost my 10,000-yen note! At this rate, my wife will realize it's missing, and we'll end up fighting over where it's gone!"

This was essentially what accruing bad debts were. If people wanted something, the price would be raised artificially: but without a buyer, that price fell again. Ichijou had also shown how wide the margin between an item's book value and market value could get.

"And so, I take my 10,000 yen, earned by suspicious means, and give it to you so that you don't end up arguing with your wife."

"Precisely, my lady! As you can see, even a 10,000-yen pudding has the power to cause strife between a married couple. Now think about how much worse debt, in the form of land and shares, can be." Ichijou's expression was suddenly grave. This man was on the front lines both during the bubble and after it burst, giving his words a profound weight. "Even Far Eastern Bank, as a smaller regional bank, still had debts in excess of 45 billion yen. It was work enough getting them that low too. At their highest, they were close to 100 billion. While one of the smaller establishments, Hokkaido Kaitaku Bank is still a metropolitan bank, I wouldn't doubt that their bad debts far outweigh those of Far Eastern Bank."

Thus, the question was whether I could secure one trillion yen in funds. With time, it might be possible if I took advantage of the dot-com bubble. Thanks to market flooding though, Hokkaido Kaitaku Bank would go under in the fall. I clearly didn't have the time for that.

"There's only one solution then." I kept my expression serious as I ate my pudding. "A special loan from the Bank of Japan. We need to come up with some plan that will convince the Ministry of Finance to grant us that."

Money. Value. Credit. Perception. Economics. A nightmarish chain of collapsing financial institutions. These were the ill-fated debts those institutions currently possessed:

Sankai Securities: 80 billion yen.
Ichiyama Securities: 260 billion yen.
Hokkaido Kaitaku Bank: 2.3 trillion yen.

Hokkaido Kaitaku Bank's debts were clearly on a whole other level. If I really wanted to avoid damaging Japan's economy, that was the institution I would need to save. The problem was I didn't have the means of securing such insane amounts of money as 2.3 trillion yen. There was only one place in this country that could: The Bank of Japan. The state itself. I would need a special loan from there.

These loans were a last resort, granted only when the financial system itself was in danger, and to maintain faith in that system. They were granted to struggling financial institutions by government request. It wasn't an overstatement to say that the fate of Hokkaido Kaitaku Bank rested on whether we could get it one of these special loans, which were both unsecured and unrestricted.

"Let's begin by making use of the special loan we already have."

Sankai Securities was already receiving a special loan because of its buyout by Far Eastern Bank. Because the loan was unsecured and unrestricted, confidence in Sankai Securities was low even after the buyout. It was still hemorrhaging funds, and the huge loan was currently being distributed to the firm in chunks. It was like a bath being continuously filled with hot water while the drain was unplugged, and you were losing the water from the bottom. The loan wouldn't stop coming until the hemorrhaging was plugged, and the tub was filled with water—i.e., cold hard money—again.

"Which is why we can afford to be a little *reckless*."

Ichijou's expression stiffened, and he hesitated as he opened his mouth. He'd learned by now that when I said things like that, it meant I was about to do something unwise, to put it mildly. When I answered his question, both he and Tachibana were lost for words.

"I'm not sure I want to know, but what exactly are you planning...?"

"If you want to achieve anything, you need to start at the

bottom and then move to the top. So, to buy out Hokkaido Kaitaku Bank, we're going to start by buying out Ichiyama Securities."

"Sankai Securities has announced a merger with Ichiyama Securities! Both firms have their head offices in Tokyo, with Ichiyama Securities being larger than Sankai. The parent organization of the surviving company will be Sankai Securities. It is expected that the resulting firm will keep the name of Sankai Securities. Not only has Ichiyama Securities been struggling with a heavy load of debts, but it had also been discovered that there was a payoff to corporate bouncers, leading to a mass resignation of management ranks below and including the president, and causing chaos within the firm.

According to some weekly publications, on top of its losses, there have been rumors of a tobashi scheme within Ichiyama Securities. Since the merger with Sankai Securities is being spearheaded by the Ministry of Finance's securities division, it is effectively a bailout. The situation has drawn criticism from the opposition party."

"Ahead of its merger with Sankai Securities tomorrow, the former management of Ichiyama Securities is going to be indicted for the proclaimed tobashi scheme and will be investigated for the resulting mass resignation.

According to the announcement, a total of 260 billion yen was caught up in the scheme. The entirety of the firm's debts, including this amount, are to be sold to the Resolution and Collection Corporation and will be treated as an extraordinary loss.

In response to the news, Sankai Securities held a press conference and made it clear that this had no effect on the merger. The Ministry of Finance also commented that it intended to continue providing Sankai Securities with its special loan for the sake of financial security."

It wasn't hard to seek out Ichiyama Securities' internal whistle-blower. Tachibana and Ichijou used the Keikain family's diplomatic immunity as a bargaining chip to get the information they wanted and used that information to establish some new Keika rules for the buyout. Once the groundwork was laid with the Far Eastern Bank, they applied for the merger of the two security companies.

The payment to the corporate bouncer—and a complete change in its management—staff had left Ichiyama Securities dysfunctional. As its supervisor, the Ministry of Finance's securities division couldn't let things go on as they were, and so they had no choice but to agree to my conditions without question. The decisive blow was the tobashi scheme the firm had been covering up—dealing with that loss would have pushed them into insolvency. The firm collapsing as a result of that was the one thing the securities division couldn't let happen.

Tachibana offered to bail out Ichiyama Securities, so long as they agreed to follow the Keika Rules. In the end, all they could do was sigh and nod, especially when he added one final thought.

"You wouldn't want the securities division to have to interfere and save you from collapse before the banking division, would you?"

Thank God for the Ministry of Finance's divided administration.

One of the nice things about a smaller firm swallowing up a larger one was that Sankai Securities got to keep its special loan, and fairness aside, Ichiyama Securities was still legally entitled to its bailout money from the Bank of Japan. We could now also visualize all the assets we had in one place so that we could deal with every bad debt we had. That was a huge advantage for us. To explain, when financial institutions merged, the surviving company ended up with all the assets of the two. The assets of the other company could then be recalculated for their current market value. In other words, the dominant company took over the assets of the other company at a reasonable price from that point in time, thus preventing those assets from becoming bad debts.

Anything horrendous left after that was sold off to the Resolution and Collection Corporation, and anything that could affect the firm's credit, such as the closing of bank accounts, was covered by the special loan.

The media paid no attention to this line of reasoning, instead going back to snap at what was on the surface: the mass resignation, the prosecution of the firm's former management, and the fact that the company was no longer called "Ichiyama" post-merger.

We were therefore graced with fantastical coverage about the "fall" of Ichiyama Securities—but that wasn't necessarily a bad thing, since it meant we didn't have to find somebody to blame ourselves. Either way, Ichiyama Securities was saved.

August.

With the bailout of Sankai Securities and Ichiyama Securities, the market had its sights set on Hokkaido Kaitaku Bank, and was mercilessly being flooded. Its negotiations of a merger having broken down, the bank no longer had the strength to fortify itself against the onslaught.

Their stock prices had fallen below a hundred yen, which was when insolvency started becoming a genuine risk. I waited for very moment they hit 59 yen a share before playing my final card.

That was when I put in a takeover bid for Hokkaido Kaitaku Bank.

"The California-based Moonlight Fund announced a takeover bid for Hokkaido Kaitaku Bank at noon today. It has offered a purchase price of 74 yen a share and intends to secure a third to a majority of the company. The fund has given the company until October 31st to make a decision."

It was time to throw away my tens of billions of yen and save both Hokkaido Kaitaku Bank and Japan's economy itself.

"The news of the Moonlight Fund's takeover bid for Hokkaido Kaitaku Bank has raised concerns among people involved in the financial markets. No one has been able to identify a motive for the bid. Should the takeover succeed but the bank then fail, the funds put toward it would have been wasted. Moreover, even if the acquisition means collapse is avoided, the loss of capital linked to shareholder responsibility cannot be avoided.

That is why such takeovers normally involve the issue of new shares via a third-party allotment to pass the right of management to the acquirer.

Those doubts aside, several investors have welcomed the bid as the only means of escape for the bank's current situation. On the other hand, there are some local shareholders who feel the move comes too late to mitigate the bank's losses significantly..."

"We have currently managed to purchase nearly 36 percent of the issued stock, spending a little over 20 billion yen in the process. I believe we'll have no trouble securing a majority stake at this rate." Ichijou narrowed his eyes slightly. "Though I must say this seems a waste of your easy money."

It would take around about four billion yen to secure a majority of the shares. I had planned for that money to simply blow away on a breeze. The interesting part of the charade was yet to come.

"It's about time for the press conference. Turn on the television, would you?"

Naomi-san, who was standing next to me, picked up the remote and followed my instructions.

The show was a special broadcast managed by the state. On the screen was Moonlight Fund's representative—a foreigner—taking the media's questions and answering in fluent English. The whole thing was being simultaneously interpreted into Japanese.

"Please tell us Moonlight Fund's intention with this takeover bid."

"We, the Moonlight Fund, are a turnaround management fund and as such, our aim is corporate revival. We revive financial institutions to maintain close relationships between their local economies and banks. Local businesses don't just hold shares in banks; several of them use those shares as collateral. The bank's revival depends on the revival of the local economy, yes, but what would happen if several companies no longer had the collateral available to borrow anything? Thus, we believe our takeover bid is a necessary expense."

"Do you really think revitalizing Hokkaido Kaitaku Bank is possible, given its mountains of bad debts?"

"To be frank, we have judged it impossible to revitalize the Hokkaido Kaitaku Bank by ourselves at this point in time. For now, I will only say that we are considering our options for eventual mergers."

"If I may, there are rumors that Moonlight Fund is a foreign vulture fund. Can you offer any comments on that?"

"I can see why some might say that, but such rumors are deeply rooted in a misunderstanding about who we are and what we stand for. We promise to reveal more about ourselves and our intentions in future, starting with this press conference."

"The US is so big. Big enough to have actors with *law degrees*."

"That's why our bluff will work. Having a Japanese actor in there would make things too obvious," Ichijou remarked.

We'd hired our spokesperson to play the part of Moonlight Fund's legal advisor and hold this press conference. As both a lawyer and an actor, he was able to keep his cool during the questioning, and anyone who looked him up would find his genuine legal qualifications. They'd then have no reason to doubt him.

The Ministry of Finance knew who was behind Moonlight Fund, but it seemed the information hadn't made it to the press yet. They still didn't know what the purpose of the takeover bid was, and if they were able to poke their noses in too deep, I might have to withdraw and then Hokkaido Kaitaku Bank would collapse after all.

"Do you think we'll be able to keep the Ministry hush-hush for the time being?"

"Yes. The banking division agreed to the same rules we wrote up for the Sankai Securities and the Ichiyama Securities takeovers."

We weren't just endangering ourselves for the desperate Hokkaido Kaitaku Bank; we were using the takeover to pay even more money than necessary to reduce the damage to Hokkaido's local economy. That much left a good impression on the MOF's banking division.

Of course, the fact they knew about our successes with the securities division, combined with the fact that they could not afford to fail, meant it was only a matter of time before the banking division also agreed to our conditions.

"Are you sure about not claiming the right of management?"

"Why, do you think I look like I know how to run one of Japan's *largest* banks?"

One of the reasons the banking division agreed to our buyout was because we wouldn't be claiming right of management. We were offering Far Eastern Bank, Hokkaido Kaitaku Bank and our merged Sankai Securities to the Ministry of Finance as a collective. Without going that far, we had no hopes of securing a special loan worth trillions of yen in return.

At the same time, we let talk of our good bank swallowing this bad bank to clean it up spread all about, setting a good example for the Long-Period Credit Bank of Japan and the Nihon Credit Bank, which were likely to merge next. Now, we were ready to do what we needed to in order to deal with Hokkaido Kaitaku Bank's bad debt.

"They're probably perfectly happy with us spending money just so they can do whatever they want with their new financial institutions," Ichijou mused.

What it was getting might not have been the major players, but the Ministry *was* picking up a bank comprised of three metropolitan branches and a second-tier regional bank, as well as a financial institution made up of a large security firm and a slightly smaller one. Both were something the MOF could make an extra arm out of.

It was a prime example of something that happened a lot during Japan's Big Bang, a period of financial deregulation.

"Let them live in the moment. As long as it's a national bank, it'll end up being auctioned off under the guise of being privatized before the big bang anyway. We have a memorandum promising we can take part in that auction, which is enough for now."

The memorandum had two components to it. One was permission from the Ministry of Finance to participate in that auction, should the new bank be sold as a whole. The other was the assurance of equity equal to Far Eastern Bank and Life Insurance and Sankei Securities combined. The state wasn't fiendish enough to use nationalization to seize back the assets we'd worked so hard to patch up for them.

I probably didn't need to mention that the support of the MOF's securities division, which helped tidy up Ichiyama Securities for us, was of great aid too.

On the television, a regional newspaper company was asking its final questions.

"...Your concern for our regional economy is most appreciated, and as a representative one of those regional firms, please allow me to thank you. However, I cannot shake off my concerns about these vulture-fund rumors and I am sure many residents of Hokkaido feel the same way. Is there anything you would like to say to those who are hesitant about accepting the Moonlight Fund's helping hand?"

"Your concerns are very reasonable and understandable. After the economical and political unification with Northern Japan, Hokkaido has become the biggest cosmopolitan area in the country after Tokyo. That is exactly why our fund's owner wishes to help."

"Fund's owner?"

"Yes. I think I'm permitted to tell you this much. The fund's owner has Russian blood. Perhaps they wish to help out their countrymen who still reside in Japan."

"I don't remember saying that."

"No, but you did give him permission to ad lib, to an extent," Ichijou pointed out. "I'd say that statement qualifies."

"I suppose I do *look* Russian. I could always give to charity or something, if it came down to it."

I didn't know then the full impact that single "ad-libbed" line would have. Both on me and the world at large.

"The Far Eastern Bank of Sakata in Yamagata Prefecture has announced a merger with Hokkaido Kaitaku Bank of Sapporo.

Far Eastern Bank will be the surviving company, taking on the new name Far Eastern Hokkaido Bank.

The Hokkaido Kaitaku Bank has struggled with several bad debts, and now, the foreign company Moonlight Fund will be taking on the right of management as a result of the takeover. Moonlight Fund aims to purge the bad debt through the merger with Far Eastern Bank, a bank over whose management it holds influence.

All of Hokkaido Kaitaku Bank's management staff below and including the president have resigned, and the bank's bad debts are to be sold off to the Resolution and Collection Corporation.

After using capital reduction to hold the shareholders accountable, the Moonlight Fund has issued new shares via a third-party allotment to inject new funds into the bank. To tackle the credit uncertainty in the meantime, they have applied for a special loan from the Bank of Japan..."

"It has come to light that the foreign Moonlight Fund received funding from the domestic Keika Group. The Fund has confirmed the allegations.

The Moonlight Fund was a key player in the creation of Far

Easter Hokkaido Bank, a corporate merger between Far Eastern Bank and Hokkaido Kaitaku Bank. The fund held notable sway over the former Far Eastern Bank, which was also affiliated with the Keika Group, leading to long-standing rumors about the relationship between them.

When asked in the Diet by a scathing member of the opposition party, whether the Ministry of Finance was really planning to sell part of Japan's domestic industry to a vulture fund, the banking division responded that while Moonlight Fund may be an overseas fund, it was established with domestic capital, and that the bank's new president was to be appointed from the Ministry itself. It was this comment that brought to light the true nature of the relationship.

The Moonlight Fund has subsequently announced that the new bank shall now instead be named Keika Bank..."

"The metropolitan Long-Period Credit Bank of Japan has announced a merger with the recently established Keika Bank. Although the surviving company will be majority owned by the LPCB, the name will remain the Keika Bank. The head office is slated to move to Tokyo, essentially making this a relief merger.

The market has continued to target banks that are struggling to deal with their bad loans, and since the bailout of Hokkaido Kaitaku Bank, the LPCB had been the market's next target. As part of its convoy system that deals with bad debts, the Ministry of Finance is considering whether Keika Bank can be used as a good bank, and all management staff below and including the president of the former LPCB have resigned. Its bad debts have been sold off to the Resolution and Collection Corporation. After using capital reduction to hold the shareholders accountable, Moonlight Fund has issued new shares via a third-party allotment to inject new funds into the new bank..."

"The metropolitan Nihon Credit Bank has announced a merger with Keika Bank. The announcement comes hot on the heels of the confirmation of Keika Bank's merger with the Long-Period Credit Bank of Japan, eliciting surprise from market experts.

While Nihon Credit Bank will come out as the dominant bank, the name of the resulting bank will be Keika Bank.

This merger will not take place until Keika Bank's merger with LPCB is complete, once again making it effectively a relief merger.

The situation is complicated. While the dominant bank in the Keika Bank collective was initially Far Eastern Bank, the first merger has LPCB takes its place ahead of this new merger, which will immediately hand dominance over to Nihon Credit Bank. In this case, the smaller company has taken over the bigger one. To proceed with dealing with the bad debts all at once, all management ranks below and including the president of Nihon Credit Bank have resigned, and the bad debts have been sold off to the Resolution and Collection Corporation. After using capital reduction to hold the shareholders accountable, Moonlight Fund has issued new shares via a third-party allotment to inject new funds into the new bank, just as it did with LPCB.

With these mergers, Keika Bank's debt in special loans from the Bank of Japan is said to be close to eight trillion yen. Market experts

*have expressed doubt on their ability to repay the loan, even going
so far as to call it an effective nationalization."*

"It appears I will be appointed as corporate officer next month."

It was late fall, and the storm that was our effort to restructure the financial industry had calmed down somewhat.

Ichijou came to my house, bringing Katsura Naoyuki with him. The market favored the Ministry of Finance's enforcement of the settlement of our bad debts, and stock prices had regained their stability. I'd lost hundreds of billions of easy money, but at that point, I was glad I'd done so.

"Oh."

"You don't seem particularly pleased when it is thanks from the Ministry, my lady."

"Well, it's not as though *I* am being promoted. All of this was purely to satisfy myself in any case." Ichijou smiled wryly at my indifference.

Investing into mergers and then reducing capital to punish shareholders—rinse and repeat. Those cycles meant that most of the money I'd thrown into this restructuring was gone. For Ichijou to become a corporate officer was pretty exceptional, but I'd call it an apology rather than thanks, though the gains I made from the dot-com bubble more than made up for the losses anyway.

"Katsura is to be placed underneath me, and I am sending him to the private bank division of the head branch. It will be difficult for me to keep an eye on your fund in the capacity of a corporate officer as I have done, so I intend to entrust him with the practical matters."

Katsura bowed his head. He looked much better than he had before, and I didn't miss Naomi-san crying covertly.

"Very well. I'm counting on you. Don't let your mother down either."

"I won't." Katsura smiled awkwardly.

I picked up the remote and turned on the TV. The financial news was currently raving about the new IT company on the stock market.

"The initial stock price of the newly listed browser company is two million yen and is expected to rise further. Other Information Technology companies are waiting to be listed, and they are expected to be the most popular investments now that the stock market has steadied.

An American operating systems company is also slated to release the 1998 version of its OS, raising expectations of further activity from the IT industry..."

This was how we would pay back our loans.

The Moonlight Fund had investments in several Japanese and American IT companies, and we'd make plenty of profit if we sold when they became listed, or their stock prices jumped. Enough profit to pay back the many, many loans we took out to ensure our capital in one fell swoop. It probably wouldn't be a bad idea to pay back the Bank of Japan either. Those special loans were mostly just to show that we had money to play with, and if we could restore our bad credit, we wouldn't need the loans anyway.

I switched off the TV. "Why don't we have some tea for now? Both of you will join us, won't you? Ah, and you too, Naomi-san, right?"

I stepped out into the garden while I waited for the tea, and looked up at the clear, blue sky.

"I made it..." I murmured.

I got through it—I survived the tragedy, made it through the misfortune. I hoped my actions would make this world just a little kinder to its people.

"The tea is ready, my lady," Naomi-san called. "Today, I have that cherry cake you love so much!"

"Coming!"

I turned and raced back inside.

GLOSSARY AND NOTES:

HIGH SOCIETY: The stratum of society comprising the nobility and those who work directly for them.

PACIFIC WAR: In the real world, Japan's surrender was unconditional.

BANK OF JAPAN SPECIAL LOAN: The Bank of Japan's trump card.

SPECIAL HIGHER POLICE: A notorious police organization synonymous with the word terror. Communism was its biggest enemy.

COCOM: An abbreviation of Coordinating Committee for Multilateral Export Controls. There was a famous scandal where Toshiba Machine broke these rules.

BALANCE SHEET: A summary of an organization's balances. Reading these along with income statements has the power to change the world.

JUSEN PROBLEM: The main cause of bad debts in real estate. Jusen Corporations fought with the Diet, leading to hesitance on their end. That delay was one of the fatal triggers for the economy.

INTERNET AND BROWSERS: Nowadays indispensable; some of the most famous services come from a company named after glass-paned fixtures and a company beginning with the letter Y.

JAPAN PREMIUM: A premium applied when lending to Japanese banks struggling with bad debts. Simply put, a higher interest rate put in place to protect the lender. A sign of how dire the market situation was.

FOREIGN EXCHANGE MARKET: FX for short. Runa's tricks would have been impossible without the 80 yen to one dollar exchange rate in 1995.

MOF CLERK: A clerk with the task of negotiating with the Ministry of Finance. They now exist as FSA (Financial Services Agency) clerks.

CONVOY SYSTEM: A way of administration that levels the playing field by equalizing everything down to the level of the bank in the worst position. The name comes from the convoys that used to protect transport ships from German submarines during the Second World War. The system is on the brink of collapse due to the relentless attack of foreign money.

ACTORS WITH LAW DEGREES: They exist. You just need to do some research.

HOKKAIDO: Currently split up into 80 percent Japanese, 10 percent Russians, and 10 percent Chinese.

THE NEWLY LISTED BROWSER COMPANY: November 11, 1997. These stocks would jump up to 167.9 million yen in February 2000.

"Smile, my lady!"

Flash!

Naomi-san took the photograph of me in my uniform with an instant camera. On my face was a look that stood somewhere between embarrassment and excitement.

Today was the kindergarten entrance ceremony. Apparently, my kindergarten education had been a source of conflict for the main Keikain family.

My blonde hair stood out, and I was an adult in a child's body. The main family feigned concern about me being bullied and stated that they would rather Tachibana and the maids took care of my education until elementary school. It wasn't the hair or anything though; what they were actually worried about was me getting picked on because of the scandals my father was involved in.

But I said I wanted to go, and so I was going.

"I wanna make friends!"

Imperial Gakushuukan Academy. That's where I'd be going to get my education from elementary school until I was college aged. Everything would be about connections and cliques and who liked you—and who didn't—for over ten years. If things went poorly, it'd end up a living hell. So naturally, I needed to know who my friends and enemies were—and more importantly, I needed to make some allies.

It was that level-headedness that made my maids into allies as I lisped and whined my way into their hearts. They found me a kindergarten that would let me into its senior class. A kindergarten in Den-en-choufu, full of rich kids.

"I'm going now!"

"Goodbye!"

"Bye!"

"My lady, be careful!"

My three maids saw me off as I got into the car. Tachibana was going to drive me to my first day of kindergarten. Even with my former memories, I was still excited to see what this new experience would bring.

I was coming in as a transfer student on the day of the entrance ceremony.

"My name's Keikain Runa! It's nice to meet everyone!" I smiled as I made my greeting in a loud voice.

Even though it was the start of the semester, I was still a transfer student, so naturally I was in the firing line for a ton of questions.

"Where do you live, Keikain-san?"

"What's your favorite food?"

"What picture books do you like?"

"Do you have any dolls?"

"I like your hair! Can I touch it?"

Children. They didn't know the meaning of privacy and personal space at all.

It was the start of spring, and I was busy enjoying my time at kindergarten. I was reading picture books with some other kids when a girl with ponytails came up, carrying a box. Another girl with a bob came following her, a similar box in hand.

"It's Asuka and her mandarins!"

"I told you to call them '*oranges*'! I got some *oranges* from home, and I wanna eat them with everyone!"

"Yay!"

...What?

I stared as the other kids glanced at me and made for the boxes the girls had. Taking out the mandarins nestled inside, they began to eat them together. Then suddenly a mandarin appeared right in front of me. The girl with the ponytails was holding it out to me.

"Here, you can have one too. It's good!"

"Thanks. But this isn't—"

"It's an orange!"

Right. I took the "orange," peeled it, and took a bite. "It *is* good...!"

"See? Have as many as you want! We had a lot of them leftover at home."

I realized now. This was around the time that Japan liberalized imports of beef and oranges, which had been causing friction between itself and the US. I heard it made a lot of mandarin farmers go bust. That didn't make the mandarin I was eating any less sweet or delicious. I'd eaten the whole thing before I realized it. A second was held out in front of me. This time it was the girl with the bob.

"Can I really have this?"

She nodded. I took it gratefully, earning a smile from her. She was cute and looked like a Japanese doll.

"It's nice to meet you! My name's Keikain Runa."

"I'm Kasugano Asuka. This is Kaihouin Hotaru. Nice to meet you too!"

I asked about the mandarins. Apparently, their grandparents sent a whole load to them, and they didn't know what to do with so many, so they started handing them out. People really enjoyed them, and so it became a regular thing. That explanation brought a natural question to mind as I continued eating my mandarin.

"Why are these oranges then?"

"Obviously because it sounds *cooler*! Oranges are in right now! Mandarins are *out*!"

Makes sense to me.

In other words, something in her past caused her to have a deep-seated grudge against mandarins.

Her dad was a member of the Diet, and his electoral district was in Ehime Prefecture, which was famous for its mandarins. It made perfect sense that they had so many.

Hotaru-chan smiled and chomped away at her mandarin as we spoke. She didn't speak much; that much I'd already worked out from her expression. Thankfully, Asuka-chan was there to help her out.

"Hotaru-chan might not talk much, but she's my friend. I was scared she'd be left out at first, so I gave her a mandarin, and then we became *best* friends. So now we're super close!" Asuka-chan hugged Hotaru-chan and nuzzled her.

Hotaru-chan didn't protest, so it seemed they were as close as Asuka-chan claimed.

"I want to be that close to you too."

"Of course you can! Everyone who eats my oranges gets to be my friend!"

Hotaru-chan nodded her agreement, took my hand, and placed a third mandarin in it.

They were good. But three "oranges" was a bit too much.

As I went about my life in kindergarten, I soon noticed the existence of several "rules," one of them being the following:

"Miss! We can't find Hotaru-chan!"

When you played hide-and-seek and Hotaru-chan was the hider, you couldn't win. It might have sounded like a fact more than a rule, but I stood by my definition. It was a rule.

She'd then just appear before time was up, which seemed a little mischievous to me.

But you could be as determined as you liked and use whatever tricks you wanted, but you would never find Hotaru-chan.

She was so good at hide-and-seek, that I wondered whether she was even human at all.

"She's gotta be human, or she couldn't eat my oranges! They're oranges from the generous fields of the Grand Master Tanuki!"

Asuka-chan's constant talk of "oranges" wasn't fooling anyone, so in my opinion she was better off dropping it before she regretted it. There was something else about what she'd just said too.

"The Grand Master Tanuki...?" I asked.

"Yup! He's really strong *and* he can kill any evil spirits with a single blow!!!"

I asked her about it. The Grand Master part came from the famous Koubou Daishi Kuukai, the monk who established the Shikoku Pilgrimage. That much I'd guessed, but the Tanuki part was more mysterious. It apparently referred to a certain tanuki spirit. There was already a famous tanuki spirit in Shikoku, but Ehime apparently boasted one that was even *more* powerful. Long story short: a lot happened, and that tanuki was sealed away in a place that held a connection to Koubou Daishi. The mandarins harvested from the fields nearby were therefore known to have The Grand Master Tanuki's protection.

"And Hotaru-chan *loves* these oranges!" Asuka-chan proclaimed, while Hotaru-chan nodded her agreement.

That was presumably why she assisted with "distributing" them.

"Couldn't we lure her out with those mandarins then?"

"We tried that already. The orange disappeared, but Hotaru was nowhere to be seen!" Asuka-chan frowned and put a hand to her cheek, while Hotaru-chan nodded her agreement.

I wondered if Hotaru-chan even realized we were talking about her.

Hearing all of this was bringing the child within me to life. I wanted to find Hotaru-chan myself. The many thoughts from my previous life had a tendency to weigh me down when it came to other things, but right now I didn't want to worry about that. What good was having a second chance at life if I wasn't going to enjoy my childhood?

I chuckled. "In that case, *I'm* going to find Hotaru-chan!"

I didn't know then that, twenty minutes later, I'd be majorly dispirited, only for Hotaru-chan to appear out of nowhere in front of me.

I chuckled again. "I'll find her using the power of science and money!"

"That's not very mature of you, Runa-chan!"

So, the next day, I came in with a home video camera. It cost a few tens of thousands of yen, so it wasn't cheap, but I *was* a noble lady—that was the kind of money I could spend without a second thought.

Tachibana bought it for me, and then my three maids found it. I made the supreme sacrifice of allowing them to film me for their amusement, and then got it set up in the kindergarten yard.

"Could I get a mandarin, Asuka-chan?"

"You mean an *orange*!"

"Sure, sure."

I placed a sheet in the middle of the yard and put the mandarin on top of it. When Hotaru-chan wandered out of her hiding place to get it, the camera would pick her up. The other kids pointed out that Hotaru-chan might not come out at all. We ignored them and hid, ready for our perfect trap to spring.

"No way! Why isn't she on the tape?!"

"The mandarin's gone!"

One second it was there, the next it was gone. We'd inadvertently filmed a horror movie. Needless to say, we were all terrified. Except for Hotaru-chan, who was happily munching away at a mandarin.

"There's got to be some way to beat her."

I'd failed several times already and ended up with an extra three video cameras in the process. Hotaru-chan didn't show up on any of the film, which was terrifying for sure, but I was now used to it. I was seriously starting to struggle when Asuka-chan, who had known Hotaru-chan for much longer, clapped her fist on her palm.

"Hotaru-chan loves singing! If we sing, maybe she'll join in!"

It was hide-and-seek, not Marco Polo, but I gave it a shot anyway, singing the first thing that came to mind: a song that played on one of those kid shows on public television.

I loved singing in my previous life. I would have loved to do it professionally, but the economic situation meant I didn't get the chance. When I grew up, I forgot all about singing, and then I...

Asuka-chan started clapping next to me, interrupting my train of thought.

"Wow! Amazing! You're such a good singer, Runa-chan!"

Encouraged by her praise, I enthusiastically sang another two or three songs. It wasn't long until the other kids nearby and even the teacher were listening as well as Asuka-chan. In that moment, I remembered just how much I loved singing.

I finished my songs, and suddenly noticed Hotaru-chan in front of me, clapping.

She smiled at me. "You're a really good singer, Runa-chan!"

"*Hotaru-chan spoke*!" everyone cried in unison.

Kindergarten included a daily scheduled nap. Whether it was because kids needed a lot of sleep or because it gave the teachers a break, I wasn't sure.

I may have been in a kid's body, but my mind was totally grown up, so there was...no...way...I'd...*zzz...Ah!*

The blanket on top of me was just so comfortable that I'd fallen asleep, and I woke up to something clinging to me. Actually, some*thing* would've been terrifying—it was more likely to be some*one*. I moved the blanket to one side to see who, but I didn't recognize them.

"Who's this?" I asked the teacher.

It was apparently Amane Mio-chan, a girl in the class below mine. Apparently, she'd wandered off to the bathroom, and the teacher was looking for her because she hadn't come back. Well now we'd found her, but since she was clinging to me and sleeping peacefully, the teacher was waiting for me to wake up. Granted, Amane Mio was clinging to me pretty tightly. The teacher put her hands together and winked at me with a quiet, "sorry," so I gave up and decided to wait for Mio-chan to awaken.

"Hmmgh...?"

"Good day to you. Who are you?"

"Amane Mio. Goodnight, dolly..."

Dang, kids sure had it easy, getting to go back to sleep the second they woke up. The teacher abandoned me with another wink.

And excuse me, I wasn't...a doll...*zzz*...

After that, Amane Mio-chan would come and hug me during nap time every once in a while. She also called me "dolly," largely because she said I looked just like a doll she had at home. I let her get away with it because perhaps I was a bit soft. Her dad was a trader, and the doll she mistook me for was apparently imported. She couldn't sleep without her doll, so she took it with her to kindergarten. The reason she got me mixed up with it was, of course, because of my hair. There was nothing I could really do about that; I was the only girl with blonde hair in the class. And she was only human—and a child at that—so naturally she became curious about me.

"Runa-chan! Let's sleep together!" Asuka-chan said brightly, while Hotaru-chan stood next to her with a pillow.

Come on, you two. If you cling to me while I sleep, where's Mio-chan supposed to go?

Asuka-chan ended up sleeping next to me anyway, but Hotaru-chan clung onto her instead as though she didn't want to leave her side.

"You smell like the sun, Runa-chan!"

"And you smell like mandarins, Asuka-chan!"

"They're *o-ran-ges*!"

"Zzz..."

Asuka-chan was still insistent on her mandarins being "oranges." Hotaru-chan was already fast asleep in the land of dreams. Honestly, I...*zzz*...

I woke up to a heavy weight on my body. Both Mio-chan and Asuka-chan were clinging to me, and Hotaru-chan was clinging to Asuka-chan, so I had the weight of all three of them on me. This time, of course, I cried out to the teacher for help.

"...And they lived happily ever after!"

"Now read this one, dolly!"

"Okay."

Reading to Mio-chan was, of course, going to win her affections, but truth be told, I was happy to dote on her. I was an only child, and Mio-chan felt like a little sister to me. I'd also been playing with Asuka-chan and Hotaru-chan.

But that was when the *incident* happened.

"Waah! Dolly!"

We were playing when Mio-chan suddenly came up to me, wailing and immediately clinging to me. She claimed the boys had been teasing her for being unable to sleep without her doll. To say I was mad was an understatement.

"How dare they?! I'm going to give them a piece of my mind!"

"Wait! If this is about Mio-chan, *I'm* going with you!"

The other one nodded in agreement.

This was what friends were for. Asuka-chan, Hotaru-chan and I charged towards Mio-chan's class.

I cried out, my hands on my hips. "Who was it that made my Mio-chan cry?!"

That was the start of the event nicknamed "Incident of the Pine Corridor, A Battle Against Five Boys," a moment that would become legendary in our kindergarten. It was utter chaos. I got in a fight with some boy, then he got his brothers and friends involved.

I took advantage of the fact they wouldn't fight back so as not to hurt me and went hard on them to teach them a lesson. I managed to get three boys crying and two running in fear before the teacher pulled me away. Their parents were called, and I ended up getting lectured by Tachibana and Keiko-san. After I explained myself, Aki-san shot me several thumbs-up from behind them, and later, brought me some cake as a just reward.

The next day, Mio-chan approached me and dipped her head. "Thank you, Runa-oneechan."

I had to work hard not to burst into tears of joy right then and there. When I graduated from kindergarten, Mio-chan cried and told me she didn't want me to leave, saying she'd held it in for a whole year. But at the very end, she sent me off with a wave.

"It appears Amane-sama's father's trading company isn't doing particularly well," Tachibana mumbled to me on the way home.

I understood what he was trying to say. Imperial Gakushuukan Academy was a private school with an elite program. It was expensive—I wouldn't get to see Mio-chan anymore.

"Do you think I'd be able to save her father from misfortune?"

"It would depend how much you care for Amane-sama, my lady."

Mio-chan was going to have to go to a different school because of her parents. It hit harder because we were so close. I turned to Tachibana and frowned to let him know I wasn't pleased with his answer.

"Since you've looked so much into it, the rest depends on how I feel about it. Is that right?"

It was probably that one incident that pushed Tachibana into researching her and her family. Apart from their business troubles, everything else seemed to have come up clean.

"Tachibana...I want a doll."

"An imported one? That might be difficult. We will probably need to find a proxy who can purchase one for us."

Living meant severed connections. It could also mean using money to *repair* those connections. This connection was one I didn't want to lose. I turned around. Mio-chan was still waving, even though she was nearly out of sight.

"She's like a sister to me. Naturally, I have to look out for her."

I waved back at her. Mio-chan kept on waving until the teacher told her to come back inside.

I made a little space in my bedroom for imported dolls after that. It made Mio-chan incredibly happy whenever she came over to play.

The word "party" in high society essentially meant "battle-ground" though a girl as young as me wasn't usually taken to them. The fact that there was an exception made for me went to show how far removed the main Keikain family considered me.

I was at a Keika hotel in Shinjuku. It was originally a Far Eastern hotel, but as a result of cutting out all the bad debt, several large hotels were rebranded as Keika. This location as well as the ones in Osaka, Kyoto, Nagoya, Sendai, Kobe, Hiroshima, Fukuoka, Hakodate, and Sapporo, received the same treatment. Its resorts, too: the ones in Hokkaido, Karuizawa, and Okinawa. We'd also started developing some smaller resorts, such as the Kurokawa Hot Springs and the Yufuin Hot Springs.

The party was being held on the top floor of the hotel: it was to celebrate the fiftieth birthday of the Keika Group.

"It would be of great aid if you could participate and just give a greeting."

I stood in the waiting room, looking at the invitation to the party, sponsored by the Keikain family. Tachibana was very politely filling me in on the invitation conditions. He said I just needed to stand there, but at this point the main family couldn't really ignore me: thanks to Tachibana and Ichijou's hard work, my investments had grown exponentially. It would only take a minimum of digging to find out that those investments were in my hands. By having me debut this early, the main family were probably looking for a chance to interfere.

"I can do that. I don't need to stay until the very end, do I?"

"No. The master has said you may leave after the greeting and dinner," Tachibana said.

This wasn't just my debut, but a symbol to show that I was

forgiven for my father's transgressions. These sorts of pardons were best to get done sooner rather than later.

"Excuse me, Tachibana-san. There are two guests who have come to see you." Keiko-san appeared then.

"Oh? What are their names?"

Keiko-san looked at the business cards in her hand. "From the Fellowship of Constitutional Government, the minister of finance Izumikawa Tatsunosuke's secretary, and also from the government, Secretary-General Katou Kazuhiro's secretary."

It was clear why these secretaries had come to see him. Everything looked like Tachibana was the one with the power, and these politicians likely wanted to forge some connections with him. The secretaries weren't here to make appointments— they were here to preface the politicians' entrances.

The Ministry of Finance was here because of Keika Bank's work to eliminate various bad debts, while the secretary-general was here because Sakata, where my dad tried to build the base of his operations, was his electoral district. They were in the same party too. While Dietman Izumikawa was the boss, Dietman Katou was his second, and there were rumors that Dietman Katou was pushing his superior to retire for the sake of "generational change."

"I don't know whether they're clever or just lack integrity."

"Elections cost money. Next year's House of Councilors' election is an important one for the ruling party. It marks an opportunity to recover their power. They're likely looking to gain all the allies they can to make sure everything goes to plan."

Both Minister Izumikawa and Secretary-General Katou were listed as candidates for the next prime minister and party president respectively, so this would also be a case of picking which one to back.

"We have enough money to hedge our bets and back both of them," I said. "Would that be acceptable?"

"That is not a bad suggestion, but it would likely lead to neither of them considering us their ally in full."

To simplify Japanese political parties and think of them as merely socialism or liberalism was bound to lead anyone into a sticky situation. Basically, it was more about whether a politician favored military power or naval power—opinions that then *manifested* as socialism or liberalism. Those who lived on Japan's west coast had a long relationship with the mainland, so they were more likely to favor the former. That said, allying with America after the war made the latter—liberalism—mainstream, and so most Japanese political parties had a mix of both sides among their politicians.

As for the two we were seeing, Dietman Izumikawa favored naval power while Dietman Katou was more in favor of focusing on the military side of things. Dietman Katou had more influence than the other. He had the support of the currently largest faction within the Fellowship of Constitutional Government: The Hashizume Faction, known as the "corps," and a group with Japan's political world in its grip.

"I think we'll have a better idea of who we favor after I debut. Try to keep things vague with them for now in order to avoid upsetting either of them."

"Certainly, my lady."

It was almost time for the event to begin when there was a knock at the waiting room door.

"Who is it?" Aki-san called out.

"Pardon the interruption. I am Katou's secretary, from the Fellowship of Constitutional Government. I came to see you earlier. Mr. Katou has expressed his desire to meet the young lady."

The secretary stepped in with Secretary-General Katou. You could tell he was currently at the peak of power because of the spirited vitality he exuded. He met my gaze. There was some sort of deep emotion in his eyes.

"A pleasure to meet you, my lady. Your father did a great deal for me. Please allow me to apologize for being unable to save him." He lowered his head to me. Me, a preschooler. I took it as his way of atoning.

"Not at all. Please, raise your head. I should be the one bowing to *you*."

The construction of the chemical plant at the root of the scandal had backing from the prefecture and city authorities. As a dietman, it would have caused Katou a lot of work both out in the open and behind the scenes. My father practically threw mud on his name, and the names of others like him.

"Children cannot choose their parents. And do not worry. I fully intend to properly atone for what happened," I said.

By atone, I meant provide financial support. Secretary-General Katou looked reassured by my words as he left. He also mentioned that he wanted to attend as much of the party as he could.

"Is there some sort of fancy public works project going on in Yamagata?" I asked Tachibana.

He said that the Yamagata Shinkansen line had just started being extended to Shinjou, and that Keika Bank was among those financing the new construction. Apparently, the funding was already being discussed back when Far Eastern Bank still existed. With all the twists and turns, mergers, Far Eastern Bank's name change, and the new focus on its bad debts, there were those within Yamagata who were worried the bank would pull out of funding the project. That was why the prospering secretary-general showed up and lowered his head before me: all so that he could check my stance on the matter.

"Contact Ichijou. Please ask him to send a message from the bank to Yamagata and reassure them that we will continue financing the shinkansen line construction. If the bank can't afford it, we'll finance it with the Moonlight Fund."

People gathered wherever there was money.

The party hadn't even started yet.

I was properly dressed—properly smiling, properly prepared.

I gave my cheeks a light slap before leaving the bathroom. My outfit was the uniform I would be wearing to my elementary school. This was a *formal* event, after all.

"Announcing Keikain Runa-sama, of the Keikain Dukedom."

I walked through the doors to a round of applause and several indescribable stares. I strained my ears to the voices in the crowd.

"Runa-sama, hm? I heard she only received the Keikain name because the family had no direct female descendants..."

"I doubt she'll be welcomed by anyone who knows about the Far Eastern Group scandal..."

"Yes, and did you know it is the remnants of the *same* Far Eastern Group that is backing her?"

"Why ever for? I understand she is a legitimate successor, but wasn't the Far Eastern Group so laden with bad debts that it was to be disposed of?"

"I heard her butler is *quite* the skilled manager. It was he who pulled off the successful merger between Far Eastern Bank and Hokkaido Kaitaku Bank."

"Ah, yes. That unusual merger where the smaller bank swallowed up the larger one. They called it a clutch homerun, as I recall. It even granted Far Eastern the glorious Keika name: Keika Bank. Didn't the same thing happen to Sankai Securities and Ichiyama Securities so that they're now *Keika* Securities? I don't think Far Eastern Bank will be in trouble after all that, and now that they have special loans from the Bank of Japan."

"*Especially* since they dealt with the bad debts that arose from those mergers."

"Far Eastern Developments filed for corporate rehabilitation, and Far Eastern Hotels renewed their entire management staff, so they were able to unload their debt to the Resolution and Collection Corporation to deal with. The decent resorts that belonged to Hokkaido Kaitaku Bank are now being managed under the Keika Hotels, and not Far Eastern Hotels. This party is to unveil Keika Bank and Keika Hotels as new core parts of the Group. It's no wonder the Far Eastern affiliates would want to put in some effort, and back Runa-sama."

"I doubt the head family and other branches are going to be amused though..."

If they were trying to keep their voices down, they were failing. It wasn't the sort of conversation they should be allowing a bright-eyed grade-schooler to overhear, but I put it down to them thinking I wouldn't understand any of it.

Thanks to my grandfather Keikain Hikomaro's debauchery, there were seven families aside from the main Keikain House. My father's known to carry his blood, resulting in about twenty children. Dividing property among them would require dissolving the zaibatsu and things would end up in family squabbles, so like most larger zaibatsu, the Keika Group formed a company to manage its assets, which handed out funds to descendants in the form of dividends.

As someone on the fringe of the family, I didn't receive any of those dividends. My money didn't come from the family; it came from the Far Eastern Bank, or rather, the Moonlight Fund.

"That's the girl who dreamt up the Keika Bank?"

"That's her. Keikain Runa-sama. It's her butler and the Far Eastern Bank's executive who handle the management side of things, but she is the bank's *owner*."

"I know times are desperate, but to think a child built up a huge finance conglomerate... There's a regional bank, some low-level metropolitan banks, a couple of big securities companies, and even some insurances companies in there. It's incredible to think of, if not downright terrifying."

"I've heard the Ministry of Finance plans to use them to try and test the waters on lifting the ban on holdings companies."

"Keika Holdings. I know, I know. Though it'll really be under the *Ministry's* control."

"Which is why everyone's so hungry for it—and precisely why we're here."

Those seats were occupied with several people related to the Iwazaki Group. The family head's late wife had connections to the group, which was why they were in attendance. What with the current economic big bang encouraging the settlement of bad debts and drastic changes in financial administration, Keika Holdings must have looked like a particularly delicious piece of meat for them to set their sights on gobbling up. They probably saw me as the stepping-stone to get to it.

I gave a precocious, ladylike greeting to the man at the center of this party.

"It has been a long time, Kiyomaro-ojisama."

"Congratulations on your new school, Runa. You certainly are a fine young lady."

Duke Keikain Kiyomaro—the current head of the Keikain House. He was just over fifty years old and looked like a well-mannered gentleman at first glance. His suit was put together by a first-rate tailor, and the glass in his hand was filled with Macallan whiskey. Mild-mannered though he seemed, Keikain Kiyomaro was the leader of the Keika Group, which all started with Keika

Pharmaceuticals, a company boasting over one hundred billion yen in sales. There was definitely something more to him than meets the eye.

"I heard you appeared before Ichijou-san one day and caused him somewhat of a headache."

"I'm sorry, Uncle. I just wanted some grape juice so, so badly. And all Tachibana and Ichijou-san would talk about was complicated matters."

Tachibana was the face of this operation. Everyone else must have seen me simply as the motive behind his actions. I wondered what they'd think if they knew the truth.

My uncle laughed. "Ha! That must have been strenuous indeed. Although I would like them to get into even *bigger* matters myself."

I plastered a smile on my face, but beads of cold sweat were springing up beneath my uniform. I shouldn't have been surprised: with their track record thus far, it should have been no wonder that my uncle wanted to put them to better use.

"No, Uncle! No! Tachibana is *my* butler!" I spoke like a toddler whose favorite toy was being taken away. I doubted it would be enough to reverse my uncle's plans, but it should at least elicit some measure of consideration from him.

"I know, my dear. Runa, it is not my intention to relieve him from that role. But Ichijou-kun seems to have a high opinion of him. That is why I wish to prepare a suitable position for him within Keika Bank. I shall ensure you have extra staff to make up for the loss."

What was I supposed to think about that?

As far as the main family was concerned, I was nothing more than a pawn to be married off for convenience. They probably wanted to prevent other people from targeting my wealth, which they could do by sending staff to me. Likewise, they probably preferred to have people they could use at the center of the group's operations. Currently, they didn't have anyone directly linked to the main family in the newer parts of the Keika Group.

As a grade-schooler, there was only one answer I could give.

"Please don't make Tachibana work so hard. I should like to ask for more confectionaries too!"

"Of course, my lady."

I pretended to get mad, at which point I was offered a plate of desserts by Keikain Nakamaro-oniisama. He was the sole son of Kiyomaro-ojisama, who had graduated college this spring and was now working in Keika Pharmaceuticals. His gentle smile was only heightened by the glasses on his face, which gave him an intellectual air. His glossy, dark hair was in vibrant contrast to my own—and today, he wore a brown suit. In the game, Runa saw him as an elder brother, but I knew when it came to my eventual ruin, Nakamaro-oniisama would be nowhere to be found. With what I knew about the internal situation of the Keika Group, it recently occurred to me that my "ruin" might have been a purge of those associated with the original Far Eastern Group.

"Yummy! This dessert is absolutely *delicious*!"

"I believe that one is called a waffle. Since you have finished your greeting, would you like to come and eat it over here, Runa?"

"Yes, Oniisama!"

Naturally, I knew it was called a waffle. I was the one who brought these treats over from Belgium. They were to be the centerpiece of Keika Hotel's dessert selection. But that was irrelevant right now; I put on my best smile and let myself be lured in by the delightful scent of the waffles. I let Nakamaro-oniisama lead me away, at which point the next guest entered.

"Announcing the head of the Teia Group, Teia Shuuichi-sama, and his son, Teia Eiichi-sama."

That was when I realized: this was the evening I was to meet *him*.

The Teia Group was a young zaibatsu formed after the war, growing by trying its hand at everything from textiles to automobiles. At present, Teia Motor Company dominated the global automobile market as a top-class manufacturer. As for its position as a zaibatsu, it placed on the outskirts of the Futaki Group, a major zaibatsu that had been around since the pre-war era. In terms of profit, the Teia Group had been doing excellently as of late.

There had been constant rumors of reshuffling within the group ever since the burst of the bubble caused its damage. If I remembered correctly, it was either Teia Shuuichi's grandfather, or his great-grandfather, who married a woman from the Futaki Group. Other rumors mentioned the Teia Group attempting to take the initiative by teaming up with Shibaura Electric Co., Ishihari Shipbuilding Co., Fusoufilm, and other affiliates of the Futaki Group.

The Group's big three—Futaki Honsha, Futaki Bank, and Futaki & Co.—were said to be against these alliances, according to the high-class grapevine. With such intricate rumors as these, I wouldn't be surprised if they were all somewhat close to the truth.

"I thank you for your invitation, Your Grace."

"I hardly deserve such a title, but it certainly doesn't displease to hear it in a place like this."

There were still scraps of the nobility system left after the war, at which point it went through several reforms. Thus, the granting of lifelong peerages and the acquisition of noble blood through marriage meant nobility was very much still alive.

That was how the Keikain family was still considered part of the nobility, and a powerful part at that, thanks to the businesses it owned. Whether for prestige or profit, there were several people who were hungry for Keikain blood.

Teia Shuuichi looked in my direction. Unsurprisingly, as my blonde hair was a rare sight here among so many with solely Japanese heritage.

"A pleasure to meet you. My name is Keikain Runa, sir."

"What a pleasant young lady you are. Judging by your uniform, you will be attending the same school as Eiichi."

Eiichi-kun was indeed wearing my school's uniform, which I'd anticipated from my knowledge of the game. Furthermore, Imperial Gakushuukan Academy was a prestigious school in one of Tokyo's top districts, offering classes from kindergarten age right up until college age, while at the same time accepting excellent students from outside who passed the entrance exams at their time of switching schools.

"Eiichi, I need to speak with His Grace for a while. Why not go and enjoy yourself with Runa-san?"

"Are you sure that's all right?" I asked. "People have a lot to say about me."

Time seemed to freeze.

I was referring to the scandal regarding the Keikain family. Everyone among the class of people in attendance should have known about it. And yet I knew the adults hadn't expected *me* of all people to bring it up so boldly.

"Runa... Where did you hear about such things?" Kiyomaro-ojisama asked, eyes dimming and losing their kind smile.

In return, I gave him my most radiant, childlike smile. It was clear from his expression that he was concealing how furious he was at my behavior.

"I can't remember," I said, glancing at where the members of the branch family and those close to them sat. My uncle and cousin picked up on what I was implying immediately.

"I see. Let us speak about it later. Go and spend some time with Eiichi-kun over there for now."

"Yes, Ojisama!"

Eiichi-kun looked a little confused. I took his hand and led him quickly to one end of the room. He didn't speak until I let go.

"You're..." he paused. "Weird."

"I'll take that as a compliment, thank you very much! The grown-ups can talk about the difficult matters now. Why don't we go on an adventure and have some fun?"

In the game, Teia Eiichi received a privileged education, which resulted in him becoming an arrogant character who was good at everything. Of course, he wasn't quite that arrogant at this age.

"Huh? *Hey*! Where are you going?" Eiichi-kun followed me out of the hall.

He had an escort with him, who I called over to whisper in his ear.

The escort smiled wryly once I was done. "That is usually something one would ask the wait staff."

"Well, I can't ask them. They would just say it's bad for me and not let me have it. Which would be *incredibly* rude, don't you think?"

"Hey. What exactly are you trying to do...?" Eiichi-kun asked, looking a little anxious.

Luckily for them both, help arrived in short order.

"What is going on here?" Nakamaro-oniisama asked with a dubious frown.

"My Lord. Miss Runa..."

I pulled out a 500-yen coin from my pocket, showing it to my cousin as though it were a precious gem.

I placed a hand on my hip and smiled smugly at him. "Oniisama. I want to get a juice box from the first-floor vending machine!"

All three males stared at me. It was Nakamaro-oniisama who said what they were all thinking.

"Runa. You could simply ask the escort to get it for you, or even better, ask one of the wait staff."

"No one understands! Not even *you*, Oniisama!" I put on my most adult voice to give a most childish explanation.

In the game, there was a scene between Eiichi-kun and the heroine where they went shopping together, and Eiichi-kun struggled because he didn't know how to use money. For the most part, I'd been planning to leave Eiichi-kun alone, but I did feel bad for him. So I decided to at least teach him a thing or two about how to function as a normal person, especially since I was here anyway.

Also, I just wanted some juice.

"I want to *buy* something *from the vending machine*. That sort of thing is important because I'm going to elementary school already!"

Sometimes, it was as though my soul took its cues from my body, turning my mood completely childish. Then again, I was happiest as a child, and I wanted to cherish my second chance at childhood.

Nakamaro-oniisama sighed and took my hand. "If you insist. I shall accompany you. Please come with us, Eiichi-kun. That is, as long as you are all right to comply with Runa's *selfish* request?"

"I'll come along," Eiichi-kun said, his expression suggesting he'd rather do anything else.

Nakamaro-oniisama led me to the elevator. Eiichi-kun and his escort got on after us, and the doors closed behind them.

"Eiichi-kun," Nakamaro-oniisama began.

"Yes?"

I listened closely, pretending I was more interested in the Shinjuku nightscape through the glass.

"You can see what sort of girl Runa is. She has always been somewhat of an outcast, both within the family and at kindergarten. It would be more reassuring if you promised to be her friend."

"...I'll think about it."

Hey! At least pretend you'll do it.

We made it down to the first-floor vending machines without me voicing my thoughts. The juice I was after was proudly situated at the very top row of the machine, with the button to select it just below. At the time, I was only 120 centimeters tall.

"I can't reach it...!" I hopped up and down with tears in my eyes. I suddenly felt Nakamaro-oniisama lifting me up. "Ah!"

"Which would you like?"

"This one! Grape juice!"

It wasn't solely juice; the drink was only 30 percent grape juice, which was what made it so sweet and delicious. I'd loved that nostalgic taste in my past life when I was part of the ordinary masses. Nakamaro-oniisama lifted me up so I could press the button on the machine for my grape juice.

"Yay!"

"Well done. Now you need to put your money in."

"Wait! Don't put me down yet!"

I pressed three more buttons: two coffees and one cola. When Nakamaro-oniisama placed me down, I handed one coffee to him and another to the escort. I passed the cola to Eiichi-kun. They were thanks for coming down with me. I guessed that Eiichi-kun didn't have cola at home, which was why I was giving some to him now.

"Thank you for coming with me. Let's all drink together. Cheers!"

"Cheers!"

"Wow! This has *bubbles* in it!"

"Yes, and you can drink them!"

Eiichi-kun's eyes widened as he took a sip of the cola and tasted the carbonation. I smiled in satisfaction. It seemed I'd given him a taste for it, because from then on, I saw him drinking it every now and then.

"Why are there two grade-school kids here?"

"They've even got the little backpacks! They shouldn't be here!"

"Wait, so if we fail this, does that make us less capable than grade-schoolers?! That'd be humiliating!"

"It is time. Please begin."

It was Sunday and we were in an examination hall. The room was filled with boys and girls in suits, and then there was us two in our elementary school uniforms. We stuck out like a pair of sore thumbs.

I wanted to get some qualifications under my belt, just in case I couldn't avoid my downfall. There were three particular level three qualifications, which, if you applied for jobs with, were said to be of no use whatsoever.

They were as follows: Bookkeeping, level three. Secretary, level three. English, level three.

There was a very simple reason.

Even without the qualifications, your skills in these areas could be assessed via a written exam, something taken by every current candidate regardless. This wiped out the difference between those with and without those three qualifications.

I was enjoying my exciting second childhood, but right now, the classes were at the level where I could sleep through them and still keep on top of things, no problem.

Which was why I'd found some free time to get myself some qualifications. I never imagined there to be a boy of similar age to me who'd been thinking along the same lines. He was wearing the uniform for Gakushuukan too.

"Hey, can I talk to you?"

I was putting my stationery away in my backpack after the exam when he came up to me. Although he was still a grade-schooler, I could already tell he was the intellectual, mild-mannered type. I stared at him. I knew that face from somewhere.

"Is something the matter?" I asked.

"I'd think you'd want to talk to me too. We're both elementary-schoolers who had the same idea of taking these exams."

"Yes, you're right."

Our conversation didn't make it sound like we were in grade school at all—but you just needed to simply look at our appearances. This would be a good time to mention that I had

Tachibana waiting outside in the hallway, while this boy had his own attendant there who also seemed to be his butler.

Suited students were shooting us curious looks as they rushed past us to leave, as though we came from another world.

"Since I managed to catch you, why not speak with me a little?"

"Certainly. Although it might be easier if we knew each other's names." I extended my hand out to him to introduce myself, like you see in romantic dramas.

He took my hand and began to lead me as we walked. And we were still just elementary-schoolers wearing our backpacks. There was no sight more surreal, but we both had the dignity and background to justify it.

"My name is Keikain Runa."

"Might you be from *that* Keikain family? My name is Izumikawa Yuujirou."

Ah, Izumikawa Yuujirou—he was another potential love interest.

With the Kanto region as its base, the Izumikawa family had produced generation after generation of big-name dietmen for the ruling parties, strengthening the Izumikawa's influence. One of those dietmen was this boy's father, Dietman Izumikawa Tatsunosuke, the minister of finance and a man who was influential enough to give a greeting at my party the other evening. He, along with the Ministry of Finance and the politicians associated with it, were currently facing heavy criticism over the current bad debt situation. However, the fact that the Ministry was still sticking to the convoy system earned praise from Nagatachou and Kasumigaseki.

In reality, all that had happened was that the struggling banks were passed over to a zaibatsu: i.e., our bank. Not that I had anything to complain about.

That achievement spurred rumors that he had put himself forward for the race to become Japan's next Prime Minister, throwing his political faction into the center of a maelstrom.

"Would you like to get some juice while we are here?" I asked.

"Yes, that sounds good. I shall treat you to some. Although a 120 yen is hardly much for a treat."

"Oh? A 120 yen is a lot of money to an elementary-schooler. That's enough to buy yourself 12 pieces of ten-yen chocolate at a small candy store!"

"Hm?"

It could also buy you twice as many five-yen chocolates: 24 pieces, in fact. This was the stage of life where arithmetic's main purpose was for working out how much candy you could buy from the store with the hundred-yen coin you were given—although you didn't see many of the candy stores I was referencing these days.

"What would you like, Keikain-san?"

"Grape juice!"

"And I'll have my usual," Yuujirou-kun informed his butler, who returned shortly with some grape juice and a bottle of milk tea from the vending machine.

We unscrewed the caps from our bottles and knocked them together. There was nothing like the sweet taste of grape juice after an exam. Yuujirou-kun seemed to be thinking along the same lines in regards to his tea.

"I was curious about these vending machines. A friend of mine was bragging about them recently, so I decided to try out some of these drinks myself. This was my favorite. I always crave something sweet after an exam, probably as a result of concentrating so hard."

"I know what you mean." I paused. "Oh? Would this friend of yours happen to like cola?"

"Oh, I didn't realize you knew Eiichi-kun."

"It's more than that. I was the one who gave him cola for the first time!"

We'd placed our backpacks down on a nearby bench to drink and chat together. There was nothing unusual about that...as long as you discounted the fact that this was a high-level exam venue, there were students in suits constantly walking back and forth, and there were two butlers standing in front of us elementary-schoolers as if to protect us.

"Which qualifications are you hoping to get, Keikain-san?" Yuujirou-san asked.

Again, we were elementary-schoolers.

"Bookkeeping, level three. Secretarial Skills, level three, and English, level three. Perhaps also Office Specialist Computing and a Class B license for Group Four hazardous materials."

"Group Four hazardous materials?"

Materials with high combustibility were classified as hazardous materials under the Fire Service Act. The qualification covered the handling of materials like gasoline, diesel oil, and kerosene.

The qualification was in high demand for jobs at gas stations and the like, and so it was a multiple-choice exam. That didn't make the exam easy to pass, however.

"There are no pre-conditions to sitting the exam. The local fire station offers short courses for it too, which definitely are useful."

"Hmm... I suppose I might try for it too, then."

"Which exams are you sitting?"

"The same as you, save for the hazardous materials one. And perhaps the real-estate broker exam."

"Real estate?! I thought you had to be an adult to take that one?"

You couldn't officially call yourself a real-estate broker without passing said exam, although it was a qualification which had changed names over the years. It was also a qualification currently in high demand and was required for starting your own real-estate agent. For that reason alone, it was difficult.

"You need to be an adult to *become* a real-estate broker. Not if you simply wish to sit the exam. I'm the youngest child of four siblings, but as my father is a dietman, I need to do something related to law, and real-estate brokerage is a good starting point. My intention is to pass the exam now and do a training course once I'm an adult. I'm also planning to earn the license to be an administrative scrivener, of course."

"Are you also going to take the tax accountant exam or the

judicial scrivener exam to someday become an attorney then?" I asked, watching my butler recycle my empty can of juice.

A smile unbefitting of an elementary-schooler appeared on Yuujirou-kun's face as he looked up at the ceiling.

"That would be ideal, but I'm sure the election will interfere with things. It doesn't matter if you're running for prefectural assembly member or city councilor, when you're running for a district, whether you have a family or not can change everything. That's why being born to a dietman is so tough."

"Oh? It sounds to me as though being born to nobility is even tougher. Twice as tough if you're part of a zaibatsu that's currently under heavy criticism."

"It would seem we both have a lot to deal with."

"Indeed."

I'll say it again and again: we were elementary-schoolers. *New* elementary-schoolers—mere first-graders.

We passed our respective qualifications and went on to study together in the school library from time to time. Eiichi-kun would go on to join these sessions, much to my amusement. He listened to us talk about our qualifications, spurring him on to go out and sweep up his own at incredibly high speed.

Otome game love interests really were something else...

Somehow, Teia Eiichi, Izumikawa Yuujirou, Gotou Mitsuya, and I came to be known as the Gakushuukan Quartet. By whose curious naming, I don't know. The following describes how we met our final member, Gotou Mitsuya-kun.

There was a certain café in a quiet residential neighborhood in Tokyo. That café, which was a hideaway of sorts, was called Avanti. I wasn't just a small girl who drank nothing but grape juice; sometimes I liked having a suitable dessert to go with it. Eiichi-kun and Yuujirou-kun, who were studying with me in the library, were eager too; at that age, kids don't give romance a second thought. It's all about the food.

"This is the place. The desserts here are some of my favorites."

"*More* food? Didn't you just have a ton of popcorn at the cinema?"

"Eiichi-kun, there's something you should know about girls. When it comes to sweet things, they're bottomless pits!"

"Yes. Until they get on the scales and start *screaming*."

"Are you sure you want to start this fight with me, Yuujirou-kun?"

"Fine, fine. I shall leave it there."

We stepped into the café with our respective butlers, who acted as our guardians. Before this, we had been to see a movie. I had insisted that movies looked better on big screens and had confused the boys by not booking out the entire theater for ourselves. I wanted to teach them what it meant to go see a movie like the rest of society.

The film we saw was an animated—anime—movie, one that broke several records in Japan and would become popular even with non-anime fans later on. I'd seen movies several times on TV, but there really was nothing like watching them on the big screen with friends. That was where movies truly shined.

"I realized while watching that I'm actually descended from the side who wanted to get that thing's head, so I kind of understand how she felt. Oh, I'll have a tiramisu and a cream soda."

"I've never seen you order anything except grape juice," Eiichi-kun remarked. "I dunno about the movie's ending. I get that the environment's important, but with what all happened, the people of the Irontown wouldn't be able to work and make a living anymore. Ah, I'll have a Sacher torte and a cola."

"You're rather confident in your beliefs, aren't you?" Yuujirou-kun said. "My family is descended from samurai. Therefore, I cannot ignore the way the protagonists and the villagers chose to live. Actually, all three of us are descended from the protagonists' enemies. Mm, I'll have a royal milk tea and a panna cotta."

We exchange our thoughts on the movie with enthusiasm as we sat at the sunny table, all wearing age-appropriate clothing. The delectable desserts soon arrived, and we prepared to eat.

I was suddenly struck with the realization that this was a very normal way to spend one's day—out with friends after a trip to the cinema. It was something I hadn't done much of in my previous life.

"*Ahem!*" A forced cough from the next table over caught my attention.

"Oh, sorry. Were we being too loud?"

The boy who turned around was no other than Gotou Mitsuya-kun. He was there by himself reading a book, his glasses positioned firmly on his nose. In front of him on the table was a steaming café latte.

"Hm? Doesn't that kid go to Gakushuukan too?" Eiichi-kun said.

"Yes, I believe his name is Gotou Mitsuya," Yuujirou-kun said.

"How do you know his name?"

It was Eiichi-kun who answered my question, and by all means it was an answer I should have come up with myself.

"Exam results table. He's always above you, right?" Eiichi-kun said to Yuujirou-kun.

"Oh."

It all made sense. The three boys always got full marks and were at the top of the tables. I tended to make a few careless mistakes, and generally came in fourth. It was normal for boys at this age to form rivalries based on close test results.

"I've met him several times at his father's dinner parties, largely because his father is a budget analyst."

More specifically, a budget analyst in the Ministry of Finance's budget division. Essentially the head of the main budget division, which was the most bureaucratic of the Ministry's divisions. He was practically guaranteed to become the next vice minister. Nepotism was the name of the game in the upper echelons of the Ministry, and you were sure to find a connection between any two people.

With that in mind, it might not be a bad idea to make a connection right now. We were destined to have such a connection in the future anyway.

"Excuse me. Why not come over and speak with us?" As a girl, I was in the best position to offer an invitation.

But Mitsuya-kun was arrogant—and a bookworm. He merely glanced in our direction. Trying to get him to open up was an interesting challenge, in terms of the game—but I already had the trump card I needed in my possession.

"I'm reading that book too. Wouldn't you like to discuss it?"

Interest flashed in Mitsuya-kun's eyes. Not to be left behind, the other two read the title of the book he had in his hands.

I smiled. "The characters have slightly mysterious powers, and while they don't perform any fantastic feats, it's a satisfying read. I hope this won't spoil you on anything, but I particularly liked the story in the middle about the time slip, and the one near the end about the musician with good ears."

"Don't worry. This is my second time reading. I like the one about the musician too." There was a hint of surprise in Mitsuya-kun's eyes. I smiled at him.

"Order me a copy of that book."

"And me too."

The other boys gave their respective butlers their orders. Since I was here, I figured I might as well sell him on another book I liked.

"Let me give you a book recommendation. I think you'll like it. It came out very recently."

"Hey, Runa," Eiichi-kun began. "That ending made no sense whatsoever!"

"I quite liked it, especially when the old lady used the ticket," Yuujirou-kun said.

"The first part was almost *too* impactful. But I believe this part is what you liked about it, Keikain."

A few days later, there were four of us sharing our thoughts in the school library. These were the three boys would end up condemning me later, but we were so close right now. In my small world, the game's tragic resolution didn't make any sense.

"Wait, Aki-san! Stop that! It's *embarrassing*!"

"But my lady, you've bought it now, so it would be a waste not to use it. Go on: smile!"

"I only needed it briefly at kindergarten."

"Don't worry. I already took as many videos as I could while you were still at that age!"

"Wait, what sort of video are you trying to take right now?! Keiko-san! Stop her!"

"I'm afraid I still do not agree with your motives to buy three video cameras in the first place, My Lady," was Keiko-san's response.

"It was a mistake..." I replied.

"My lady! This is a *momentous* occasion! The open day at Imperial Gakushuukan Academy! Please, smile!"

"Naomi-san, I am hardly in the mood for smiling right now," I protested. "I am trying to take a photograph myself! You smiling people over there, please get in the shot! That's an order from Lady Keikain herself!"

"Yes, of course. My name is Sone Mitsukane. I will be driving the young lady to school."

"I am also assigned as her driver. My name is Akanezawa Saburou. We will both be taking turns driving her to school."

Aki-san giggled. "And this is just why I've bought a new car!"

"Aki-san, wouldn't the old car have been good enough? I'm not particularly fussy over what sort of car I'm seen in."

"It is about more than appearances, my lady," Akanezawa-san explained. "A fancy car deters ignorant people from driving into it. It is all a part of keeping you safe."

"That's right. Additionally, as Tachibana-san becomes busier, he will be required to drive more often. As such, it is important he has a comfortable vehicle in which to do so," Sone said.

"I remember now!" Aki-san said. "It was because you mentioned that before I bought this Benz specifically!"

"I appreciate the concern for my health. Now, I think it is about time we get going."

"*What*?! Oh, it's so late already!" I exclaimed. "See you later, Naomi-san! Bye, Akanezawa-san!"

"Have a nice time," Akanezawa-san said.

"I'll take care of the house, so don't worry about a thing!" Naomi-san reassured me.

"Wait! My lady, what are you doing?" Keiko-san asked quickly.

"You have to be in the frame too! I can't just have a video of me by myself in front of the school gates, can I? You're dressed well enough for it!"

"I'm dressed this way because I am acting as your *guardian*."

"Oh, don't make a fuss!" Aki-san said. "This is a special occasion! And this way, we can keep a memory of you in that suit for all time!"

"You too, Aki-san?" Keiko-san sighed.

"It's a fantastic suit! You can't even tell how old—wait, I didn't say anything!"

"All right..."

"But seeing her in a branded suit after all this time is definitely excit—*Wait*, I didn't say anything either!"

"My lady! Aki-san! Remember that silence is *golden*!" Keiko-san playfully rebuked us.

"Of course..." Aki-san replied. "Since you're here too Tachibana-san, you should get in the frame as well!"

"...I would find it a little awkward."

"Come on! Do it for the sake of our lady! This is an important time in her life!"

"That's right!" I added. "You should be in the video too!"

"If I must..."

"You know, Keiko-san, I think you must be frozen in time or something," I said. "No matter how far back I try to remember, I feel like you haven't changed a bit."

"Interestingly enough, my lady, I feel much the same way," Aki-san agreed.

"Yes. She is eternally beautiful."

"Tachibana-san! What are you saying?!" Keiko-san cried.

"You wear that suit so well," I said. "I hope I can grow up to be a lady like you."

"Oh! Good morning, Runa-chan!"

"Asuka-chan! Good morning! Attention, everyone! This is my friend from kindergarten, Kasugano Asuka-chan!"

"Huh? What's this? We're on *TV*? Oh, um! I'm Kasugano Asuka! Nice to meet you all!"

"Where's Hotaru-chan?" I asked.

"She should be here—"

"Ah!"

"My lady! That little girl just appeared out of nowhere!"

"Don't worry. She's our friend too: meet Kaihouin Hotaru-chan."

Hotaru-chan nodded.

"She's rather quiet," Keiko-san remarked.

"*This* was the girl I wanted to catch on all those video cameras."

"Oh, this is her?"

"What are you guys doing?"

"Eiichi-kun! Hello! We're taking a video, as you can see. Come on. You can be in it too!"

"Why? I'm not your family or anything..."

"Who's this, Runa-chan?" Asuka-chan asked.

Hotaru-chan, meanwhile, was just watching the proceedings with a smile.

"Hello, to the adult Runa," I began. "You haven't fallen to ruin or anything yet, have you? You're not breaking your back at some silly job that was forced on you by society, are you? My future still has a spark of hope in it, right?"

"Please don't say such pessimistic things with such a straight face, my lady..."

"I'm just giving my future self a warning so I don't end up in a sad state. At present, I'm incredibly happy. Adult Runa, are you happy? Even if you're not, I hope you'll remember the times when you once were. Remember the times when you used to smile like I do. To my future self... You may have forgotten how to smile, so I'm sending you my smile so you'll find your happiness again."

"You're such a weirdo," Eiichi-kun muttered.

"Ah! The battery's low! Where's the—"

That was when the video cut to black.

GLOSSARY AND NOTES:

THE LIBERALIZATION OF IMPORTS OF BEEF AND ORANGES: A process that started in 1991. The Kasugano family, with its position within the Ministry of Agriculture, Forestry, and Fisheries, strongly opposed the move. Their daughter was a frontline witness to their opposition. The Kasugano family have large mandarin groves at their family home in Ehime prefecture.

THE MASTER TANUKI: A legendary monster tanuki, in our reality sealed away by the power of the Usa Hachimanguu Shrine, but in this story sealed away by Koubou Daishi.

MINNA NO UTA (TRANSLATION: EVERYONE'S SONGS): A short television program featuring songs. Runa's favorite songs are: Makkuramori no Uta (Song of the Dark Forest), Tsuki no Waltz (Waltz of the Moon), and Metropolitan Museum.

THE DOLL: An antique bisque doll. Expensive, naturally.

MILITARY AND NAVAL: Based on the geopolitics of Mahan. They are more commonly known as land power and sea power respectively.

YAMAGATA SHINKANSEN SHINJOU EXTENSION: The construction of the Yamagata route lent itself nicely to an extension to Shinjou, but that same construction meant that the route went no further.

MERGERS IN WHICH A SMALL COMPANY BECOMES THE DOMINANT ONE: This has the advantage of avoiding losses from the merger and the includes the possibility of minimizing the deficit.

KARUIZAWA: Hosted an event at the 1998 Winter Olympics, which took place in Nagano.

KUROKAWA HOT SPRINGS: Became popular in 1998.

WAFFLES: Became popular in 1997.

MACALLAN: An expensive single malt whiskey for the discerning drinker.

IWAZAKI ZAIBATSU: One of Japan's biggest zaibatsu. There are several companies bearing the Iwazaki name, all under the three umbrellas of heavy industry, commercial business, and banking.

TEIA GROUP: A car manufacturer.

FUTAKI ZAIBATSU: A zaibatsu surviving from an Edo-period draper's shop.

LIFELONG PEERAGE: Similar to life peerages in the United Kingdom.

THE PRICE OF JUICE: During this time, it was still 120 yen per can.

NAGATACHOU AND KASUMIGASEKI: Jargon for political circles and government officials respectively.

THE MOVIE RUNA AND HER FRIENDS WENT TO SEE: Princess Mononoke by Studio Ghibli.

THE BOOK MITSUYA-KUN WAS READING: Hikari no Teikoku (Empire of Light) from the Tokono Monogatari (The Story of the Tokono) series by Riku Onda, published by Shuueisha.

THE BOOK RUNA RECOMMENDED: Tenmu Koukai, or Far Journey, by Yuki Taniyama, published by Asahi Sonorama.

WHY MY HAIR IS BLONDE

IT WASN'T UNCOMMON to receive a lot of "visitors" when you found yourself suddenly rich.

"Please! Just a small donation!"

"Trust me, I can make you even *richer*!"

"Please help! We're related, *aren't we*?!"

I was crowded by the masses, their inhibitions clouded by greed. I already knew what was about to be explained to me.

"I've been keeping them at bay, but we hired you a pair of drivers partly for this reason too."

It used to be Tachibana who took care of the petitioners for me, and now Keiko-san filled in for him when he wasn't around. She used to dominate Ginza by night and was by no means a pushover—but there was always a risk she'd be seen as an easy target because of her gender. Hence the hiring of two male drivers to help back her up.

"I've also hired a detective to investigate not only the people of this house, but those around Ichijou-shi as well."

"Why?" I asked.

"Some of these people may target those around you," Tachibana replied simply.

When the Yodoyabashi Bank of this world found itself recording an unprecedented 500-billion-yen loss, the daughter of the powerful bank president suffered a horrendous assault in the art store she worked in. The gentlemen of the bubble, or rather the influential characters in the society's underbelly, were not the type to miss out on preying on such weaknesses.

"Am I really being targeted that much?" I asked.

"It would be stranger if you *weren't*. There is need to make contingency plans, both in response to your earning of the money and the management of it." Tachibana smiled, though there was no heart in the gesture. It was clear why in his next words. "It has been difficult for anybody to reach you up until now. Various parties have been looking out for you, including the Cabinet Intelligence and Research Office."

Now things made more sense. I was probably wearing the same smile on my face as he was. I was being observed because of what my father did—but that surveillance was also to *protect* me. If Tachibana now needed to take measures to protect me, then either that surveillance had been loosened, or it was gone entirely.

One of the two.

"This was either due to my uncle, Minister Izumikawa, or Secretary-General Katou, wasn't it?"

"Correct. My guess would be that it was because of your apology to the secretary-general."

It was a favor I could have done without. But seeing as I didn't even know I was being watched up until now, I couldn't really complain. Whether Tachibana knew what I was thinking or not, he continued delivering the bad news in a simple tone.

"There is also the matter of the Long-Period Credit Bank of Japan and Nihon Credit Bank, which merged with Keika Bank. There was something of Pandora's box with all the finances related to certain politicians. I am sure it was a blessing to several of those politicians that those loans were dealt with before being announced as part of the collective bad debts."

Initially, those two banks were deemed special under national policy, but had now transformed back into regular banks. That was why there were plausible rumors of politicians having so many loans wrapped up in them, to the extent that some even called them the politicians' personal piggybanks.

I remembered from my previous life that one of the two banks was bought up by foreign investors who were able to do completely outrageous things once the deal went through, using the quieting leverage they had through the ruling politicians' loans. At least, that was the cause attributed by rumors. I didn't know whether that was true or not for my previous world, but it certainly seemed true in this one.

"We'll have to discuss that, and include Ichijou as well," I said.

"In that case, why not set up a weekly dinner meeting? Make some time to eat together. There will be no ignoring the connection that forms between us then."

I nodded my agreement. I was only a grade-schooler at this

if Tachibana and Ichijou betrayed me, I was done. It was vital that I constantly worked to keep them loyal to me.

"That sounds good. When would be a suitable time for these dinner meetings?"

Even if not necessarily on the same day, these dinner meetings would end up becoming a weekly occurrence: one where the senior staff of my companies and myself could meet, and the most productive meetings in terms of decision making.

Tachibana didn't know then how important they would become, and so he didn't put much thought into his answer.

"Given that you have school, I believe Saturday evenings would be the wisest choice."

And so the first of these dinner meetings came around.

There were three participants: Tachibana, Ichijou, and me. On that night, we were sharing in some of Keiko-san's homemade Hamburg steak. She even put a flag in mine, which was most appreciated.

It was as we were making our way enthusiastically through our meal that I learned a shocking truth.

"Moonlight Fund isn't a *company*?!" I ended up spitting out my food, my mind totally numbed from the shock.

Ichijou smiled wryly before explaining the trick to me. "There is a corporate body called 'Moonlight Fund' in the US, which deals with asset management. However, when we say 'Moonlight Fund' among ourselves, we are talking about a bank account in your name, my lady."

It was apparently a desperate attempt of theirs to try and cover up a glaring flaw of mine: that being the fact that I was just a child. Something to build up a few layers of security so that I wouldn't be caught if everything were to go wrong. The account was set up for me by the Tokyo branch of the former Far Eastern Bank, and in it was the 500 million yen I'd previously mortgaged the estate for. The mortgage itself had already been repaid by a shell corporation named "Moonlight Fund" in Panama.

The 500 million yen itself had been channeled through various funds to be sent to a private Swiss bank, before being lent to a "Moonlight Fund" in the Bermuda Islands—another shell corporation—which then invested the money into high tech industries. The Bermuda "Moonlight Fund" was owned by a Moonlight Fund that existed on the Isle of Man. The Isle of Man's Moonlight Fund was funded exclusively by my private Swiss bank account, as was the Moonlight Fund in Panama.

As for the Moonlight Fund in America—which was investing in IT companies there—it had a branch office set up in Silicon Valley by a legal entity of the Cayman Islands and was owned by the Panama Moonlight Fund. It was *that* Moonlight Fund that dealt with the business relating to the Bermuda Moonlight Fund.

I wasn't sure I'd ever heard anything more complicated.

"Why does it have to be this complex?" I asked.

They'd drawn me out a map, but it wasn't much help since everything on it used the same name.

With another strained smile, Ichijou explained the situation to me. "The biggest reason is the people after you and your money who Tachibana-san has been worried about. With so many companies spread out and sharing the same name, your average person shouldn't be able to make heads or tails of it."

And though we had all these shell corporations and funds being sent every which way globally, all that tricky business was taken care of by the staff in a single building in Silicon Valley. It made it difficult to work out our profits or where they went, though they all eventually ended up in my account in the private Swiss bank. That account was the nucleus and hub of the Moonlight Fund.

"We also wanted to spread our debt out across several companies. That way we could borrow more."

In finance, there was a term called leverage. If you didn't have as much capital as you would like, you would borrow to prepare yourself large sums of money. We borrowed using our various international Moonlight Funds and used the hundreds of millions of borrowed dollars to invest in the American IT industry. Thanks to the bubble, we had returns of *billions* of dollars. We'd now paid off the worst of our debts and were working on securing our profits.

"Hmm...I understand that we've brought the money we made in the US over to Japan, but what do we do about converting it to yen? And what about taxes?"

I didn't miss the way Tachibana and Ichijou exchanged a glance. I wondered if my selfish quest to save Japan's economy had set me on a dangerous path.

"All the money we've used within Japan has been borrowed."

That was the secret.

When the Japanese Moonlight Fund was set up, it borrowed from the Far Eastern Bank, and all that borrowing was done in *yen*. When the Far Eastern Bank became part of the Keika Bank, we began to borrow from a different metropolitan bank, which agreed for us to pay our debts back in dollars. That was the key to all of this.

The yen had been borrowed at a high rate due to exchange rate risk, but the Moonlight Fund had paid the entire debt back all at once. An investment bank in New York had prepared the dollars for us, and they were happy to do so because they knew of the immense holdings the Moonlight Fund had in the booming IT industry. We used those shares as collateral to borrow dollars from the New York bank and pay the Japanese metropolitan bank back through its New York branch.

International finance was a true blessing from above.

"To be perfectly honest, I doubt even those at the very core of the Ministry of Finance fully understand all the details of the Moonlight Fund yet." Tachibana explained. "They're still struggling with regulating the rescued Keika Bank and Keika Securities."

"We heard the regional tax bureau was looking into us until they had an order from above to hold off. Minister Izumikawa and Secretary-General Katou apparently made a secret agreement that they would pay out should Keika Bank get involved with any more banks that are in dire straits. The bureau itself currently has its hands full with its battle to raise consumption tax," Ichijou added.

When it came to administrating finance, the Ministry was clear: banks were regulated by its banking division, and securities companies by its securities division. It took no time at all for the fight for dominance between Keika Bank and Keika Securities to become a fight for dominance between these two divisions of the Ministry.

Meanwhile, the regional tax bureaus were caught up in all sorts of things, not least their fight to raise consumption tax to five percent, leaving them unable to intervene. Minister Izumikawa and Secretary-General Katou won their case in the end, saying we'd lost more in bailing out the financial institutions than they were trying to collect in tax, and therefore shouldn't be punished.

"Are you sure they won't come to pick a fight with us when they're less busy?" I asked anxiously, picking at my pudding with a spoon.

Ichijou shrugged, following it up with what I expected: the very thing that made it worth being nobility in this world.

"The regional tax bureau will have no choice but to give up when they come against your impunity to arrest. Tax evasion is the crime for which that impunity is most often invoked. We fully intend to stick as close to the white side as possible when it comes to gray areas, but if something *were* to happen, you can trust the Keikain Dukedom to stamp it out—which is why the regional tax bureau will likely keep their distance."

"Additionally, since you are underage, I am acting as your guardian for the purposes of these account," Tachibana said. "We have also made it so that no funds may be moved between accounts without the agreement of both Ichijou and myself."

I was sure he was trying to reassure me that they would be the ones taking the blame if something happened, but I instead was a little frustrated that it was impossible for me to take any responsibility at all because of my age.

"It still isn't ideal for the two of you to continue putting yourselves at risk like this," I said. "Let's come up with a legal way to get the money into Japan and put it to use."

Having finished eating, I put my hands together, leading Tachibana and Ichijou to follow suit and give thanks for the meal with me.

A child is destined to inherit their father's regrets—whether they like it or not. The dispelling of those regrets was a moving tale that was sure to become my shield. This is that tale.

At least, I think it is.

"They're talking about the chemical combine construction in the Port of Sakata again?"

"Yes. Discussions were once deadlocked, but the land is still there. It is only natural that they are thinking of ways to reuse it."

I studied the documents outlining the plans for the combine's construction as Tachibana gave his report.

My father's downfall all came about from the use of Russian oil—or as it was then, the Soviet Union. The Union was struggling economically in thanks to the perestroika deadlock while Japan was riding the highs of its economic bubble, meaning they had more than enough money to buy Soviet oil.

The reason Sakata was chosen for the location of the combine out of all the western coastal towns was because it would benefit from being between the oil fields of Niigata, Akita, and others. There was also an oil stockpiling base there, which the combine could rely on in case of emergencies. Not many people knew that it was actually Secretary-General Katou who insisted on having the combine in Sakata rather than Niigata. At the time, he was a politician with a lot of promise who was steadily rising to the top.

"I finally understand why the secretary-general came to apologize to me."

"It is your decision whether that apology was enough for you to forgive him or not, my lady."

Secretary-General Katou was the one who made use of his impunity to arrest to obscure the details of the scandal of collusion with the East. That wasn't enough to wrap everything up of course; my father needed to be sacrificed for that. Sakata may have been on the coast, but that wasn't the only reason the whole thing smelled fishy.

"I don't feel that much obligation to a father I've never met that I intend to hunt down his enemies. But talk of this combine should have died along with the bubble; why is this discussion coming back now?"

Tachibana pointed to a location on the map: Karafuto.

"Karafuto is in the process of rebuilding its economy, and at the moment is holding out thanks to its exportation of weapons and resources. And yet its unemployment rate is likely to surpass 20 percent. The prefecture's most prolific resource is natural gas, which led to a discussion on constructing a thermal power

generator to make use of it. Discussion on constructing a combine is proceeding alongside that."

Karafuto wasn't the only part of this country struggling
with unemployment, but natural gas was a potential solution,
thanks to lack of competition. Kickstarting Karafuto's economy
again would be vital to get Japan out of this economic funk,
and power generators were a simple way of making use of that
natural gas.

"This is all part of a public works project that Karafuto is in-
volved in, that will be handled by the government. Hokkaido and
Niigata were also invited to put their hats in, but it was Sakata in
Yamagata that won out in the end."

"I suppose this is Secretary-General Katou's way of apologizing."

The Keika Group had a subsidiary that dealt with chemicals:
Keika Chemicals. If our chemical company put a bid in, we were
almost guaranteed to be accommodated—in exchange for funding during the next House of Councilors election, of course.

"As I mentioned before, everything comes down to *your* decision, my lady." Tachibana's words were blunt, but I was certain he
felt abandoned by the main Keikain house. His obligations to
them were finished once the Far Eastern Bank was saved.

"This is something I'd like to speak to a professional about," I
said. "Do you know anybody knowledgeable in petrochemistry
or natural gas?"

Tachibana paused to think. I remembered Keiko-san telling
me that he had more personal connections than I knew—which
was probably why the suggestion he gave was positively perfect.

"Keika Corp has a certain advisor. He used to work for a zaibatsu-owned general trading company, which broke up due to political dispute. Resource trading is his specialty, as I recall."

"He sounds good. Please set some time aside for me to speak with him. Then I will make my decision."

"A pleasure to meet you. My name is Toudou Nagayoshi. I used to be the head of resources supply for the Iwazaki Corporation. I am now a quasi-advisor to Keika Corp, thanks to Tachibana-san's introduction."

He was one of the staunchest businessmen I'd ever seen, but he had lost out due to some internal company politics, which was why he was taking a quieter job now as an advisor of sorts. In his previous role, his job was to jet all over the world and bring resources back to Japan, which was small and had few of its own. It was a job that often kept him out of his home country, never mind the office itself, so there was no way he could win against those internal politics. That was around the time Tachibana picked him up.

"What are you doing now as an advisor?" I asked.

"Well, a little trading in resources with the company's money. I give advice too, just you have called me for today."

He shot me a stirring smile—but I'd heard rumors that Keika Corp's finances were in great shape compared to the rest of the Group's subsidiaries, and it was mostly down to this man's trading. Its smaller size as a trading company was exactly why this top-class trader was able to come in, work at it, and bring the company out of the red and into the black. The fact that Keika Corp gave him

a title as wishy-washy as "advisor" just went to show that they weren't above company politics and keeping cliques themselves either—but I digress.

"You wanted to speak about the combine construction in Sakata, yes? I've already been investigating it to some extent, and I have to say things aren't looking particularly good."

Japan didn't have a public intelligence agency: there was a time during Toudou-san's previous employment when he did a lot of foreign information gathering. It seemed he hadn't lost the knack of gathering and analyzing information even now.

"Do you mean the combine isn't likely to make any money?" I pressed.

"Correct. Ever since the crisis around South Asian currencies, the price of natural resources, starting with crude oil, has been slumping. If you buy into Karafuto natural gas now, you'd be buying at the top of the market, and setting yourself up for trouble."

Natural gas had always been expensive compared to crude oil, but the current slump meant the gap was widening further—that was essentially what he was saying.

It didn't matter that this was a government venture; there would be no profit to be gained from buying the gas at a high price and using it to generate electricity when the demand simply wasn't there because of our economic slump.

Any private company that ignored the cost and assumed government-backing made it a safer investment would then be in trouble if the government backed out due to the lack of profitability—something it might very well do.

"It looks like coal-powered generators are starting to be replaced, what with all these concerns over the environment. But if it were me, I'd be building a coal generator *along* with the chemical combine. If resources become cheaper, you could rely on Russian crude oil to prop you up, as those prices would likely crash as well."

I narrowed my eyes at Toudou. He knew the current currency crisis would end up spilling over into Russia due to previous experience. The chance to purchase incredibly cheap crude oil, something lauded as Japan's lifeblood, was fast approaching.

"That sounds good. Shall we do that, then?"

"You're being very casual about this. Go into this alone, and you'll be set to spend hundreds of billions of yen," Toudou warned me, though I could tell by my eyes he wasn't doubting my sanity. He likely already had an inkling of my money-making activities with Tachibana and Ichijou. He would've done a general background check when Tachibana told him we were coming. If so, I had every intention of working him as hard as I could.

"I already have billions of dollars from our IT dealings abroad. I want to bring that money into Japan."

Toudou picked up on what I meant immediately—he was a talented trader for sure.

"I see. You mean to say that Ichijou-san will have a lot of responsibility on his shoulders if you do nothing, so you want to unload that burden onto me. However, Keika Corp is too small a company to deal with this."

Up until now, we had brought the Moonlight Fund's foreign

earnings into Japan in the form of debt. The trick was making use of Keika Bank's position as a financial institution. We were playing a dangerous game, and I wanted to have access to a different method just in case we lost Ichijou for any reason whatsoever. The most convenient method was oil: something Japan needed but was reliant on other countries for. Using large amounts of money on not only the combine's construction but tankers and the like too was perfect an opportunity.

Having worked out the full extents of my intentions, Toudou made me a proposal. "Right now, trading companies are struggling. Perhaps you should think about buying one, even a small one."

I had no idea where the conversation was going to lead me at the time Little did I know I was about to get involved in Russian oil and be baptized into the greasy world that was global society.

It happened while I was on my way in a limousine to Keika Bank's head office.

"The Asian currency crisis isn't looking too good. What if it reignites the bad debt problem...?" I murmured to myself, reading a report in the back seat. Thanks to the government's convoy system, Japan had just managed to come out of the problem, but the currency crisis originating in Thailand threatened to create credit uncertainty all over again.

"There are some convenient aspects for you however, my lady," Tachibana pointed out.

"You realized that, did you?"

Trading companies were the ones taking the hit from this crisis. There were several Japanese firms that had expanded into Southeast Asian markets, and this crisis was a cause for political instability that simply could not be ignored. It was the trading companies—the glue holding the firms together—that was bearing the brunt of the crisis.

What's more, the new five percent consumption tax had slowed the Japanese economy further, filling the country with talks of credit uncertainty, especially for places that hadn't yet recovered from the bubble's burst. That was why I could now afford to buy a trading company of my own, something I'd had my eye on for a while.

"I wonder whether 200 billion yen is actually a bargain. Toudou-san seemed pretty keen on this..."

It wasn't an amount of money that should ever have been heard from the mouth of a grade-schooler, but I guess you could say I was used to seeing purchase prices in financial publications.

"It has been announced that the Matsuno Trading Corporation, which has its head office in the Shibaura district of Tokyo, is to become a subsidiary of the Moonlight Fund. It will receive capital from the Moonlight Fund to wipe out its bad debts and work towards stabilizing its administration.

Meanwhile, the Matsuno Trading Corporation has made little progress on its bad debts after the burst of the bubble. There were rumors of struggling management with the onset of the Asian currency crisis. That is why the Moonlight Fund has purchased all the credit

*loaned to the Matsuno Trading Corporation by its main banks and
is now intervening in its management.*

*The trading company has had its capital reduce to hold the
shareholders accountable, has had its debt converted to stocks, and
the Moonlight Fund has also allocated it new shares via third-party
allotment.*

*The entire upper management of Matsuno Trading Corporation
has resigned, and..."*

This was different than the previous buyouts and bad debt
settlements. Keika Bank was no longer the lender; the Matsuno
Trading Corporation was a *borrower*, and it was separate banks
that had lent 180 billion yen to the pot.

When all was well, Japan's main bank system allowed the
lending banks to take care of the lender and manage its large
sums while lapping up the irresistibly juicy benefits. When things
went poorly, the lender ended up with nowhere else to turn, and
nothing else but heaps of bad debts.

The banks were then at risk of credit uncertainty, and in
this case, were unable to classify their unpaid loans to Matsuno
Trading Corporation as "bad," continuing to borrow to them
even when the cracks in the management started to show publicly. Any breathing room the banks may have had despite this
was wiped out by the currency crisis. On top of that, two of
MTC's main banks underwent a merger, forcing them to tidy
up their public appearance, something that was quickly approaching a dead-end thanks to a corporate blackmail incident,

which worked to put all this management trouble out into the open.

"Perhaps you should have tried to haggle," Tachibana suggested.

"If I had, the banks wouldn't have been able to reclaim their debt. They were relieved too, since these won't turn into bad debts. It was easy enough to make this money. Easy come, easy go. All in all, it's no skin off my nose."

The business of buying out MTC had all happened between banks. Moonlight Fund had purchased the debt that MTC owed to its main banks. With all the debts in one place now, Moonlight Fund had proposed changing those debts into shares, and a third-party allocation of shares in order to bring MTC under its control.

Unlike our similar operations in the past, this time we made the dealings at each bank's New York branch one by one. Keika Bank was able to finance Moonlight Fund thanks to its massive unrealized gains in the American IT industry, allowing it to buy MTC's debts in American dollars.

The main banks would risk losing out on the exchange rate when they went to change those dollars into yen, but they were happy to agree seeing as I didn't haggle them down when buying up the debts. Of course, once all the business was said and done, the loan from Keika Bank would be repaid.

"The reason Japan's financial institutions have accrued so many bad debts is because they have come to a point where they cannot afford to be prudent when it comes to value or rather, to discrepancies in credit. If a bank lends out a million yen in credit but only received 500 thousand back, it has made a loss of 500 thousand. They will, of course, have collateral in the form of real estate or shares, but those assets will also be depreciating, to the extent they will be unable to retrieve their original million yen That is why they are struggling as much as they are."

I thought back to what Ichijou had told me.

It explained why, when a bank wrote off its borrower's debt in order to save it, they suffered an extraordinary loss—it was because they would never see the money they'd lent again. That was how Japan's industries had found themselves bathing together in a swampy pit of bad debts for so long.

Which got me to thinking: what if there was a way for all those abandoned loans to be repaid, in full? The banks wouldn't suffer any losses, and businesses could set themselves to work clearing their bad debts to other lenders. The borrowing companies could also carry on without worrying about the banks demanding they pay back their money.

The peculiar thing about Japan's bad debts was that businesses were actually quite good at making money. It was when the bubble burst that those same businesses struggled to pay off their enormously inflated bad debts: excessive loans from banks that had been used to purchase real estate.

That was the situation—there were many companies around that would recover if those excessive bank loans were repaid. The Mitsuno Trading Corporation was a perfect example.

"Let's send in Toudou-san as the new president of MTC. How are we doing on selecting the rest of the board of directors?"

"I have already completed the preparations," Tachibana replied.

I was going to Keika Bank's head office to speak with Ichijou make sure everything was in order and start things progressing. While MTC was a subsidiary of ours, it was still one of ten major general trading companies. It was likely to play an important role in the reopening of the Sakata combine project.

"May I say something, my lady?" Tachibana's question interrupted my thoughts. It looked like he had just finished speaking to the driver, Sone-san. I could never have predicted what he was about to say next. "It appears we are being followed. I have used the car's phone to contact the main family and call on my subordinates. I have also contacted the Metropolitan Police's fifth section of its security division. I'm afraid we will have to cancel our plans for today."

The Keikain family were dukes: it was only natural we had private bodyguards. Aside from Sone-san and Tachibana, there was one female guard with us in the limo. Driving ahead and behind us were two bulletproof Benzes, each with two guards inside.

What did it mean then that we were still being followed despite all that?

"All right," I agreed with a sigh. "Regarding these people following us. Do you think they're outsiders or not?"

Tachibana merely shook his head in response.

There were plenty of reasons that those on the inside—that was, the main Keikain family, or one of the branch families—would target me. The simplest was the Moonlight Fund, which was at the center of Keika Bank's profits, and yet the only one who knew the full extent of its inner workings was me. The exorbitant money it had made from the dot-com bubble was no secret, and there had already been attempts on my life as well as attempts on luring Tachibana and Ichijou away from me.

But they each had a reason they could never be bought.

"The master asked me to take care of you."

Tachibana's loyalty to my grandfather, Keikain Hikomaro, was greater than his loyalty to me. The Keikains were a relatively young noble family, yet it had already been half a century since the Pacific War. The family had already produced successive generations, and it seemed that time was all it needed to create a loyal servant too.

"I had made it to branch manager at the Tokyo branch of a modest regional bank. I had assumed my only choice for the future was to transfer, and yet I ended up as a corporate officer at a head office. It was all thanks to your schemes, my lady. Keika Bank is dominated by retired officials from the Ministry and metropolitan bank executives. Without your support, I would have been dismissed immediately. How could I betray you after all of that?"

I hoped Ichijou would never find out that his reasoning made me laugh.

It was important to note that corporate executive was treated as an important role, but technically, was little more than a hired executive. In other words, they were not a board member and didn't have a say in corporate decision making.

A certain electronics company, which had just released a games console and increased its influence because of it, had introduced the position, and Keika Bank had then followed suit. Tachibana was also selected for the post by Ichijou and my uncle, who wanted to take him away from me.

The rest of Keika Bank's management, including its president, was half made up of former Ministry officials. The rest was a mix of the more talented executives from Hokkaido Kaitaku Bank, the Long-Period Credit Bank of Japan, and Nihon Credit Bank. Most of the management of the former Far Eastern Bank hadn't survived this game of high-class musical chairs, with some being kept on to live out the rest of their years as advisors to Far Eastern Life Insurance. Tachibana and Ichijou, meanwhile, had my backing—they were special to me. While there were those who wanted the two out, Ichijou was one of the very few people who had access to the Moonlight Fund, and Tachibana was a loyal servant of the Keikain family going back generations. In true Japanese political fashion, Keika Bank introduced the title of corporate officer to create a place for the pair of them.

The reason an outsider would want to target me was more obvious—I was a good target to be kidnapped for ransom.

"We will change our route and head for Keika Pharmaceuticals' head office."

"Wait," I said. "I don't mind if we go there, but it could get dangerous if we don't think carefully about how to change our route. It will be safer to go the bank's head office first and *then* head for Keika Pharmaceuticals. We can make use of the bank's security personnel and get on the subway at Kayabachou to get to Kasumigaseki. That way will be faster too."

In saving the banks we did, we also acquired several buildings in Tokyo, which allowed the Keika Group to move headquarters.

The central company of the group, Keika Pharmaceuticals, had moved headquarters to Hibiya, where the former Long-Period Credit Bank of Japan had its head office building. Keika Bank, meanwhile, had concentrated its management operations in Kayabachou, where the former Ichiyama Securities had its head office building.

"There is a problem with that plan, my lady. There is quite some distance between Keika Bank's head office and the subway station."

A distance of four hundred to five hundred meters, to be exact. It was a practical invitation to whoever was tailing us to attack, if that was what they were after.

"I have an idea..." I told Tachibana, a sweet smile forming on my face.

Eitai Bridge.

There was a suspicious car that, after its driver spotted us, made a move eastward, as though trying to avoid being questioned by our guards. I watched from atop the boat.

"When did you think up this plan, my lady?" Tachibana asked.

"A little while ago. Tokyo has a lot of rivers. I just thought that moving by boat would be an easy way to shake off anyone tailing us." The salty wind rustled through my golden hair as I answered him. The Nihonbashi River flowed behind the former head office of Ichiyama Securities, where there was also a small harbor. That was our only way out of this situation.

I'd ask Ichijou to prepare a single boat with a sailor to moor there; it was there just as I'd asked. It was lucky that there were leisure boats planned for the resorts that were planned before all this bad debt business.

"Head for Takeshiba Bridge, please. Keika Pharmaceuticals had prepared a car to meet us there. We'll go ashore as soon as they're ready for us."

The nice thing about boats was that nobody could come aboard as long as you stayed away from the shore, and you could equip them with radios to make communication easy. We had an overwhelming advantage against our followers right now.

"My lady, I've received a report from the bank's security personnel. They got the car's license plate, and it's not good news." I grimaced. I'd never seen such a grave expression on Tachibana's face. When he said it wasn't good news, he meant it. "They checked the number with the metropolitan police. Apparently, the car is registered to the Russian embassy."

Once we made it to Takeshiba Bridge, Tachibana and I got inside the waiting limo. There was one Benz in front and one behind to escort us again, as well as an unmarked police car.

"This has gotten serious. Now, who might this be?"

The plain-clothed police officer who was riding with us showed me his ID and introduced himself. He had a fishy smile if I'd ever seen one.

"I'm from the National Police Agency's Public Safety Bureau, Foreign Affairs Section. My name is Maefuji Shouichi. I'll be responsible for your protection and will also be explaining the situation to you."

"Oh my. Is it so bad that a renowned member of the Special Higher Police has gotten involved? What on earth have I done?"

As a governmental organization, the loss of the war dealt them a hard blow, but they, along with the army and navy, were part of the Home Ministry, one of the top bureaucratic organizations in Japan.

After the war, the ministries and government offices were disassembled, and police organizations were moved into the Cabinet Office. One of those, which changed its name, was the Special Higher Police, which was now calling itself the Public Safety Bureau. Moreover, it was the Ministry of Finance that now reigned over these bureaucratic organizations since the post-war reshuffle.

"You haven't done anything, my lady," Inspector Maefuji explained. "Rather, it appears there are those out there in the world who *think* you have done something. They are targeting this 'Moonlight Fund' of yours."

He went on to explain that the Russian economy had slowed due to the aftermath of the Asian currency crisis—something that I already knew. What I didn't know was what that had to do with the situation at hand.

"Forgive me for asking, but how much do you know about your origins, my lady?"

"Inspector Maefuji," Tachibana warned, but I raised a hand to silence him.

I looked the inspector right in the eye as I spoke. "I am aware that my parents had links to the East in their pasts. Could you explain what that has to do with the current situation?"

Inspector Maefuji looked a little taken aback by my tone; one that was far beyond my apparent years. His fake smile disappeared to be replaced by a serious expression.

"Hmm, I see now. The quality of education within a dukedom is exceptionally high. Very well. I will lay out everything I am permitted to you. Do you know that your grandmother was related to a Russian Grand Duke?"

The Romanov family. It was then that I realized that blood ran through my father's veins too. I nodded, and Inspector Maefuji directed his gaze away from me and outside the window as he continued.

"By studying documents from Northern Japan, we learned that your mother was also nobility. And you, my lady, are closely enough related to a *certain house* to claim inheritance."

Ah.

A terrifying thought popped into my mind. Something about a promise from an ancient romance novel.

"Do you mean the House of Romanov...? I've heard certain rumors. In terms of the inheritance, I believe there is still somebody before me."

Inspector Maefuji shook his head coldly. "The inheritance itself isn't important. It's the *security* for that inheritance. There are those who would only see you as a Romanov successor once you get ahold of the House's inheritance. That is the logic they are using to come after the Moonlight Fund."

"I see. Russia is under the impression that Romanov treasure is funding the Moonlight Fund."

They thought there was a chance there was imperial Russian treasure hiding away in that private Swiss fund. There was some suspicious talk of the Swiss becoming such a financial power because of assets such as those, which didn't get withdrawn. If they just did some investigating into the Moonlight Fund, they'd see they were wrong, but private Swiss banks had a tendency to protect their customers' information very thoroughly. It was because there was nothing to disprove those rumors that I was in trouble now.

I was born in Japan after the East began to collapse with the fall of the Berlin Wall in 1989. At that time, Japan was thriving in its bubble while the East and the Soviet Union were suffering from destruction.

The East was in enough trouble then both to spy on Japanese technologies and go after strange rumors like these.

Inspector Maefuji opened his notebook and began to read aloud. "The first signs of suspicious Russian activity came with the talk of Sakata's combine, due to Russia's involvement with the plot of land there. They were likely keeping an eye on it already when the recent news broke, so it's only natural they would make a move."

"It still seems a little soon," I said. "The news only came out *today*, didn't it?"

The inspector began to explain things to me. At least he wasn't treating me like a simple child in any of this.

"When news of projects such as this breaks, it means the plans are already more than 50 percent complete. The Sakata combine will not be able to make a profit without natural gas or crude oil from Karafuto or Russia. They clearly started there and did some tracing before arriving at your name." Inspector Maefuji smiled in bemusement, before catching himself and quickly pressing his lips together again. "Russia's economy is in poor shape at the moment and there are whisperings of political instability. To that nation, the blood that runs through your veins holds a special meaning. We don't know whether they are after money or fame yet, but those are our top two contenders."

"I understand. Then, what must I do?"

Inspector Maefuji smiled. It was a smile that sent a chill running down my back.

"Nothing at all. You are a protected person. That's all you need to know. You can leave the rest up to the adults."

I pretended not to pick up on what he'd purposely left hidden. These lowlifes who were after me were being supported by the Russian government. It was even possible that the Russian government was spearheading the entire operation.

"I'm so glad you're safe, Runa." Nakamaro-oniisama swept me up in his arms.

We'd made it to the executive suite of Keika Pharmaceuticals' head office, which had a view of Hibiya Park. Nakamaro-oniisama was holding me a little too tightly, and it hurt.

"Nakamaro-oniisama, I'm fine. Please don't worry."

"Ah, sorry. I owe you thanks too, Inspector Maefuji."

I didn't know if Nakamaro-oniisama was genuinely worried about me, or if he was just worried about losing my money and noble blood. Still, I needed to be careful assuming the worst about people like that, just in case the paranoia broke me. I decided he was worried about me because I was only a child. That was the most mentally healthy conclusion.

Nakamaro-oniisama let go of me, which was when I spotted Ichijou and Toudou. With everyone here, my cousin would require an explanation—to some extent, at least. And so, Tachibana, Ichijou, and Toudou began to fill Nakamaro-oniisama and Inspector Maefuji in.

"The Moonlight Fund manages stocks in both Japanese and American IT industries, but the account that manages the funds is set up with a private Swiss bank. That account has links to Russian imperial assets, which is one cause of this situation."

Both Ichijou and I were thinking along the same lines, and it made sense. To have confidence in a private bank, it needed a good, long track record. That meant a trustworthy private bank at this point was likely to have existed at the same time as the Russian Empire.

"The worsening Russian economy brought attention to the Moonlight Fund. It would not take much investigation to discover that the Fund was only set up recently, but I believe the economic situation means they do not feel they need a watertight excuse." Toudou's tone was light while his words were anything but.

There was no doubt that the currency crisis had caused problems for Russia as it progressed. Asia had been at the front of the recent economic growth that had pulled up the price for resources. It was that growth—and its oil and natural gas exports—which were at the center of Russia's economic recovery. That growth had stalled when Asia was hit with the currency crisis, damaging expectations and causing resource prices to slump, which hit Russia as a nation whose economy was dependent on exporting those resources.

The world was already connected economically at this point in history, but humans had yet to learn how much devastation economic fallout from other places could actually cause.

"Due to the economic crisis in Russia, wages are going unpaid. There have been strikes across the nation, starting with the coal miners." Again, Toudou spoke smoothly, but his words made me feel cold inside.

A company's inability to pay its workers' wages was a sign that it was close to bankruptcy. I knew this would lead to the nation's collapse, and I was terrified of the upcoming economic crisis.

"I think I understand what's happening. There was a time when miners and other workers would gather in the darker corners of society. I would wager that this situation has something to do with them," Tachibana said.

The Soviet Union, a state synonymous with socialism, collapsed as a result of its planned economy and the mafia who were running the black market made a fortune as part of newly formed conglomerates. It was as though the same confusion that happened in Japan after the war was now being repeated in Russia— and our illustrious Keikain family had now been upgraded to Russian nobility, as far at this suspicious group was concerned.

Tachibana's tone was a little wistful. He had lived through the post-war years and through the following era of economic growth. It was easy to see the person in front of you in the present moment, but people tended not to seek out the past of that same individual.

"This must be big if the Russian embassy are involved," Nakamaro-oniisama said.

Toudou replied to him—and it was because I understood the meaning of that reply that I realized the situation was worse than I thought.

"There can only be one reason for the embassy's involvement. It means that, whoever's idea this is, they have a *lot* of money to spend on it. And with that much money involved, it likely means there is something more to this than just money."

A long silence fell over the room.

It was broken by a quiet cough from Inspector Maefuji. "I understand it will be inconvenient, but I ask that you allow the Security Division, Section 5, to stick to the young lady for a while. I promise the Foreign Affairs Section will do everything we can to solve this case."

The Security Division was the shield, and the Foreign Affairs Section was the sword, as well as the leaders of the whole operation.

I had to speak up then. "Um, how are you planning to solve the case? Didn't the bad guys have a car from the embassy?"

The Public Safety Bureau was moving too fast. All they had was a tip that I was being followed, and yet the talk about Russian involvement had come this far. They must have been holding on to this information for a while.

I kept those thoughts from Inspector Maefuji, who went on to explain simply how the Bureau would put an end to the case. "Our intention is to make sure nobody can get too close to you. The rest is a job for the diplomats."

The door opened quietly, and Katsura Naoyuki appeared with a note for his boss, Ichijou. Ichijou read it and then, his expression unchanged, showed it to Tachibana and Toudou.

"If I may, my lady" Tachibana, who usually wouldn't interrupt anyone in a place like this, handed me the note.

I froze the moment I'd read it.

I knew this was going to happen.

I just didn't know it would happen with such awful timing as this.

"What's wrong, Runa?"

I passed the note to Nakamaro-oniisama then, whose face quickly turned to a reflection of my own feelings.

Based on everything we'd heard so far, this note was the trigger that would lead to the collapse of Russia's economy. The Russian financial crisis was due after the Asian currency crisis.

Simply put, the crisis depended on the availability of funds to purchase currency. There were huge unrealized profits from tech companies lying within the Moonlight Fund that would be available to do just that. Tachibana knew that, which was why he'd passed us the note.

"May I see that?" Inspector Maefuji asked, at which point Nakamaro-oniisama passed the note on to him.

This was what was written on that devastating note:

From: Bangkok.
The Thai government is changing to a floating exchange rate. Its currency's crash is expected to have a knock-on effect on other Asian countries.

"So that's the situation," I explained.

"You sound way too unconcerned," Eiichi-kun sighed.

The three boys and I were having a study meeting in our school's library. Even here, there was a plain-clothed, female police officer standing guard at the side of the room.

Yuujirou-kun glanced at her. "Does that mean you won't be able to attend tomorrow's boat party?"

Despite the latest explosive development in the Asian currency crisis, the minister of finance was throwing a party—or perhaps it was precisely because of the crisis that he wanted to keep everyone united. The truth was that it was to collect funding for next year's House of Councilors election, and Dietman Izumikawa Tatsunosuke's bid to run for the next party leader.

"No, if you think about it, I shouldn't be invited regardless."

The current minister of foreign affairs was also running for next party leader, and his ministry was one of nobility's strongholds. Diplomacy with other places where nobility had survived, such as Europe, could be wrought with complications.

If the Ministry of Foreign Affairs was our stronghold, then our headquarters was the Privy Council. It had survived the postwar period in this world, and that was because nobility was even more protective of it than the House of Councilors.

"After what happened with Keika Bank, shouldn't your family *want* to get on the minister of finance's good side?" Mitsuya-kun pointed out, sounding a little fed up with things.

Due to my grandfather's arrogance and the scandal surrounding my father, the Keikain family were outcasts within noble society, despite the family's high position. That was why it devoted itself entirely to its businesses, an attitude to which it owed its current prosperity.

"Oh, I don't think anybody is going to be making a big deal out of banking business. But I suppose I will be forced to go anyway, to fill in for the family head."

There was probably a lot of strategizing going on among the adults at the moment.

I put down my pen and sighed. "It is so, so inconvenient not being able to make my own decisions in life."

The next day, I was indeed escorted by a guard to the boat party. Since it was a black-tie event, I was in my school uniform.

"I really was hoping to give this one a miss, considering the recent incident." Inspector Maefuji gave a wry smile. He was also in a suit.

It had been Dietman Izumikawa who insisted on my appearance. He and his supporters in the party must really have had some sway.

"Announcing Keikain Runa-sama, of the Keikain Dukedom."

I stepped out to a round of applause. Applause—and more whispered rumors.

"I heard that much of the Thai cabinet has resigned..."

"Indonesia's crash isn't showing any signs of slowing..."

"It's all linked. You really don't want to see their domestic exchange and stock markets right now!"

"Apparently our midrange zaibatsu, which have expanded into Southeast Asia, have run out of options and are asking the Ministry of International Trade and Industry for help..."

"That's not good. If those zaibatsu go down, we're looking at even *more* bad debts. We're already getting blamed for struggling to deal with them, and the recent consumption tax increase."

"That's why we invited Keikain Runa-sama. Keika Bank and Keika Securities, both from the Keika Group, are part of the Ministry of Finance now. We need the Keikain family on our side if we want to break up the zaibatsu and deal with the bad debts."

"If we're going to keep up this deregulation, we will need bank holding companies. I'm happy to butter up a small girl if it means we can make a success of this combined bank and securities company—and it will set a good precedent."

Did they seriously think I couldn't hear them?

I kept the question in my head, instead thanking the party's host as a prim and proper young lady of my standing should.

"It was an honor to be invited, Minister Izumikawa."

"Well, aren't you a cute young lady? Yuujirou speaks about you a lot. I hope you'll carry on being friends with him." After my greeting, Minister Izumikawa had me stand next to him as he made his opening address. "Once we have weathered this storm of bad debt, Japan's financial institutions will once again be ready to take on the world. A financial big bang awaits us! The first step will be to lift the ban on bank holding companies, something I am currently aiming for in the Diet. The first chosen companies for this project are all subsidiaries of the Keika Group, where young Lady Keikain Runa comes from. They are Keika Bank, Keika Securities, Far Eastern Life Insurance, and Keika Maritime Insurance," Minister Izumikawa announced proudly, as though he had forged those companies himself. "Keika Holdings: that name will lead the way for Japanese financial institutions to launch themselves back onto the world stage!"

His words were met with thunderous applause and a raucous toast, at which point the magnificent party really got under way.

It was all well and good that I'd been invited, but because of my age I couldn't really talk the talk with the adults. My choices were eating or drinking juice in the corner.

This floating restaurant flaunted herself as a Tokyo Bay cruise ship. Her name was Actress, and in reality, she used to be a source of bad debt. Now she was under the ownership of Keika Hotels and what she should be used for when she had nowhere to go was another topic of discussion at this party. The venue was practical in that sense, if nothing else. Since the ship technically belonged to me, I felt safe leaving my guard behind.

"It really is a bother, having to come to a place like this at my age," Mitsuya-kun lamented. This was his first party like this.

Apparently, news of the Gakushuukan Quartet had reached our parents and guardians, meaning we'd all received an invite. I felt bad for Mitsuya-kun in particular: Eiichi-kun, Yuujirou-kun, and I were all used to this sort of thing, and we were happily munching away on sweets and gulping down juice from the children's table.

"You can say that again. With no games to keep us entertained, time seems to drag."

"You play games, Keikain-san?" Yuujirou-kun asked.

As the host, he must have felt it his duty to make sure we were having fun. Eiichi-kun seemed interested in the topic too.

"I play them to relax," I said. "Although I can't play them for long when my butler, Tachibana, or my maid, Keiko-san, are watching."

"I get you. I always get stopped just when I get to a good bit too. What games do you play?" Eiichi-kun.

"That popular RPG that's being advertised right now. No spoilers, please!"

I had played it before long ago, but I'd forgotten most of it. The save function was a great new feature. I think my generation would have suffered a lot more stress without it.

"Oh, that one," Mitsuya-kun said. "That huge company that features in it; it's got to be a zaibatsu!"

"I agree. Do you play too, Mitsuya-kun?" Yuujirou-kun asked.

"I played it, yes, but it seemed I made the wrong choice somewhere as it made me restart from my last save point."

Poor guy.

"Excuse me a moment."

I got up to head for the bathroom. I took a female guard with me, but all of a sudden, she stopped in front of me.

"My lady! Get back!"

Something flashed before my eyes, and I lost consciousness.

When I woke up, I found myself tied up and locked away in a dark space. If I had to guess, I'd say it felt like a largeish box. I expected to be trembling from fear, but I wasn't. Maybe I'd been drugged; I couldn't move my body at all. Something was tied around my eyes, and there was a gag in my mouth, so I couldn't make a sound either. I had no idea where the guard was. I worked hard to suppress my fear and forced myself to think as clearly as possible. It was immediately obvious to me that somebody had betrayed me—otherwise this kidnapping would have been a much messier affair.

Whoever had taken me, they needed *me* for some reason. If they were only after the Moonlight Fund, then kidnapping me shouldn't have been worth the trouble; if I died, it would be distributed among the Keikain family. They needed me, and they needed me alive. There was only one reason for that: Romanov treasure. Legendary treasure that I'd never even touched, but that required me to be *alive*.

There was something else I noticed only then: the noise of an engine, and a vibration. I was probably still aboard Actress. That meant there was still a chance of rescue. At the same time, while I was confident that I would be searched for, it would probably be kept quiet. If word of my disappearance got out, the reputations of both the Keika Group and the party's host, Minister Izumikawa, would be politically damaged. The ship was essentially a locked room mystery, lending itself to the delicacy of the situation.

"Hello? I don't feel too good. Could I get some anti-nausea medicine please?"

I recognized that voice! It was Eiichi-kun.

"Me too!"

"And me too!!!"

That was Yuujirou-kun and Mitsuya-kun. I was relieved that they hadn't been caught as well. Did this mean I was being held in the sickbay? I had to communicate with them somehow. I tried to move my body, but I was bound so tightly that even making any sort of sound was difficult.

"Please keep it down if you can. There's somebody sleeping in here."

That must've been the doctor. For a second, I thought they'd heeded his instructions, but then I heard Yuujirou-kun speak again.

"Would you happen to know where Keikain-san is? She has yet to return from the restroom."

"You know how girls are. I'm sure she'll be back soon if you just wait for her outside," the doctor said.

"Huh. You know, I feel sorry for you, doc. Having to hole yourself up here because someone got sick," Eiichi-kun said.

The doctor scoffed slightly. "That's my job. Now, here's your medication."

I heard the sound of something falling, as though somebody had thrown something into a trashcan.

"Thanks. I'm guessing this used to be a storage room or something? They've still got the nameplates up and everything..." Eiichi-kun remarked. "Looks to me like they just stuffed the bed and medicine cabinets in afterward."

"I was called here last minute for the party," the doctor replied. "I work for the Keika Group."

I see now. I'm locked in the storage room.

But where *within* that storage room?

"Thank you for the medicine. I'll leave my cup here. Do you know how long we have to stay on this boat for?" Mitsuya-kun asked.

I heard what sounded like paper passing hands. "Just hold on a little longer. The party will be over in an hour or so."

"Oh, I'm afraid there's been a change," Yuujirou-kun said. "Father has said he would like to extend the party by another two or three hours, since he's enjoying himself so much. He discussed as much with the captain, and suggested we come to get some medication before we suffered too much from the seasickness."

There was the sound of somebody drinking, and then a door opening.

"Thanks very much, sir. And I hope the rest of your duties go well," Eiichi-kun said.

Then the door closed. For a long time, there was silence, and then voices again.

"What do we do now?! We can't hide her for another two or three *hours!*"

That was the guard who escorted me to the restroom.

Ah: so she and the doctor were behind this.

"Calm down. We've prepared a smaller boat for situations like this. We can pass her over to that one if we need to."

I mulled over my chances of getting saved before then. And if I did end up on that smaller boat, what would happen to me then?

I could feel the terror steadily growing inside me. Suddenly, there was a hissing sound.

"Is that *smoke*?!"

"Don't move! This is the police! We are arresting you on suspicion of kidnapping and other charges!"

It was Inspector Maefuji. The noisy thumping made me think he must be here with several of his subordinates.

"I've found it! An underfloor compartment under this bed!" Something clicked, and I could see light filtering through the blindfold. "It's her! She's safe!"

I was untied, and my blindfold lifted. I spotted three familiar faces in front of me, and relieved tears started streaming down my face.

"I'm so sorry for allowing you to fall into such danger, Lady Runa," Inspector Maefuji said.

Just as I thought, it turned out the doctor really was the culprit. He worked for the Keika Group but had connections to one of the branch companies, which was struggling with debt due its failing business. The guard had been the victim of a honeytrap, which revealed that there were sinister parties even closer to the center of the Keikain family. They'd suspected the guard, since she was the one closest to me, and when they checked the map of the sickbay where she was recovering from her "injuries," they noticed a compartment beneath the bed where she was sleeping.

"I see. But why did you three come to the sickbay? Wasn't it dangerous?"

"Nope!" Eiichi-kun replied with a confidence that I knew would stick around as he grew up.

"There was no risk of them going after us if they were after Romanov treasure," Yuujirou-kun explained with a reassuring smile, something that wouldn't change as he grew older. "If they wanted a ransom for you, that would be another story, of course."

"We were the ones who asked to help. We wore a wiretap so our conversation could be used as evidence, and left a small smoke device behind," Mitsuya-kun concluded. That explanatory tone was something he would use a lot when he was older too.

"We controlled the conversation," Eiichi-kun said. "When he wasn't looking, we put the bug in the trash, and the smoke device in the cabinet with the cups. Lucky for us the guard had the curtain drawn around the bed, so she didn't see a thing either!"

Watching the way they smiled as they boasted about their victory, and the fact that they walked right into danger to save me, made my heart thump.

The former Nihon Credit Bank's head office in Kudanshita.

The bank's main facilities were now being offered at Keika Bank's head office, leaving this building out of use. It had already been selected for reconstruction too, so the insides were totally deserted.

Eiichi-kun, Yuujirou-kun, Mitsuya-kun, Tachibana, and I were in the building's reception office, giving a stress interview to our visitor.

"I do hope you will be able to explain this."

There was a newspaper in front of that visitor, Inspector Maefuji, and the front page screamed in large font: "Minister of Finance Izumikawa Resigns! After a Ministry member was arrested for corruption, the Minister..."

Roughly speaking, the corruption started from payoff to a corporate bouncer. The case was investigated and revealed two more people involved in the corruption: A banker who acted as an intermediary between the Ministry of Finance and a bank under its control, and a Ministry bureaucrat.

Both the minister of finance and the Bank of Japan Governor

had resigned, and some among the arrested had died by suicide. The Japanese finance administration was being left braindead in a situation that was already bad enough but worsened by the Asian financial crisis. Needless to say, Minister Izumikawa's plan to allow holding companies had come to a spectacular *stop*.

"I'm afraid the explanation might be simpler than you'd like. If somebody has done something bad, it's the police's job to arrest them." Inspector Maefuji smiled.

"I understand that. I'm asking for the details and background on the decision to use me in order to further your investigation."

The inspector kept the smile plastered on his face, but his eyes were no longer warm. Myself aside, these three boys were smart to an unfair degree: I knew they would be able to follow this logic of these proceedings, so I had them join in on the interview. Eiichi-kun didn't have a horse in this particular race, but Yuujirou-kun's father was not only forced to resign; he could no longer put his name forward in the vote for the Bank of Japan's next Governor. Mitsuya-kun's father was on the very edge of the investigation, so nothing had happened to him personally, but the budget division itself had taken a heavy hit, and its future was looking bleak.

In my case, I'd been put through a traumatic experience, and my uncle and Nakamaro-oniisama were now working hard to clear things up after the scandal within the Keikain family.

I was here because I wanted to know what was behind all of this.

"The Public Safety Bureau was investigating those two fairly early on, wasn't it?"

The Bureau had come to an agreement with the Keikain family not to make that particular aspect of the investigation public, since it was seen as family business. I couldn't help but think that the Public Safety Bureau was behind this whole thing, including the deal with my family.

"My evidence is that you immediately showed up the moment my car was followed. Romanov treasure and the Moonlight Fund—those are just two of many reasons why I might be targeted. But there's been someone *setting* these people on me," I laid out my logic plainly, a young grade-schooler playing detective. "You're the Public Safety Bureau, yes? You knew the Tokyo Prosecutors Office had its sights set on the Ministry of Finance. First, there was the situation with Keika Bank and Keika Securities dealing with the bad debts, and then the enormous finance politicians got for their dealings through their piggybanks: the former Long-Period Credit Bank of Japan, and The Nihon Credit Bank, both under Ministry control. If the Ministry lost power through this scandal, it would give the Bureau the opportunity to dig the knife in and investigate these finances. It was all a ruse." I paused to gulp down some grape juice and continued speaking without waiting to enjoy the aftertaste.

"The problem is the perpetrators were seriously planning to sell me off. The enormous money tied up in Romanov treasure and the Moonlight Fund twisted the fake kidnapping into a *real* one. That was why everything has ended up how it has." I glanced at the three boys. They seemed to be following, but they didn't seem to know how to proceed. They didn't know that adults fought with words. "That was why you had to rescue me on the boat, no matter what, and that was why you got these three involved. Because you orchestrated the kidnapping, it would have put them on guard if you showed up first. I was already tied up, and when you realized you'd underestimated the two kidnappers, you had no choice but to use the three boys."

That much was obvious from the fact that neither Minister Izumikawa, nor Mitsuya-kun's father, a budget analysist next in line for administrative vice minister of finance, had received any direct punishment. If the Prosecutors Office had managed to arrest those two, it would be praised for cinching a surprise victory. It must have been Inspector Maefuji and his Bureau who stopped that from happening, because they were behind the fake kidnapping. Though I wasn't about to explain that much.

So why was Eiichi-kun here?

He insisted: Eiichi-kun's arrogance meant he couldn't stomach being left out.

"That would make a good plot for a detective manga. But I'm afraid all your evidence is circumstantial." Inspector Maefuji almost sounded criminal in his response, or as though he was simply humoring what he considered to be nonsense.

Even if I blamed him for everything, it had already been decided that this whole thing was the Ministry's fault. I knew this because this scandal was the trigger that would lose the Ministry of Finance much of its control over monetary policy.

"The Handover of Hong Kong and the planned Asian Monetary Fund." The smile faded from Inspector Maefuji's face completely: I'd struck gold. "Thanks to the Ministry's convoy system, Japan was able to make it through its bad debt crisis. Any action against the Asian currency crisis is sure to instantly drag the country back down. Keika Holdings was supposed to be the Ministry's trump card against the crisis."

The Asian Monetary Fund was a grand plan proposed by a senior member of the Ministry of Finance, one who had worked for the prime minister himself. The plan was not only to defend against hedge funds by lending money from a fund with Japan at its center, but to provide economic support.

If the Asian Monetary Fund could provide enormous capital for every country in Asia and supposing the ban on holding companies lifted and Keika Holdings could provide support for the Fund, history would change, if only a little.

But I wouldn't have played a part in it.

"Did you know that much of the underground money in Hong Kong found its way to other Asian nations after the handover, only to be sucked up by American hedge funds? Meanwhile, there were those who saw the Ministry and everything in its grip as shameful. The Ministry of Foreign Affairs, for example."

"My lady. Whether you are speaking seriously or not, I should warn you that there are some things it's better not to talk about."

It was around this time that America-based hedge funds were really about to lash out—something that was set to align with the USA's current national interests. The interesting thing was there were several conservative dietmen who *wanted* Japan to be weaker. We still had those from the wartime generation among

WHY MY HAIR IS BLONDE

our government who, after losing the Pacific War, didn't want Japan to have to face off against America again. But their time was coming to an end.

Despite that, America had opposed the Asian Monetary Fund, saying its duties were too similar to the IMF's, even if it was limited to Asia.

Secretary-General Katou was a former bureaucrat of the Ministry of Foreign Affairs, and once represented it in the Diet. Now that Minister Izumikawa was forced to resign, The secretary-general was working hard to poach his followers. The Minister and those around him had taken the fall to preserve relations between Japan and America. The Keikain family was chosen specifically for me: a symbol of its former collusion with the East.

"Very well. Thank you for lending this grade-schooler your ear."

"Not at all. It was a very interesting tale, my lady."

The three boys had followed everything. Yuujirou-kun and Mitsuya-kun were seething with rage—or perhaps, bloodlust. Eiichi-kun was glaring at Inspector Maefuji coldly, as though he thought himself above our visitor.

The reason I got these boys involved was because of my arrest at the end of the "game." I wasn't sure, but I seemed to remember that the inspector who would come to arrest me was Maefuji. He was never named, and only shown in a single image, but I got the same vibe from him. Unbeknownst to the boys, part of this had been to damage their perception of Inspector Maefuji to try and change the course of my prison-bound fate.

"It was interesting *indeed.*"

Inspector Maefuji had opened the door to leave the room, only to find Nakamaro-oniisama standing behind it. He stepped inside. His expression was free of its usual noble indifference, instead replaced with burning emotion.

Thump!

Nakamaro-oniisama punched Inspector Maefuji directly in the face. The inspector fell to the floor.

"How dare you get my precious little sister wrapped up in something so filthy and *disgusting*?! You and your bureau will never step foot in the Keikain household again! You can tell that directly to your superiors!"

Inspector Maefuji wiped the blood from his nose and stood up. He said nothing more and left the room with a single, perfunctory bow.

I already understood.

Nakamaro-oniisama swept me up into a tight hug.

"I'm so sorry, Runa. You must have been so terrified. But you can relax now. No matter what anybody says, you are a Keikain like any other. You are my precious little sister!"

I could feel his tears dripping down my cheeks.

To become a police inspector, you were made to learn a martial art to aid in arrests—and yet Inspector Maefuji allowed Nakamaro-oniisama to hit him without resistance. I was forced to come to terms with the realization that Nakamaro-oniisama's rage and his attack on the inspector was all part of the deal between the Public Security Bureau and the Keikain family. The Bureau used its knowledge of my late father's scandal with the

East to force my family's hand into allowing it to fabricate my kidnapping.

"Don't cry, Runa. Would you boys say something to help her cheer up?"

The four boys in the room looked panicked when I started to cry.

No. You don't understand.

Keikain Runa, are you there? You spent so long being afraid of everything and everyone. After all of that, what did you think the protagonist had that made you so jealous of her?

GLOSSARY AND NOTES:

VARIOUS MOONLIGHT FUNDS: A similar scheme played out with a Japanese tour bus company, leading to a change in administration.

SWISS BANKS: A sniper from a famous seinen manga series makes use of them. In this case, Swiss bank does not refer to a singular bank, but is a general name for the private banks in Switzerland. They were best place to protect Runa's assets from the masses, and held a deep connection with the Romanov family, so much so that there were nonsensical rumors that the Romanovs had left a secret fortune in these banks before they fell, which was the main reason Swiss banking became so successful.

RISE IN THE CONSUMPTION TAX RATE: It was raised in 1997, something that caused the ruling party to take huge damage in the following years' Upper House election.

ASIAN CURRENCY CRISIS: A large-scale financial crisis that started in Thailand and spread throughout the ASEAN nations.

CHANGING DEBT INTO SHARES: Also called a debt/equity swap. When a company needs to pay back a debt, and it repays in the form of shares instead. A way for a company to reduce its debt without paying in cash. Some disadvantages include stock dilution (where the company ends up with more shares) and a moral hazard (for example, management just deciding to use stocks irresponsibly to repay debt). These were avoided in the story via capital reduction to take shareholders responsible and having the management ranks resign.

SECURITY DIVISION, SECTION 5: A fictitious department that is responsible for protecting nobility in this universe.

DIPLOMATIC IMMUNITY: Special rights afforded to diplomats that may include legal impunity and protections against having their dwellings searched without consent. That is why it is common to see spies driving embassy cars in spy novels.

FOREIGN AFFAIRS SECTION: A department within Japan's security police which investigates the activities of foreign intelligence agencies and international terrorism. It wasn't touched much during post-war reforms, so some older laws such as anti-spy laws are still around.

FLOATING EXCHANGE RATE: A system wherein a currency's value changes in line with supply and demand. A fixed exchange rate is the opposite of this system.

ASIAN FINANCIAL CRISIS: Investors sold vast amounts of currencies with a fixed exchange rate, and then profited by buying the currency back once it was forced to float and lost much of its value. Thailand, Indonesia, Malaysia, and South Korea were all countries that fell victim to such tactics, and the success only encouraged the offending hedge funds to keep going.

PARTY LEADER ELECTION: In the novel, this is the leader election for the Fellowship of Constitutional Government. Harsh reality means the person who wins the leadership election of the ruling party generally becomes prime minister. Those who become prime minister after aiming too high suffer for it.

PRIVY COUNCIL: The Emperor's advisory committee, also known as the Watchmen of the Constitution. Though abolished in our reality, in this world, the Privy Council lives on along with nobility, and has likely evolved into something similar to the British House of Lords, when it still held powers similar to the Supreme Court. There is a possibility that dissolution of the zaibatsu and nobility is becoming a problem in the Japan of the game world.

MINISTRY OF FOREIGN AFFAIRS: The highest position involved in noble diplomacy is likely the UN Ambassador. The EU Ambassador also probably has noble blood and several people doing the actual legwork underneath them.

CORRUPTION WITHIN THE MINISTRY OF FINANCE: Also known as the "no pan shabu shabu incident" (literally: hot pot without panties). While researching the incident again for the book, I came across a very interesting quote: "No-panty hot pot places are treated as restaurants, so unlike sexual establishments, the bill can be covered as food expenses, which is why they were used to entertain bureaucrats." Clearly, the bill was the real issue all along.

CORPORATE BOUNCERS: A group that buys a company's shares in order to make a profit. They technically differ from activist shareholders but are generally considered the same thing by most people.

TOKYO PUBLIC PROSECUTORS OFFICE: There was a time when an investigation by its Special Investigations Department invariably meant there was a political scandal going on.

HONG KONG HANDOVER: Hong Kong was handed over to China in 1997. I once heard that basing stories on conspiracy theories just makes them less realistic, because they get too complicated.

ASIA MONETARY FUND: A proposed Japanese version of the AIIB (Asian Infrastructure Investment Bank). The potential success of this project is a key point in this fictional record of economics.

THE ATONEMENT OF KEIKAIN NAKAMARO

RUNA LIVED AWAY from the Keikain's main residence, which was divided into a western-style building that acted also as a reception hall for esteemed guests, and a main building where the family lived. Keikain Kiyomaro was currently reading a book in the main building's living room.

"Pardon the intrusion, Father. May I have some of your time?" Nakamaro stepped into the room with wine and two glasses in hand. He sat down once his father allowed the interruption by lowering his gaze.

"This is a rare wine," Kiyomaro remarked.

"It's Tokachi wine. Keika Hotels sell a lot of it. It's apparently very popular paired with meals."

A maid brought in some smoked salmon and cheese as a snack. Like the wine, those also came from Hokkaido. Keika Hotels was taking advantage of the recent rise in wine's popularity by selling fresh food products and wine from the region. While there was the company's connection to the former Hokkaido Kaitaku Bank, it was the financial support of Keika

185

Bank that was the real reason the hotels were making use of the prefecture's products.

"It's good. She would've liked it. Let's serve it at our next party."

The father and son enjoyed their wine and food in silence. The woman Kiyomaro referred to was his wife, Ruriko: Nakamaro's mother. It had been a long time since her death.

It was a while before Nakamaro broke the silence. "She's a clever girl. Runa, I mean. She saw through most of our set up."

Runa was seen as somewhat of a hot potato by the family, and the recent incident meant dealing with her had just become even more difficult. If she had remained ignorant, they would be able to keep using her like their puppet until the time came that they could marry her off to the son of some zaibatsu or another.

But this incident had proven one thing to the two of them: Runa was the mastermind behind the Moonlight Fund.

"We don't have anybody. If we take Keika Bank back from the Ministry, we're stuck with Tachibana and Ichijou. And Runa isn't about to start seeking independence." Kiyomaro raised his gaze to the ceiling. There had been calls from the family for him to remarry after Ruriko's death but, perhaps because he'd loved her so much, he ignored them.

Nakamaro was their only child, and Kiyomaro was proud of how he'd raised him. In the not-so-distant future, he would likely take over the Keikain family.

On the other hand, Runa's father was Keikain Otsumaro, an illegitimate son who wouldn't inherit anything, and instead formed the Far Eastern Group. It had a lot of unrealized profit in land at the height of the bubble and survived just to the point before it would have taken over the Keika Group. Kiyomaro had avoided following its ruin too closely.

Either way, the Keika Group and its main pharmaceuticals company had survived without being carried away by the bubble economy. They were under the thumb of the Public Safety Bureau, but that had now been settled with the recent farce.

"Why not gift her a prince out of one of those three boys? I think it might do us well too."

Marrying her off to the son of the Teia Group would form an incredibly tight bond between the two zaibatsu, but other families were unlikely to just let it slide.

Cabinet ministers received peerages and were on par with lifelong nobles. Dietman Izumikawa was a baron, so a marriage between two noble families might not have been so bad either.

Gotou was a budget analyst and would be the easiest option of the three. Marrying Runa to his son would take very little preparation. And if he happened to become administrative vice minister of finance, even better. If not, there would be a position at Keika Bank for him post-retirement; the Keika Group could use someone like him with precious knowledge of financial tricks.

"What do you think of Runa, Nakamaro? You are essentially her brother."

Those words were a declaration that he considered Runa to be his own adopted daughter. There were several cases of adopted girls being married off as though they were a natural part of their adoptive family, so that wasn't what Kiyomaro was asking. It was instead a question of Runa's affection toward them.

"I think she's very capable. She was left completely alone in the world. I wonder if her talents developed as a way to show she can be helpful too."

"My brother wasn't a bad person..." Kiyomaro murmured, with a slight tone of regret. "He just wanted our father to accept him and didn't know how to doubt people. That was why all he could do was watch when the internal strife between the Keika Group and the Far Eastern Group broke out. I don't want Runa to meet the same fate..."

The recent incident had just exposed those family troubles, and now they were quarreling about control within the family. The only way to protect Runa was to treat her as though she were a daughter of the main family.

"Don't worry," Nakamaro said, putting his empty wine glass on the table. "I shall protect Runa, even if nobody else does."

"You ought to be thinking about marrying yourself. There is a daughter to a marquess with deep connections to the Iwazaki Group, the family Ruriko came from, who was asking about you. What did you want to do about that?"

Ruriko's maiden name had been Iwazaki. The Iwazaki Group was one of Japan's most prominent zaibatsu, and she was from the family who ran Iwazaki Chemical. The marriage between the two had been one of convenience to help the two groups through difficult business conditions. To the most pessimistic, it seemed that the Keika Group had sold itself to the Iwazaki Group.

Nobody could ever have expected that Runa would form a conglomerate even bigger than the Keika Group when she was still in elementary school. It was necessary to form an even deeper bond with the Iwazaki Group in order to protect her as well.

Nakamaro looked into his father's eyes to make sure he wasn't drunk, and then gave a clear and natural answer. Such was his job, after all.

"I will accept her as my fiancée."

"Protect her..." Nakamaro murmured to himself after leaving the living room.

He looked out to the garden from the hallway, before turning his attention to Tokyo's skyscrapers.

I've come to love this view. Where I come from, we didn't have tall buildings like this, and it never got so warm.

Nakamaro couldn't remember his mother, but he did remember the woman who said those words. She was to marry his uncle, but even now he remembered his breath being taken away by that golden hair, and her almost-spiritual beauty. She may well have been his first love. It was because the memory was so vague and dreamlike that he couldn't forget.

"Please. Please, Nakamaro-kun. Protect Runa."

She died without Nakamaro being able to do anything about it. His uncle followed her shortly after, dying by suicide and leaving Runa all alone.

And the promise Nakamaro had made to her remained within his heart.

"I've changed since then. Making Runa happy is the least I can do."

Whether he truly loved her, or just regretted what happened, Nakamaro didn't know, but he wanted to keep his promise to her.

Snowflakes began to dance down from the sky over the garden.

"She hated snow. I told her it meant Christmas was near. I see... So I'm making up for that now."

That snow invoked another memory of her. But now he understood.

For a while, Nakamaro stood there, just gazing at the snow.

GLOSSARY AND NOTES:

PEERAGE: There are likely quite a few peers in this world who have earned their peerage through their position.

WHY MY HAIR IS BLONDE

A NUMBER OF NEWSPAPER EXTRACTS

"*A*FTER REUNIFICATION *of the north and south, The Ministry of International Trade and Industry has put forward a plan to restore the north's economy, sparking worries about the plan's enormous cost. On top of Karafuto's economy suffering a heavy strain on its social system due to inefficient bureaucracy, outdated facilities, and rampant corruption, swarms of talented personnel are leaving for mainland Japan, putting the prefecture at risk of over reliance on the mainland to support its economy and the destabilization of public order.*

The government are treating the issue as severely as possible, putting together a long-term plan to revitalize Karafuto's economy and outlining the points most urgently in need of improvement. The plan is to partner up with the Karafuto Prefectural Office to move the measures along, but the massive budget is..."

PUBLISHED 1994 IN THE *KARAFUTO NIPPO*.

"*It has been confirmed by government officials that they are currently negotiating a deal with several zaibatsu to hand over resources* and establishments in Karafuto in return for funding as part of the prefecture's economic restoration plans. Particularly contentious is Karafuto's competitive heavy and chemical industry as well as its natural gas, both of which the Iwazaki Group and Yodoyabashi Group are said to be butting heads over.

The government has discussed passing the former industry over to the Iwazaki Group and entrusting the latter to the Yodoyabashi Group, but as the Futaki Group has also thrown its hat in the ring, it is thought that it will take some more time before the matter is fully settled.

Then there is the matter of Karafuto Bank, nationalized to centralize Karafuto's financial institutions with large amounts of bad debts It is currently in no state to be handed over to a zaibatsu, and a government insider has stated that there is no choice but to run it as a governmental financial institution for the moment.

Despite these measures, the post-unification crash has left every zaibatsu struggling to deal with its financial affairs. The Fellowship of Constitutional Government has criticized the ruling party for failing to focus on revitalizing Japan's mainland economy before focusing on the North..."

PUBLISHED 1994 IN THE *KARAFUTO NIPPO*.

"While mainland Japan is grappling with the effects of a terrible earthquake and a terrorist attack by a new religious group, Karafuto's economy is continuing to worsen and hemorrhage workers at an even faster rate. Meanwhile, there have been reports that criminals and terrorist organizations are fleeing into Karafuto, a situation the police are treating as an immediate threat.

An anonymous government agent has explained that the Karafuto Prefectural Police is still as dysfunctional as it was when handed over by Northern Japan due to corruption and bureaucracy. The source has cited the first step as enforcing the new government's law.

The influence of the Russian Mafia in the police force is considerable, with Russians being seen to pass over the Strait of Tartary to establish drugs and weapons trafficking routes with citizens of former Northern Japan.

Given that, as well as the Cabinet Intelligence and Research Office, Interpol has also dispatched investigators, it can be thought that the organization's corruption runs deep. Interpol is after counterfeit notes made by Northern Japan's government, colloquially known as 'Super-J.' The proliferation of these notes is said to be one cause of the bubble's bursting.

Following the recent earthquake and terrorist incident, the Japanese Self-Defense forces were dispatched to Karafuto, placing the whole prefecture under martial law. Since then, public anxiety has started to ease, but with rumors of a Russian oligarch being behind the mafia's activities..."

PUBLISHED 1995 IN THE SHUUKAN KARAFUTO.

"Hokkaido's economy continues to worsen.

This is due to both the bubble's burst transforming resort developments into bad debts, and a cut to Hokkaido's public works budget after the government was forced to sink large sums of money into Karafuto. With the movement of the national border to Karafuto, the government has moved the discussion of cutting Japan's Self-Defense

Force bases of its agenda. Staff from the Hokkaido Prefectural Office have been seen lobbying Kasumigaseki and Nagatachou to reject the plans, and there are those who say Karafuto's population hemorrhage and its resulting social unrest is too much for the Prefectural Office to handle by itself."

PUBLISHED 1996 BY A MONTHLY FINANCE MAGAZINE

MARKETED TOWARD ZAIBATSU, COUNTING DOWN TO

"HOKKAIDO'S ECONOMIC COLLAPSE."

"Hokkaido Kaitaku Bank will survive. It's the truth, even though it will change its name. It's a single ray of hope in Hokkaido's dark economic skies. As a resident of Hokkaido, I would like to give my personal thanks to the Keika Group, which pulled the whole thing off.

The economy is still struggling and incidents of shootouts in banks caused by criminals with Russian-made guns are still causing a stir in the papers, but..."

PUBLISHED 1997 IN THE *RYOUDOU SHIMBUN*.

FROM THE LETTERS SECTION.

"Karafuto's Natural Resource Industry Picks Up.

A government-funded construction project to build thermal power generators that use natural gas from Karafuto has been launched. Three areas were chosen for the new chemical combines that will use these generators for their power: the estuary of Ishikari Bay in Hokkaido, Sakata of Yamagata Prefecture, and Niigata City of Niigata Prefecture. The companies going all in on this project are the Iwazaki Corporation, which is one of the big three of the Iwazaki Group and is heavily involved in Karafuto; the Yodobayashi Corporation, for which resource development is a strong point; and Keika Group's Matsuno Trading Corporation, a new addition to the group that was eager to be bought due to its bad debts.

Critics say that Karafuto does not produce enough natural gas for the project to be profitable, and that the closed pipeline across the Strait of Tartary should be reopened to enable the purchase of Russian natural gas.

Due to the Asian currency crisis, resource prices are currently in a slump, and there is talk of the Russian government teaming up with the oligarchies to purchase foreign currencies, thus forcing the zaibatsu to go ahead with the project..."

PUBLISHED 1998 IN *THE KARAFUTO KEIZAI SHIMBUN.*

"Increase of Cantonese-Speaking Chinese in Karafuto.

It is said that they are former Hong Kong citizens who fled to the prefecture at the time of the Hong Kong Handover. A network of overseas Chinese was formed in Karafuto seeking Japanese citizenship after Southern Japan took over the North.

While improvement has been made, general public anxiety in Karafuto is still high. While it looks promising as a location to flee to, it has also become a final destination for money laundered via the Asian black market. Funds made from illicit drugs, weapons, gambling, prostitution, and other nefarious means are laundered through Hong Kong before the so-called 'dirty money' is sent back to Japan through Karafuto in the form of natural resources.

This network is controlled by the Hong Kong and Russian mafias, contributing to the changing power balance since the Hong Kong Handover..."

PUBLISHED 1998 IN THE *SHUUKAN KARAFUTO.*

GLOSSARY AND NOTES:

KARAFUTO BANK: A financial institution in Karafuto, whose existence I only learned about while writing. The central bank of the former Northern Japanese government.

THE GREAT 1995 EARTHQUAKE AND RELIGIOUS TERRORIST ATTACK: The Great Hanshin Earthquake and the Aum Shinrikyo Incidents respectively.

SUPER-J: A supernote based on the real-life counterfeit dollar bills made by North Korea.

TOUDOU NAGAYOSHI'S LUCKY STRIKES

T HERE WAS ONE SCENE in Toudou Nagayoshi's life that he could never forget.

"Don't forget this. Without this, the country is dead. Take it to your hometown across the ocean, refine it, then take it wherever you need to. It is like a fine woman; it must be treated with care."

Those were the words of the man who had taught Toudou his trade, spoken almost carelessly.

But speculating was not a proper trade.

Manchuria. Heilongjiang Province. Just being inland made all the difference temperature-wise.

"Are you really sure it's there?"

"It's there. The American commission have given their authorization. The equipment is the high-performance American kind too. Not the junk they produce domestically. I *know* it's there!" It was no exaggeration to say there was a hint of insanity in his eyes.

He had come here from Japan in pursuit of oil after using his expertise from the Second World War to score a job in an oil facility in Palembang. His dream was to become a staunch speculator, and he was now undertaking his life's final gamble: developing an oil field in Manchuria.

In Toudou's opinion, developing the oil field in the midst of such political instability wasn't the sanest idea in the world. However, the Kuomintang forces—fleeing as a result of the Chinese Civil War—had nowhere to go *but* Manchuria and as a capitalist bulwark, its worth was now on the verge of increasing. If, after that increase in value, oil was then discovered in Manchuria, the profits and rights were likely to be snatched up by the west's Oil Majors. Toudou's company, the Iwazaki Corporation, was afraid of losing out, and so had come forward proposing a 30/70 joint undertaking, using its knowledge of Manchuria and its geography from the occupation as a bargaining chip.

After Japan's surrender in WWII to the Allied Nations, Japan's zaibatsu lost much of their influence, so it went without saying that a 30/70 split was a big win for the Iwazaki Group. At the same time, that rate showed that America wasn't taking the venture too seriously.

Toudou had graduated from an imperial university; the reason he was now embarking on this project and getting cozy with this speculator was because after new marriages within his affiliated zaibatsu, he had been cut off from its innermost clique. The group itself had only paid ear to this suspicious speculator because there were those among its families' newer in-laws who had left Japan and been helped out a great deal by this man. Something along those lines anyway. Regardless, none of the new elite members in the zaibatsu had wanted to come to this land, now struggling through the civil war after only just being done with the Manchurian War.

"This country was able to start importing oil from America once the war was over. With that in mind, is there really any point in looking for oil *here*?"

"That's an ignorant question. It was because those oil imports were cut off that Manchuria was forced into the war in the first place—a war it lost. If only it had its own oil fields before then, it would never have gotten involved in the conflict!"

Toudou held a cigarette in his mouth to ward off the cold. Given where they were, he left it unlit. The speculator gestured for one, at which Toudou threw him the entire box. They were Lucky Strike cigarettes—goods that America had passed onto the black market here in order to support the Kuomintang. The speculator looked at the box and laughed: the brand name was based on slang referring to miners who struck gold during the gold rush. Taking a cigarette from the box, the speculator put it in his mouth and grinned.

"They were stupid. It's always more fun to discover this stuff by yourself. Now when you go home, you'll be a hero!"

Before Toudou could respond, there was a rumble, and then a burst of black liquid from the oil well. It wasn't mud.

The speculator let out a hearty laugh as his body was splattered with dirt and oil. "Look! I really found some! Well? I did it! *I really did it*!"

Toudou was captivated by this man's victory; a dream earned through sheer stubbornness and determination.

Will I be able to laugh like that one day?

That was the start of his new career.

Though neither of them knew it, this oil field, which would come to be known as the Daqing Field, would have a decisive influence over the Far East. It was this field that would push Japan and America to chase out the Communist Party troops who pursued the Kuomintang here to Manchuria.

It was this field that would set the two men on separate paths.

Toudou would start his career here as a foreman of the oilfield, going on to get stuck transporting the oil to Japan. That was how his involvement in establishing combines in Japan and exploiting and transporting crude oil from Southeast Asia and the Middle East, would begin.

The speculator would wangle big money from Japanese and American industries, and though he claimed to be hailed as a hero on his return home, his final years were anything but heroic. He spent his newfound wealth extravagantly, and after that money was targeted by suspicious groups, he would die with nothing to his name.

The speculator would have a daughter by a woman in Manchuria. At his funeral, his daughter would be attacked by those seeking his fortune, which was long gone by then. Toudou would step in to help her, and then she would eventually become his wife. Before he died, the speculator passed an old, empty box of Lucky Strikes to his daughter. It represented nothing more than the cigarette he had in his mouth upon discovering the oil field.

The Iwazaki Group started talking about an arranged marriage for Toudou, but he rejected it, leaving him with no place to take his career. He left the Iwazaki Corporation behind him, only to get picked up by Tachibana Ryuuji.

Tachibana was part of the Keikain House. Its current head, Keikain Kiyomaro, was married to a daughter of an Iwazaki Chemical executive, through which Keika Chemicals and Iwazaki Chemical formed a business partnership.

Toudou had met the speculator and gained his expertise in oil through his exploits in Hong Kong during the time Keika Pharmaceuticals was big. That, along with his experience at the Iwazaki Corporation, earned him an invitation to work at Keika Corp, which he joined under the condition that he was free to do as he pleased.

That was when Toudou encountered his dream.

"A pleasure to meet you. My name is Toudou Nagayoshi. I used to be the head of resources supply for the Iwazaki Corporation. I am now a quasi-advisor to Keika Corp, thanks to Tachibana-san's introduction."

Meeting her—Keikain Runa—had reminded him of the oil field in Manchuria. The lady and the speculator were completely different types, and yet she had a look about her that reminded Toudou of him. Toudou found himself reaching for a Lucky from his pocket before he stopped himself.

"That sounds good. Shall we do that, then?"

"You're being very casual about this. Go into this alone, and you'll be set to spend hundreds of billions of yen."

Tachibana had told Toudou what she was up to, and he'd looked into her himself too. The decisiveness behind her smile was captivating. Her smile was identical to the speculator's.

"They were stupid. It's always more fun to discover this stuff by yourself."

The next words out of Toudou's mouth came without hesitation.

"Right now, trading companies are struggling. Perhaps you should think about buying one, even a small one."

The Matsuno Trading Corporation, based in Shibaura, Tokyo: Toudou sat in its managing director's office. His wife had barely reacted to the news of his new position, as though he were her grown-up child coming to tell her they'd increased her grandchild's pocket money. The realization came a little late that Toudou may have picked up the speculator's lack of presence.

He put down his box of Luckies on the table where he could see it. That was where all of this had started. It was a part of his dream.

"I came to congratulate you, so congratulations on becoming managing director."

"Thank you, my lady."

She handed Toudou a bouquet of flowers, after which her eyes immediately fell on the cigarette box. She also seemed to notice the lack of an ashtray on the table. Her perceptiveness was something else that reminded Toudou of the speculator, but he said nothing.

"What's that cigarette box for?" she asked.

"It's a lucky charm. Lucky Strikes. The name comes from…"

PEOPLE WHO ARE REALLY RICH don't go shopping. Department stores' out-of-store sales teams come to them instead.

But even though I was currently rich, I was just an ordinary person in my former life. I *wanted* to go shopping.

I went with Tachibana and a new guard to Ikebukuro's department stores to treat myself to a day of shopping though I wouldn't have gone if I'd known it was the scene of a certain in-game encounter.

"Wow! There are so many people!"

It was winter, and the height of the Christmas season. With good progress being made on the bad debts, Keika Bank's share prices were keeping steady around the 20-thousand-yen mark despite the ongoing Asian financial crisis. The Keika Group's survival kept those prices steady too, and as far as the public was concerned, Japan's financial convoy system was working well, which was why the bank was chosen as a safe place for money at risk from the continental crisis. While the public seemed to sense poor economic conditions due to the consumption tax increase, they hadn't gone so far as to fall into a panic.

"What might you be looking for today, my lady?" The member of the out-of-store sales team asked me with a crisp, professional smile.

I only came here for some quiet window shopping, so I didn't feel I needed a personal shopper. But I was a noble lady from the Keikain Family, and a department store that left such an esteemed guest to fend for themselves wasn't much of a department store at all, was it? Especially when said guest was a member of the bank that had saved this store when it was on the verge of selling itself off as a result of its bad debts.

As for Tachibana, I was pretending to be his puppet.

The post-war period gave rise to an excellent zaibatsu: the Teisei Rail Group. After the founder's death, the group was split between his siblings and passed down, with one of the branches developing into Teisei Department Stores. The group held department stores, supermarkets, and convenient stores. During the bubble, it tried its hand at hotels and real estate, something the original Teisei Rail Group was already involved in. It turned out to be a fatal mistake, amounting to bad debts of around 1.75 trillion yen. To make matters worse, the group's main bank, DK Bank, was unable to do anything due to the threats from corporate bouncers, leaving Keika Bank as the only possible savior.

Keika Bank judged itself unable to save the entire group, and had the bad debts sold off to an asset management company, after which it was able to buy the remnants of the group. Even after that, Teisei Department Stores remained a bigger zaibatsu than the midsize Keika Group, so the bailout was met with a lot of skepticism.

"Let's see. First, I think I'd like to look for a watch. More specifically, I'm interested in a pocket watch."

A young child with a pocket watch wasn't a particularly charming sight—but I liked the mechanical ticking noise they made. When it came to watches, people often said to pick something expensive. While partly a matter of keeping yourself presentable, in truth, a watch was a valuable asset in that you could walk right into a pawnshop and exchange it if you needed to.

"In that case, what would you say to this, my lady?" The personal shopper held out a silver pocket watch to me.

I liked its simplicity. It was made of sterling silver, and the inside of the cover could be engraved, which was a plus. It had a six-figure price tag.

"I'd like it to be engraved with my family crest. Then it can act as a personal ID."

The crest was usually used for pill boxes. It was a moon-and-flower design.

"Hey, would you consider being a model?" A man suddenly showed up out of nowhere. He ignored the way I narrowed my eyes at him, creating a square with his fingers and looking through it at me as he prattled on. "You must have a good eye for picking a watch like that, but your outfit leaves a lot to be desired. We had a princess dress around here somewhere. Could you put that on? You can keep hold of the watch though."

"Wait," the personal shopper cut in quickly. "This young lady is..."

I put up a hand to stop him. It was clear from the look on Tachibana's face that he considered the newcomer a nuisance and wasn't trying to pretend otherwise.

"What? I thought I was called here to shoot for Teisei Department Stores' winter campaign! The one that decides the fate of these stores! If it's that important, you should let me do what I want! And I'm sure this young girl has the power to save Teisei!"

Technically, he wasn't wrong, though the Keika Group was still on course for a pretty bleak future at the moment.

"What do you know about me?" I asked without thinking.

"Nothing. Only that you're going to grow up to be a *beautiful* woman. That's enough for the time being, don't you think?"

I suppressed a sigh, but I had to admit defeat here. This man was an artist, so I was sure he was very picky about the things in his world. That he spoke a lot without much concern about what his conversation partner thought gave me the impression that he had a proven track record as a photographer.

"Tachibana," I said. "We've lost."

"But, my lady—"

"Teisei Department Stores has taken a gamble on this man, and now he wants to take a gamble on me. He seems to know what he's doing, so let's take a gamble of our own."

My words were grand, but the truth was that if Teisei Department Stores failed, it'd be a burden on Keika Bank too.

There was the Asian financial crisis to worry about on top of the Ministry of Finance scandal, and I'd rather not add the blowing-up of 1.75 trillion yen worth of bad debt to that list. If everything went wrong, we were looking at the implosion of DK Bank.

Ignoring my sigh, the photographer puffed out his chest. "See? She'll be a fine woman for sure!"

A fine woman who also wanted to punch him in the face.

"Um, Runa?"

"Keikain-san..."

"Keikain..."

I already know, so please don't say anything.

I'd noticed the other students whispering and staring at me too.

I didn't have a choice, okay?!

Teisei Department Stores' Winter Campaign:

"Tell me what you want, Your Little Majesty."

That campaign earned me the nickname "Little Queen." It also ensured that there were posters in every department store, supermarket, and convenience store owned by Teisei Department Stores, featuring me on a throne in a princess dress with a smirk on my face and a pocket watch in my hand. Apparently, the campaign was a huge success, something that the group had been lacking in recent years.

That photographer showed up a few times since then to ask me to model for him, but that was another matter *entirely*.

Valentine's Day.

Some called it a conspiracy by candy companies, others saw it as a battlefield for young girls, but it was the same everywhere—and Imperial Gakushuukan Academy's elementary grades were no exception. In fact, since it was full of noble-ish families, elites, and zaibatsu-born boys, the competition was even fiercer.

"Um, Runa..."

"Keikain-san?"

"Keikain?"

Eiichi-kun, Yuujirou-kun, and Mitsuya-kun all held chocolate in their hands. I'd spent five yen on each of them. In fact, I'd given five-yen chocolates to everyone in the class, regardless of gender.

"If I gave you something expensive, you'd only be obligated to give me something expensive in return. Doesn't that sound like a bother? A game, however, is much more fun!" I winked mischievously.

It wasn't until the protagonist appeared that this kind of commoner activity would really be featured, but there were some things the boys could stand to learn in preparation for that. We'd already ended up as quite a tight-knit group too.

"I don't want anyone spending any more than three times what I've given them when White Day comes around!"

I watched as the blood drained from their faces. There was the common three-fold rule for Valentine's Day—that men were expected to return a woman's Valentine's gift three-fold on White Day. But since I'd made it very clear that each gift was worth only five yen, it became a thrilling game of intellect.

"Wait, wait, wait. Three times. You can't mean *15 yen*!" Eiichi-kun protested.

"It's an inconvenient amount," Yuujirou-kun agreed. "I can think of plenty of gifts worth 10 yen, but then what do I do with the extra five...?"

"Knowing Keikain, I doubt she'd mind a 10-yen gift."

The three boys glanced at each other. I knew from the game how competitive they were.

I puffed out my chest. "It's the thought that counts. Honestly, I'd accept any kind of gift."

I knew the ambiguity would annoy them. Boys were all about competitiveness and, when it came to girls, showing off and being romantic. The tension running between them was all but visible.

"I see. So it's a contest to see who can get you the best gift," Mitsuya-kun said.

"And you're the judge then, Keikain-san?"

"Who can get you the best gift for less than 15 yen?" Eiichi-kun mused.

I'd passed five-yen chocolates to Ichijou and Tachibana too and given them the same rules.

"If blessed adults like us do not spend our money, who is going to contribute to the economy?"

That was the response I got from them: a scolding in return for my gift. That said, they also thanked me and promised to get me something expensive. They were rather capable adults indeed.

As for Nakamaro-oniisama, I joked that his thanks alone was worth 15 yen. His reply was just what I'd expect from the son of a distinguished family.

"Remember this, Runa. Gratitude and apologies cost nothing."

I was hoping for a better response from the boys. Unlike the adults, their hearts hadn't yet been hardened by the world.

"All right. I'm in!"

"I'll participate too. It sounds like fun!"

"It'll be a good mental exercise. I hope you'll look forward to the results in a month's time, Keikain!"

I smiled at them fondly as I watched—something I knew I wouldn't be able to do forever given our future. But I honestly hoped we could get on well together until the day they came to destroy me.

A month passed.

On White Day, I got gifts like gum, candy, and cookies. The challenge really got people to thinking, and I had some kids coming up with clever ideas like giving me half of a 30 yen cookie. Some offered me "treasures" like cicada skins, which I politely declined.

Of the three boys, Mitsuya-kun was the first to approach me.

"Here, Keikain." He passed me a sheet of paper that looked like it had been ripped from a notebook.

I read the note, and in some ways, it was just what I'd expected: "Voucher for a favor worth 15 yen."

"Yes! This is the sort of thing I wanted. Thanks!" I beamed and accepted the note from him.

The interesting thing about the note was that *I* was now the one who had to consider the value of 15 yen if I wanted to use it. It would have been even craftier if he'd put an expiration date on it, but maybe that was asking too much.

"Keikain-san. Here's your present." Yuujirou-kun came next, his hand filled with marbles. His angelic smile as he presented them to me made them sparkle like gems.

"That's a clever idea. I don't know how much these cost each, but I know they're cheap, so it's up to me to determine their value."

Did one cost 10 yen? Or maybe it was three for fifteen? I picked up two marbles while trying to appraise them.

"Why did you pick those colors?" Yuujirou-kun asked, his smile never fading.

I held one of them up to the light with a smile of my own as I replied, "No particular reason. Did I choose wrong?"

"Not at all."

Now I had some real childlike treasure in my possession. Since I was still a kid, I decided I should find myself an empty candy container as a treasure box and keep the marbles in there. Even if I ended up falling to my ruin, at least the treasure I kept wouldn't judge me.

"It's my turn now, right?! I've got *the* best present you can get for less than 15 yen! Take a look at this!" Eiichi-kun showed me a piece of paper.

I gasped.

"Eiichi-kun," Yuujirou-kun said, "you have managed to *completely* miss the point."

"Teia. Technically, you didn't do anything wrong, but you kind of did at the same time..."

It was a sketched portrait of me in the classroom, complete with Eiichi-kun's signature. He'd had private art lessons, so that picture of me listening drearily to the teacher, done in art nouveau style, was actually rather well drawn.

"I hate you, Eiichi-kun!"

"Why?!"

I had the sketch appraised, and they gave it a six-figure value just like that. I would need to have very strict words with Eiichi-kun...

When you were the daughter of a well-to-do family, you were expected to learn the arts to a certain degree. The Keikain family may have washed their hands of me in other ways, but not in this aspect: I knew the villainess I had become was talented too, so now it was up to me to live up to that standard. By the way, my personal interest was in classical music.

"You're here too, Runa?"

"Speak for yourself, Eiichi-kun. I mean—ah, right."

I checked the ticket. This was a special concert by the Teia International Philharmonic Orchestra, taking place in the Teia Symphony Hall. The entire performance was put on by the Teia Group. Of course, their son would be expected to go.

"Wait, you don't have a VIP seat?" Eiichi-kun said, spotting the seat number on my ticket.

Of course I didn't. I came here for fun: I didn't want to

have to go through a proper greeting as a formal guest. I'd asked Tachibana to reserve me an expensive seat, and he'd gone the extra mile by getting me one as close to the end of the row as possible. It was also why I hadn't dressed up much fancier than what the dress code required.

"I don't," I replied. "I like classic music. I'd rather listen to and enjoy it quietly and without any fuss."

"Huh. Okay..." His face said he clearly didn't understand.

Eiichi-kun called for an attendant.

Great. This isn't looking good...

"Get her a seat next to me. She's Keikain Runa, from the Keikain family."

The attendant bowed and left without another word. Apparently, Eiichi-kun's staff knew all about me.

"Hey. Didn't you hear me when I said I wanted to listen quietly and *without any fuss*?"

Eiichi-kun put his hands together, something that was rare for him. And then, very reluctantly, he asked for my help.

"Please, Runa. I hate classical music. It's sooooo boring to me!"

It was rare to hear him whine too.

I sighed. "Okay, but you owe me one. And get me a dress appropriate for sitting in a VIP seat as well."

"My lady, I actually already have one for you."

Tachibana. You knew this was going to happen?!

Eiichi-kun's seat was a box seat right in the center of the hall. Today's performance featured suites from Bizet's *Carmen* and *L'Arlésienne*. The show was around an hour in length, and since these were opera pieces, the whole thing promised to be loud and energetic. Eiichi-kun would get bored just listening, so I gave him some commentary in between pieces.

"This is from an opera?" he asked.

"Yes. They'll be playing from two operas, *Carmen* and *L'Arlésienne*, rearranged as suites."

Both operas told irredeemable tales.

Carmen was about the downfall of a man, Don José, after falling in love with the titular Carmen. The opera ended with him stabbing her to death. *L'Arlésienne* was about a man named Frédéri, whose love for a girl from Arles pushed him into the depths of insanity and ruin. As for what was so irredeemable, it was the fact that, despite these stories being so tragic, it was all undone by the bright and lively Southern-European style of the production. That was why I didn't like opera when I first started getting into music.

"She's a femme fatale?"

"Yes, that's right."

I realized how ironic everything was. In this otome-game world, I was destined to fall to my ruin at the hands of the protagonist, the femme fatale of the story. It was no wonder I liked these pieces so much.

"I've heard this one," Eiichi-kun said.

"'The Toreador Song.' You hear it a lot."

"I could listen to it a thousand times and not get sick of it."

"It's even more interesting when you know the historical context. Bullfighters used to be stars, and..."

"Why did Don José fall in love with Carmen?"

"It was changed for the opera, but it was originally to do with her Basque heritage. There are problems related to that, women's social progress, and the Roma population in Europe today, which remain unsolved..."

I suddenly realized Eiichi-kun looked like he was enjoying the rhythm of the pieces.

"I've heard this one too," he said.

"'Minuet.' You hear it in the mornings in certain places!"

When the performance was over, the hall was filled with applause. The audience began making their way home after that, but we were better off waiting from our position to avoid being caught up in the crowds.

"That wasn't so bad." Eiichi-kun seemed satisfied.

"Right?" I knew he would end up as a classical music fan when we reached our teenage years. "Did you have any favorite pieces?"

"'The Toreador Song' for sure. And I liked the last one too. It was really vibrant."

"'Farandole' from the second *L'Arlésienne* suite. I like that one too. The opening and ending are really something."

"What were your favorites, Runa?"

I inclined my head and gave it some thought. It was hard to choose; I liked them all. "'Nocturne,' from the second *Carmen* suite. I like it so much I know all the words."

"There are words?"

"Oh, yes. They go like this:"

I was the villainess: I had the body of a Mary Sue and the talents of a Mary Sue, and I was ever so grateful for them. I forgot we were in a concert hall; my voice carried further than I thought as I sang. It was that, and the fact that people seemed to recognize the song that tripped me up. There was no turning back once the orchestra began to accompany me. And of *course* they did; this was a piece they had played within the past hour. Since the audience weren't all out of the hall yet either, they thought it was a surprise encore.

I couldn't back out now; I had to sing with all my heart. "Nocturne—Micaëla's Aria." The final three quarters felt like they lasted forever, and when I'd stopped singing, the audience erupted into applause all over again.

I didn't have the wherewithal to enjoy their response. I was drenched in sweat. My breathing was ragged. Eiichi-kun wasn't clapping like everyone else. He was clapping more slowly, his eyes sparkling with admiration. I decided my heart was beating just a little faster than usual because I'd been singing, and not because of anything else.

You only know how much somebody is truly worth once they start their decline. After resigning from his post because of the Ministry of Finance scandal, Dietman Izumikawa's next party was a more intimate affair at his family's home.

"Ah, Keikain-sama. A pleasure to see you here."

"Yes, I was invited too. Do you know where Yuujirou-kun is?"

When a politician threw a party, it was one of several types. The most well-known type was to gather funds for a campaign, and they would often end up with several times the value of the party tickets themselves. That was the kind of party the former minister threw on our ship, *Actress*.

For this party, he really only had invited those closest to him: celebrities and influential people from his hometown. This party's objective was to start refining the organization of the campaign itself.

"He's over there. I can call him over if you'd like?"

I politely declined the secretary's offer. Yuujirou-kun was the one who invited me, but this was really Dietman Izumikawa's party.

"I would like to greet Yuujirou-kun's father first," I explained.

"Understood."

I made my way to the center of the banquet hall. This place was like a samurai's mansion. The Izumikawa family was descended from a samurai family, something they were famous for in their hometown. That family was also active in politics, a contribution that earned each successive family head a lifelong barony. That this lifelong barony was effectively inherited created a problem for the Privy Council system, but that was a different matter in and of itself.

Part of my job here was to be noticed and talked about by the guests. I was supposed to be sending a message that the Keikain family considered the Izumikawa family to be important.

"Ah, Little Queen. It would appear you've been busy."

"It is good to see you again, Izumikawa-ojisama. If there was an election going on right now, I bet I'd win!"

My quip got a laugh out of both Dietman Izumikawa and the attendants. There was a House of Councilors election this year, and this gathering also served the function of deciding who from this district would give the ruling party the best chance of winning. Izumikawa Tatsunosuke was in the House of Representatives, but his eldest son, Taichirou-shi, was considering running for the election.

Two representatives were needed from this electoral district. The opposition party already had one candidate, and the ruling party had one already sitting member running, and both their campaigns were underway.

From the results I knew the opposition would score a surprise win in this election, leading to a mass resignation of the current cabinet.

"It's nice to see you so confident. When you're old enough to run, do reach out to Taichirou or myself. We'll help set you up as a candidate."

"I shall certainly consider it. But it is a little early to be thinking about that. May I ask where Yuujirou-kun is?"

"Oh, yes. He stepped outside for a bit to look at the stars. Feel free to go and see him."

"I will. Please excuse me."

I excused myself, but not before glancing at Yuujirou-kun's brother, Taichirou-shi. He was a feeble-looking man with a fierce gaze. As I recalled, in the game he lost the election, and that was a severe enough hit for his father to lose out on the party-leader election afterward. After losing so much power within his faction and the electoral district, Dietman Izumikawa would fail to appear in the next election at all and then resign, something that caused conflict between Yuujirou-kun and his brother. Yuujirou-kun would be forced to support the Izumikawa family from then on, something that would be hard on him. He was eighteen years old in the game, so couldn't do anything until he was twenty-five and could legally stand for election. His route was all about the responsibility he took on at a young age, and the stress and loneliness he went through because he couldn't be open about his struggles.

"It's cold out here. How's the stargazing?" I called out to Yuujirou-kun, who was by himself in the garden. My words came out in a cloud of white mist. Even though spring was close, both he and I were wrapped up for wintery weather.

"I was looking at Polaris. I was thinking about how lonely it must be, sitting there quietly in the sky for tens of thousands of years."

His words were poetic, but at school his grades had slipped a little. He'd had his father's resignation and the huge scandal on his mind. Children were sensitive to that kind of thing because of how simple and pure they were.

That would leave Mitsuya-kun all by himself, in terms of his family's position. Although he always used to be by himself anyway, but it was probably rude to point that out.

"I wonder if it is lonely. I'm not a star, so I wouldn't know.

Though I do shine so brightly that people avoid me. Now isn't that cruel?"

I was an illegitimate child with links to the East, left alone with nothing but bad debts when my parents died. Only when I made friends with Asuka-chan and Hotaru-chan did I join any sort of social group. Though because of my advanced mental age, it wasn't too long until I felt like the one doing all the work to settle any sort of trouble between the girls. I was so totally different compared to them that they didn't know how to treat me, and they ended up choosing neutrality over total rejection. Things might well change when we were old enough to fall in love though. When there were boys involved, girls were all too happy to sell out their friends.

"That's very like you, Keikain-san."

"What? *What's* like me?" I replied defensively.

"Sorry, forget I said anything."

We laughed together in the cold air, and then looked up at the winter constellations.

"I'm sorry," Yuujirou-kun said. "Father must have sent you an invitation using my name."

"No, I should be the one apologizing. I caused a lot of trouble at the previous party. For now, let's just say we're even."

We smiled at each other again. Noticing I was shivering, Yuujirou-kun passed me a steaming-hot drink from his flask. I recognized what it was from the smell: royal milk tea.

"Here you go."

"Thanks. Ah!"

"Be careful. It's hot."

"Tell me that before I burn myself!" I blew on my tea before drinking it. "I didn't know you were into stargazing though. Let's bring the others next time."

Yuujirou-kun smiled awkwardly. There was resignation in his voice as he said, "You being here is company enough for me. And I'm not sure anybody would want to join me out here, when it's so cold..." he trailed off.

He really was a little naïve, to think that nobody would bear the cold for him.

"Hey! We've been looking for you, Yuujirou! Oh, huh. You're here too, Runa?"

"What do you mean, 'huh'?!"

"It certainly is cold. What were you two doing out here?"

"Looking at the stars!"

I was the one who told Eiichi-kun and Mitsuya-kun to come to the party. The adults seemed reluctant at first, but likely let them attend on account of my presence. I glanced at Yuujirou-kun and noticed him rubbing his eyes.

"Yuujirou-kun's been teaching me about stars. See that one? That's Polaris!" I pointed confidently into the sky.

My cheerful and loud proclamation brought the usual gentle smile to Yuujirou-kun's lips. "Keikain-san. Polaris is over there."

What?!

"Oh, yeah, I heard Polaris moves too," Eiichi-kun said.

"No way!!!"

Seeing the way Yuujirou-kun laughed as he watched us confirmed something I realized I'd known all along.

"It's not important to be right about everything. I bet you like that sound of that, don't you?" Yuujirou-kun winked at me, and I fell silent.

He had the potential to become a great politician for sure.

Because of the kinds of kids who went there, Imperial Gakushuukan Academy covered quite a large plot of land. The gates were lined with cherry blossom trees, their flowers welcoming the students every spring. When the cherry blossom season came around, I left my house a little early one morning to go and see them. I arrived at the school gates to find somebody else who'd had the same idea.

"Good morning, Keikain. Were you here to see the cherry blossoms?"

"Yes. They're so pretty."

Mitsuya-kun was standing among the trees. It was such a beautiful sight, and he looked so ephemeral, like the flowers would spirit him away at any moment. I stood next to him to look at the trees myself. The sky was clear and the breeze just enough to gently stir our hair as petals swirled down around us. They looked as though they were dancing, and the sight made me understand why these flowers were so popular in Japan.

"They say there's something buried beneath cherry blossom trees. Did you know that?"

"*Beneath the Cherry Trees*, by Motojirou Kajii. I didn't know you'd read it." Mitsuya-kun asked.

The conversation fell into silence then, but it wasn't

uncomfortable. I picked a pink petal from my golden hair and let it fly away again.

"I'm quite the fan of modern literary masters," I said. "I admire their lifestyles, and things like that."

"Are you serious?" Mitsuya-kun looked at me dubiously.

Many of these literally masters lived lives that were seen as useless and lazy. It was the work their pens produced that affirmed them. The most influential of art held a power that transcended morality, good and evil.

That was something I learned from Osamu Dazai's work, *Run, Melos!* During his life, Dazai-sensei let a friend stay at his house when he couldn't afford to stay elsewhere. That was never cited as a source of inspiration for *Run, Melos!*, but I was confident it had some influence on the story.

But I was getting off topic.

"If I had to recommend one work from a modern Japanese literary master, it would be Ryuunosuke Akutagawa's *Tu Tze-chun*."

Tu Tze-chun was about a man who came into large amounts of money, and then became poor after spending it all. Other people's cold attitudes to him during his poor period pushed him to seek enlightenment in the mountains. While training there, he found himself unable to rid himself of the love for his mother. It was while I still partly considered this life as something borrowed that Ryuunosuke Akutagawa's *Tu Tze-chun* showed me what it meant to be human. It was particularly relevant because I was set to earn great wealth myself.

"I think I'd pick Nankichi Niimi's *Gon, the Little Fox.*"

It was a truly tragic tale of a formerly evil fox named Gon, who regretted his actions and chose to help humans instead. It was only after they shot him that his good deeds were discovered. Even more tragic was that this sort of thing happened all the time in real life.

Mitsuya-kun was a lone wolf and self-centered, so that book felt like an odd choice for him.

"Why that one?" I asked.

"Because there's no book that better describes how hopeless reality can be."

Like I often was, I was struck with how mature our conversation was, given our age. Our little randoseru backpacks just made the whole discussion even more absurd.

"Are you eager to grow up, Mitsuya-kun?"

"Where did that come from?"

"I just felt like you're acting as though... No, as though you're trying to be an adult."

Mitsuya-kun smiled a little at my words and nodded confidently. "Yes. I'd like to become an adult as soon as I can."

"But that's a waste. Your childhood is precious."

"Says the girl whose face is all over Teisei Department Stores."

Touché.

"My father's been late coming home recently. He goes to work early and doesn't come home until late at night because the recent scandal has put so much on his plate. More and more, there are days I don't get to see him at all. It's frustrating that I can't do anything about it. I wish I could do something to help my parents, but all I can really do is study."

So he wanted to grow up quickly to stop feeling so powerless. But Mitsuya-kun didn't understand his parent's point of view—he didn't understand that they would be happiest if he spent his childhood like any other child. It wasn't until I came to understand that myself in my previous life that I truly felt like an adult.

"Isn't that enough? My own parents are beneath the cherry trees, you know."

Mitsuya-kun shot me an awkward glance at my casual words. "I'm sorry, Keikain. I wasn't thinking."

"It's all right. I've always felt that my life is incomplete because of it. If I were in the same position as TuTze-chun and saw my parents suffering, would I be able to call out to my mother? Honestly... I'm not sure."

The wind danced, sending down blossoms that obscured our vision.

Mitsuya-kun looked me in the eye. "You are Keikain Runa. And the Keikain I know would definitely call out. You'd shout out that the spiritual training was boring."

"Pfft! Seriously?"

The bell rang. We would need to go in for morning assembly soon.

"Let's go," I said. "We don't want to be late."

"Yeah."

I'm sorry, Mitsuya-kun.

In some ways, I probably already was enlightened. That was something I would keep a secret from everyone, not just him.

"Runa-oneechan! This way! Come on!"

I smiled when Amane Mio-chan joined the school and came to see me like it was the most natural thing in the world. It was quite pleasant to have her trotting along behind Asuka-chan, Hotaru-chan, and me, just like she used to in kindergarten. It was around that time that Mio-chan invited me to a peculiar event.

"A doll exhibition?"

"Yeah! Daddy said I could bring some friends! So I'm inviting you!" Mio-chan puffed out her chest with a grin.

I patted her on the head as I studied the ticket. The sponsor and venue for the event was Teisei Department Stores. This was my company's event. So we decided to attend the opening day of the doll exhibition, hosted by Mio-chan's father. My arrival was apparently a big deal, because the executive staff of Teisei Department Stores and Mio-chan's father were there in a line, bowing to welcome me.

"Oh, this is impressive."

"Look how many dollies there are!"

To be accurate, this was an antique doll exhibition and part of Teisei Department Stores' cultural affairs project. I had to laugh at the fact that many of the dolls on display were ones I owned. I'd bought several expensive dolls to help out Mio-chan's family trading company, and I figured I might as well have them displayed here since I had them.

They were generally called antique dolls, but could be further categorized into bisque dolls, which were popular among the upper classes of 19ᵗʰ-century Europe. Nowadays, they were considered works of art with quite the cultural heritage. That objects with such historical and cultural significance could be lined up and look us in the face like this went beyond beautiful and ventured into scary territory.

"Oh! Look, Runa-oneechan! It's your name!"

I giggled. "I asked your father to order this one for me. I'll show it to you the next time you come to my place."

"Yay!"

There weren't just dolls on display, but accessories too. Clothes, shoes, and hats for them to wear, and dollhouses where you could play with them. I found myself drawn to one dollhouse in particular: it was based on a perfectly ordinary European mansion, but it was oddly realistic in that...

"Oneechan! Runa-oneechan!"

Mio-chan was shaking me. We weren't in the department store anymore; we were in a huge house. I blinked in confusion as Mio-chan kept on shaking me.

"Mommy said the food's ready! You're always spacing out, Oneechan!"

"You should know what you're going to get for saying stuff like that!"

"Aah! That *tickles*!"

I was confused, but at the very least it seemed like Mio-chan hadn't noticed anything. Or perhaps she was just adapting. After fooling around, I took her hand and we headed to the dining room, where a mom was sitting at the table.

"You took a while. What's wrong, Runa?" This mom's face was completely blank. This faceless doll playing our mom was worried about us. I knew it was fake, but I still replied.

"I'm sorry. I'm just a little sleepy."

"Really? Were you up until midnight reading again?"

"Runa-oneechan loves books! But reading makes me sleepy!"

"I'm sure you'll come to love books too, Mio."

The door opened, and another faceless doll stepped in. The uniform told us that doll was male.

"Morning, Runa. Mio. I'm glad you're so lively and energetic this morning."

"Runa's been up late reading again."

"Good morning, Dad! And Mommy," Mio-chan said.

This was the familial warmth that I—no, Keikain Runa—never got to have. And Mio-chan had been dragged into this too somehow. I was fine, but I at least needed to make sure Mio-chan got home.

"Good morning, Mother. Father." I gave my faceless parents a properly polite greeting.

There was bread, soup, and bacon on the table, as well as apples and black tea. I had the sense that this place was set in Victorian times.

The food was delicious. Or maybe enjoyable would be more the right word?

"Guess what? I love going to school with Runa-oneechan!" Mio-chan announced.

"You really love your sister. Is school fun?"

"It's fun!"

"Do you like it too, Runa?"

"Yes. I have friends, and I'm committed to my studies. I never expected school to be so enjoyable."

The dad laughed. "I do wonder what sort of adult you'll grow into."

"I'm sure she'll be a lovely lady," the mom chimed in.

"Like you?"

"Yes, once she finds herself a wonderful man like you."

It was almost comical seeing the dolls act so warmly toward each other. I didn't know what my own parents were like in this world. This strange setting was the only way they could have any contact with me.

I didn't want to think about my parents from my previous life. I was never very obedient, and they never ever understood me. This breakfast setting must have been something I'd wished for. That must have been why I was hoping this time of warmth could last. But fun experiences were only fun because they had an end.

Part of me wanted this to continue, but the other part was desperate to get Mio-chan home. A bell sounded from the entrance hall, drowning out my conflicted thoughts.

"Oh, it's time for you to go to school. Your friends are here!"

"Go and get ready. Have you got your bags? Your handkerchiefs? Be sure to put your hats on!"

"I'm ready, I'm ready! You know I'm already in elementary school!" Mio-chan announced proudly.

Mio-chan and I opened the door to find Hotaru-chan smiling at us. It felt like I was about to wake up from this world—this dream.

"Have you come to take us back?" I asked.

Hotaru-chan nodded. As usual, she didn't speak, but her response was enough for me to let out a sigh of relief. Still holding on to Mio-chan's hand, I turned back to the dining room. Those parents weren't bad people. That was why my next words came naturally.

"We're going now!"

"We're going!" Mio-chan repeated. There was a gentle determination in her voice.

"Have fun!"

I decided I would try to remember their voices. For the sake of Keikain Runa, whose life I'd usurped, and for the sake of her lost parents.

"What's wrong, Runa-oneechan?"

It seemed like I'd spaced out. Mio-chan looked worried, so I patted her head to reassure her.

"Hey, there you are! You went on without us!"

I heard Asuka-chan's cheerful voice, and I was sure Hotaru-chan would be right beside her. Had I really been dreaming just now?

"Hotaru-chan..." I was about to ask her, but Hotaru-chan cut me off with a finger to her lips and a mischievous smile.

I looked for the dollhouse after that, but I never found it again.

"My Future Dream by Keikain Runa.

I've never seen my parents. My mother died shortly after I was born, and my father betrayed his country and was then eradicated as a traitor. The reason I am still here is because of my wealth, which amounts to more than a trillion yen.

Money is magnificent: you can smack anyone over the head with a wad of bills and they'll bow to you, even if you are just a mere child. Now that I've learned the power of money, I plan to keep using my excessive wealth to hit these adults over the—"

"Okay, that's out."

I screamed. "What are you doing, Asuka-chan?!"

Asuka-chan and Hotaru-chan had come to my place so we could do our homework together. Asuka-chan had taken my half-finished essay and tossed it in the trash. When I tried to object, she slammed the desk.

"You don't get it, do you, Runa-chan? We're reading these essays on Parents' Day! You're gonna creep them all out!!!"

The elite Imperial Gakushuukan Academy was attended by noble children, and children from zaibatsu-owning families. That meant that almost everyone was aware of what mine had done. That was why both the adults and children treated me with kid gloves, something I didn't know if I could begrudge them or not.

I was genuinely grateful for the friendship of Asuka-chan and

Hotaru-chan, who treated me just like any other child, though Asuka-chan did have a tendency to meddle at times.

"Everyone already knows, so I thought it'd be easier just to be completely open about it," I said.

"You might look like a doll and be all mature, Runa-chan, but I guess you shouldn't judge a book by its cover!"

I winced. That one hit right where it hurt. It was my stance that you needed to give as good as you got, and so I launched a counterattack.

"Show me what you wrote then, Asuka-chan!"

"Okay! I actually wrote about a *normal* dream!"

I took Asuka-chan's essay from her and read it. Her writing was neater than mine. Apparently, she was doing a long-distance penmanship course.

"*My Future Dream by Kasugano Asuka.*

My future dream is to get married. My daddy is a dietman, so my husband will inherit his constituency. Daddy said he will work for twenty more years, so my husband will train as his secretary then become a city councilor or prefectural assembly member to follow in his footsteps.

As his wife, I will create a regional election committee, have three children, raise them..."

"Okay, that's out."

Asuka-chan screamed. "What are you *doing*, Runa-chan?!"

She was wailing, but I was just getting back at her for before; I wasn't being serious. I mean, I *did* throw her essay in the trash, but she could just go pull it out again, like I did with mine.

"It has all the same 'problems' as mine does! Asuka-chan, we're reading these essays on Parents' Day! You're gonna creep them all out too!!!"

"But Daddy said the elections have been tough lately, so I gotta find him a successor as soon as possible..."

"You're getting way too ahead of yourself. You need to write something more suitable for a grade-schooler."

"What, so hitting adults around the head with a wad of bills *is* suitable for a *grade-schooler*?!"

"Careful what you say, Asuka-chan! You're about to start a civil war here!"

Asuka-chan and I approached each other, a menacing rumbling almost visible in the air behind us. Our eyes were sparking with emotion.

"Hmph. I was thinking that I should go up against you eventually," I declared.

"How funny! I was thinking the same thing. I'm going to become an excellent woman, *waaay* better than my friends!"

"That's laughable! It'll be a hundred years before you can even hope of surpassing *me*!"

"*Might I ask what you two are doing?!*"

Asuka-chan and I froze. All my instincts were telling me not to turn around, but I did anyway, only to see Keiko-san with a strained smile on her face and a plate of cake in her hands. Smiles were originally a sign of aggression—and the cake she had with her was the secret weapon that would completely pacify us.

"Girls who fool around instead of doing their homework don't get cake."

"We're really sorry," we said in unison. "We promise we'll do our homework properly, so please may we have some cake?"

We were kids after all. We were forced to wave our white flags in the face of that cake and throw ourselves down on the floor before the adult in the room.

"Wait, I just thought of something!" I exclaimed.

"What?"

"We haven't seen Hotaru-chan's essay!"

"Oh, yeah!"

We'd hastily written up our proper essays and were now sharing the cake and tea Keiko-san had brought us. Hotaru-chan had earned her cake and tea without being scolded, and though she wasn't much of a talker, she knew how to read a situation. She held her essay out to us with a smile.

"*My Future Dream by Kaihouin Hotaru.*

I wasn't supposed to exist. To be more accurate, I always thought I was supposed to be sacrificed to the gods so that I could become a zashiki warashi. But because of the Grand Master Tanuki's generous mandarin harvest, my spirit was saved and allowed to live in this world. Because I was saved, I lost my future dream. What will I become now? What will I be reduced to?"

"Okay, that's *definitely* out."

Hotaru-chan stared at us in shock. We had to repeat the same line; that was just how comedy worked.

These are the titles of the essays we actually read at Parents' Day:

"Keikain Runa: I Want to Earn Some Qualifications and Work in an Office."
"Kasugano Asuka: A Wife with Three Children."
"Kaihouin Hotaru: I Don't Know. Let Me Think About It."

My essay was praised for its detail and vividness, but that was because I'd been through the process of getting a job in my previous life.

They say the building blocks of society are first created in the tiny environment that is elementary school. I spent my first couple years of elementary school on the fringes of that environment. It was down to my hair and my parents' actions. If I hadn't met Eiichi-kun, Asuka-chan, and my other friends, I'd probably be the class loner right about now.

"Morning."

"Hi, Runa-chan! Have you done your homework?"

"Yes. Why do you ask?"

"I'm really sorry, but please can I copy off you? Please, please, please! I packed the wrong notebook for school!"

"Can't you copy Hotaru-chan's?"

"I already borrowed a different notebook from her... Heh heh heh."

Hotaru-chan smiled at me bashfully from behind Asuka-chan. Apparently, Asuka-chan was too proud to put herself in any more debt to Hotaru-chan, and so she'd come to me. This wasn't a bad deal for me either. It was thanks to these two that I wasn't a loner.

"Okay, then. You can have my notebook for one of your mandarins."

"I'll give you a whole *box* of oranges. A whole entire box!"

For better or worse, Asuka-chan was very popular. The girls were always talking about her, and those who were into the occult were fascinated by Hotaru-chan's mysterious aura. My friendship with them saved me from loneliness. Not to boast, but I definitely made the right choice going to kindergarten.

I felt a tap of my shoulder.

"Hm? What's wrong, Hotaru-chan?"

She was pointing at the classroom door. There was a girl standing there and staring at us. She was wearing the elementary uniform, so she was either in our grade or a bit older.

"Hello?"

The girl jumped when I called out to her. She probably thought I hadn't noticed her. She focused on me then, and I noticed she was older than us, but she had the same blonde hair I did. That was unusual.

"W-wait! Ah, she's gone..."

The last I saw of her were her half-up French braids. I had a fleeting thought that it was a lovely style, and that was the end of our encounter. I soon realized she had been looking at me, and it didn't take long for everyone else to notice too.

"Hey, Runa. That girl's here again."

"Her name is Lydia-san. Shisuka Lydia. She transferred from Karafuto."

"The Shisuka marquisate is somewhat famous. It was

distinguished family in the Northern Japanese government and played a big role in the absorption of Karafuto."

I put together all the information that Eiichi-kun, Yuujirou-kun, and Mitsuya-kun gave me.

The fall of the East started with the fall of the Berlin Wall. Despite what happened after the splitting of East Germany and the pattern of war in Romania, one of the biggest reasons Northern Japan was also broken up into parts after the East fell was because of internal coups happening at the time. Like the rest of the East, Northern Japan's army rose up against its reality: the Communist Party and its secret police. The difference was that the secret police soon joined the army, and the entire revolt was a bloodless battle. The revolution happened during the time of the winter festival, earning it the names of "The Winter Festival Revolution" and "Karafuto's Springtime."

The head of the secret police at the time of the revolution was Shisuka Lydia-san's father. Realizing he was losing in the internal post-coup power struggle of Karafuto's government, he sold himself to this country—Japan—at just the right time. His leaking of secret Karafuto information to the Japanese government was part of the explanation why Japan's occupation of the prefecture progressed peacefully.

He and the powerful people who sided with him guaranteed their personal safety and the safety of their assets, and one by one, traded in their own flag for that of Japan. This country used them well to progress its rule of Karafuto, and while they were heroes in the eyes of Japan, in Karafuto's mind they were traitors who were difficult to forgive.

Shisuka Lydia-san's father was given the title of marquess and came to live here as nobility in Tokyo. I was already an example of how that sort of thing was regarded by this country's upper classes.

I bet people said all sorts of things about Shisuka-senpai, and bullied her too, but she stood up to it all. That attitude had earned her the nickname "Vasilisa." The name came from the protagonist of a Russian fairy tale. To explain it simply, she was like a Russian version of Cinderella.

After hearing all of that, I more or less understood. The reason I was safe from harsh criticism wasn't just because of Asuka-chan and my other friends; it was because of Shisuka-senpai experiencing it all before me.

"So, what are you gonna do?" Asuka-chan asked.

I smiled. The boys described this smile of mine as being like a wolf that's found some prey, a comment that led to a huge row between us. But that's a story for another day.

"First, I'm going to catch her. And then we're going to talk."

Hotaru-chan, who was going to be the plan's trump card, stared at me.

"Hello? Shisuka-senpai?"

As expected, her reaction was reminiscent of the hedgehog's dilemma. No matter how much she was bullied and fought back, there was now a new side to the whole thing. A girl in the year below whose circumstances were very similar to her own. She was obviously interested but scared to get too close in case I rejected her. So I decided to reach out to her first, but she was too scared to respond, and ran away instead. I knew she would, which was how she walked right into my trap.

Hotaru-chan was standing there, blocking the way and smiling. It was kind of terrifying how perfectly she fitted the job. Still, it was an unexpected obstacle, and now we had successfully rounded Shisuka-senpai up. Hotaru-chan's stealth skills were something I doubted you'd see in wild animals, let alone dogs. That might have been a bit of an exaggeration though.

At least, I hope it was.

"Now let's talk!"

"You're not scared of me...?" Lydia-senpai asked timidly.

I gave her a perfectly honest response. People like her were sensitive to lies.

"Oh, no, I'm *very* scared. That's why I want to talk to you, so we can understand each other." I stuck out my tongue mischievously. "It's less scary than you standing around staring at me in silence all the time anyway."

"Yes, you're right. What was I thinking...?" Lydia-san finally smiled. I held out my hand. She took it and introduced herself. "I'm Shisuka Lydia."

"Nice to meet you, Senpai. I'm Keikain Runa."

Imperial Gakushuukan Academy had several libraries. It had one for each section of the school, from elementary to the collegiate level, but those were rarely used—most students favored the communal library, which was open to every level of education.

"May I see your student card, my lady?"

"Here!"

I showed my card to the guard at the library's entrance and headed on inside. The library was huge. It had giant shelves with even more sizable closed stacks underground, seminar rooms, reading rooms, various halls, and even a decent-sized café. Its use was usually reserved for students, but on weekends and holidays, it was also open to the public. It was a common setting for dates and social events in the game too.

"Welcome, my lady. You look as sweet as ever. What kind of book are you after today?"

That was the library's manager, Takamiya Haruka. She was an older lady with reading glasses, and in any different genre of game, she might give off a kind of witchy impression. A good witch, that is—not a wicked witch. She was one of those characters who stuck around for most the game.

"I'm looking for this book in particular."

"Now where were we keeping that one? I haven't seen it in years..."

This author's newer series were probably more popular.

"I was hoping to re-read it," I told her, and it was the honest truth.

I bet she was thinking I should just buy myself a copy if I wanted to read it again, but my desire to read it partly came from it being a *library* book. Whether Takamiya-sensei understood that or not I didn't know, but she led me to the book's shelf without even consulting the map.

"I was thinking about moving these books down to the closed stacks. I'm glad someone showed up to read you before I did." The way Takamiya-sensei spoke to the books was proof of how much she loved them. There were several points when I was playing the game that I wished people like her really existed. "So many news books come in every year, and so many books are put away. The unread books go to have a rest so that they can be read again another time, by someone who comes to need them."

She had been called a friendly witch for nearly two decades, and it was no wonder when she led children around this establishment and said things like that to them with a smile. According to the older students, her appearance hadn't changed a bit in that time, and she always dressed the same, though it was uncertain whether she was aware of the nickname or not. But if you mentioned the witch at the library to anyone at the school, they would at least be able to guess who you meant.

In the game too, she showed up often as a supporting character, who used her extensive knowledge to help the protagonist identify what she was lacking.

"Here you are. The book you're looking for is on this shelf. Aren't you lucky to be sought after by such a lovely little lady like you?"

"Thank you," I said with a bow, taking the book from her.

I followed Takamiya-sensei back to the counter to check the book out.

"Learn as much as you can about as much as you can, and your life will be filled with color. Every experience, good or bad, will be dear to you once it has passed."

Takamiya-sensei grew up when the value system was on the verge of flipping. From a time when girls weren't seen as suited to education, to a time when women started working. She was one of the first to experience that.

Born as the only daughter to a distinguished count, Takamiya-san was blessed with good looks and a love of learning and reading. It was decided that she would marry into another noble family, but when faced with that family's idea that a woman's place was at home, she divorced and returned to her parents. She was almost resigned to live at home for the rest of her days, dishonored by the fact that she had been "returned" by her husband. However, this was in the middle of the war, when male labor was in short supply.

The government was urging its non-military citizens to use their skills for society, and after applying to several jobs, Takamiya-sensei became a librarian here during Japan's period of rapid growth after the war.

I remember reading about the lore of the game and thinking it'd be nice to have a life like hers, but now I realized I'd never managed it. Takamiya-sensei never found another man to marry, and though her house fell into bankruptcy, she still carried out her work at the library with a gentle smile on her face. Maybe she felt like she'd fought back against her time and won.

"So you'd like to check this book out. May I see the borrowing card?"

Borrowing cards—that was something I could never forget about her. Loans for older books were recorded on a card in the book itself. You could find the name "Takamiya Haruka" written on that card in every book in this library. In other words, this woman in front of me had read every single book inside this huge library. That alone was enough to brand her as a witch, as far as I was concerned.

Not that I would call her that to her face.

There were several amusing events revolving around her in the game too. For example, if you elected to join the library commit-tee, you could check out one of the library's new arrivals before her, which would leave her frustrated.

This book also had an entry for "Takamiya Haruka" on its card. Several entries underneath that, she wrote "Keikain Runa."

"Here you go. Please return it within one week. I hope this book becomes something irreplaceable to you." She passed me the book.

There were several people who visited this library because that witch had charmed them with her smile. I was probably one of them.

"What're you reading, Runa?"

I thought it a shame just to go straight home, so I stopped by Avanti and started reading. That was where Eiichi-kun and the others found me, and where he asked me about it. That was one of the interesting things about books.

"A book I borrowed from the library. I suppose you could call it a puzzle book."

"A puzzle book that's also a story? Sounds kinda interesting."

"Don't tell us the answers!" Yuujirou-kun warned.

"I won't. Although it's an awfully *strange* puzzle..."

Naturally, Eiichi-kun and the others also borrowed the book a few days later. When they did, I was already reading the author's next book.

Hotaru-chan had a mature personality and she loved to read. She was often in the library, but Asuka-chan and I knew she was there for something other than the books.

"Kaihouin-san. Classes will be starting soon. You should go back to the classroom."

The library's witch, Takamiya Haruka-sensei, had the ability to find Hotaru-chan, a revelation that shocked me and Asuka-chan, and instantly boosted the respect I had for her.

"Is it really that amazing?" Eiichi-kun had asked.

My expression turned grave. It always did when I was recounting an experience that I didn't want to believe myself. "Eiichi-kun, have you ever tried snatching a mandarin under surveillance without getting caught on the tape?"

"An *orange!*"

"Would I be allowed to use some kinda tool from off-screen?"

"I'm not sure. I feel like there's some sort of trick to it though."

"If such a tape exists, I would like to study it first, Keikain," Mitsuya-kun said.

So I brought in the tape and let them watch it. Their faces turned as grave as mine.

"No way! How'd it disappear like that?!"

"It didn't look edited in any way either. The mandarin just vanished."

"It seems impossible, but I now understand what you meant, Keikain."

"It's an *orange*..."

After seeing Hotaru-chan's legendary hide-and-seek skills in action, the boys naturally wanted to challenge her. Asuka-chan and I joined in, and we ended up having a hide-and-seek tournament and, of course, the boys could never find Hotaru-chan.

Having humiliated the five of us, Hotaru-chan looked at us with a triumphant expression... No, it was more a gentle acceptance that we were done playing.

"So how come Takamiya-sensei can find you so easy?"

That was the next logical question, one which Eiichi-kun came to ask Hotaru-chan the next day at lunch. Hotaru-chan didn't seem to know herself. She just tilted her head at him. Asuka-chan gave her opinion—a very girly one, in some ways.

"Takamiya-sensei's the library's witch, right? She's gotta be using magic or something!"

"Magic is unscientific."

"I'm sure there's a more logical explanation."

Mitsuya-kun and Yuujirou-kun's sharp words deflated Asuka-chan's enthusiasm. I'd already tried finding Hotaru-chan using science and money, but it still hadn't worked. Not wanting to depress anyone further, I stayed silent.

"Then the answer's simple. We just need to watch Takamiya-sensei find Kaihouin."

Eiichi-kun's suggestion had Asuka-chan frowning. Her concern was extremely reasonable. "Won't we get in trouble for playing around in the library?"

It was a library. You weren't allowed to make a noise. It was such a natural rule, that other children often enforced it themselves.

Having waited for the right time to speak, I opened my mouth. "That's easy. We just won't 'play around.'"

"You want to use the library for independent research?"

We'd passed an independent-research application to Takamiya-sensei. The title was *"Why Is Hide-and-Seek Banned in the Library?"*

We intentionally picked a title that was the complete opposite of what we wanted to do and handed it in to Takamiya-sensei herself. She smiled at the document, filled out with such a childish title, as though she were endeared rather than anything else.

"Yes. We understand it's a school rule, but we can't explain *why* it became a rule. Can we ask for your assistance?"

It the type of question that could only be asked by grade-schoolers: one that would easily be answered in a simple interview about manners or school rules. But we were after more than that.

"We'd like to do an interview, a presentation on the library and manners, and carry out an example by having someone hide in the library. We heard about children hiding in the library who then got trapped in there because the librarian went home."

The person who would hide was, of course, Hotaru-chan. The boys were busy with the interview and presentation side of things. Takamiya-sensei listened patiently to my request.

"That sort of thing doesn't happen at this library. But that inquisitive spirit of yours will surely prove important in life. So I will cooperate with your research."

That was how we ended up staying in the library after hours for a game of hide-and-seek. The game would last thirty minutes. When that time was up, Hotaru-chan would come to the library entrance.

"Go and hide, Hotaru-chan!" Asuka-chan said.

Hotaru-chan nodded and then promptly disappeared. This was the boys' first time seeing her vanish like that, and they stared in astonishment. I found their reaction amusing, but I kept that to myself.

"I see..." A wry smile appeared on Takamiya-sensei's lips. She'd probably worked out what we were up to by now. But since we'd done the rest of the things we said we would, including the interview and preliminary research, she didn't say anything.

"Please start," Yuujirou-kun said, after giving Hotaru-chan the time to hide. He was measuring the time.

Eiichi-kun had one of my video cameras and was recording this part of the room. Mitsuya-kun and I were acting as seekers, following Takamiya-sensei to see things from her point of view.

"The reason I'm able to find Kaihouin-san all comes down to experience," Takamiya-sensei said as she walked through the library. The sun had already set, and the library lights quietly illuminated the deserted shelves. It created a strange and frightening atmosphere. "This place is my castle. I've been here for decades since it was built and know everything about it. Not even the tiniest of changes escapes my notice. That's all there is to it."

She wasn't even searching. Takamiya-sensei was leading us as though she had already guessed where Hotaru-chan was. The orderly shelves seemed to bow to their master as she passed.

"Found you." No sooner had Takamiya-sensei spoken than a surprised Hotaru-chan appeared, as if out of thin air. It was seriously terrifying. I checked the footage afterward, but it really was like she and her book popped up out of nowhere. "Kaihouin-san likes fairy tales and folk tales. She's been reading that series and taking out the books in order for a while now. So I thought she was probably reading the next one while she waited. Have I answered your question?"

Takamiya-sensei smiled at us, and we could do nothing but nod in response. She even took our independent research results and displayed them in large font by the library entrance. We could do nothing but smile a little awkwardly about the good reception we got.

GLOSSARY AND NOTES:

TEISEI DEPARTMENT STORES: A department store group. Logistics industries at this time naturally had debt to the tune of hundreds of billions. As well as department stores, supermarkets, and convenience stores, the group also owns other businesses such as beef bowl restaurants.

THE KEIKAIN FAMILY CREST: Also acts as the Keika Group's company badge. Based on a traditional moon-star design, the star is replaced by a mountain-cherry flower.

CICADA SKINS: When I was a kid, there were a few kids I knew who kept them as treasures.

MARBLES: Jewels for children. Similar to the balls from Ramune bottles but not the same; both are equally treasured.

ART NOUVEAU: An art movement involving artists such as Alphonse Mucha.

BASQUE: A territory between France and Spain whose independence remains uncertain to this day. But then there's what happened in Catalonia...

ROMA: A traveling people. Their persecution comprises a dark part of European history.

MICAËLA'S ARIA: She was Don José's fiancée and sang this determined song to get him back from Carmen.

BENEATH THE CHERRY TREES: The place where dead people are buried.

RUN, MELOS!: Tired of waiting for Daizu-sensei to return home, his friend went to see what he was up to, only to find him playing shogi. I would've punched him and flipped the board.

TUTZE-CHUN: Because of enlightenment training part of the story, it was apparently very tough to write.

TOUGH ELECTIONS: A phenomenon occurring within a single ward. In smaller wards, only one representative can be elected. In urban areas, swing voters have a large sway on voting behavior. It was around this time that they flowed to the opposition party in urban areas, gaining wins for the opposition one after the other.

THE BOOK RUNA CHECKED OUT: Poppen-sensei no Nichiyoubi (The Sunday of Professor Poppen), by Yoshihiko Funazaki, published by Chikuma Shobo. My recommendation from this series would be Poppen-sensei to Kaerazu no Numa (Professor Poppen and the Swamp of No Return). The anime left an impact on me, so I borrowed the books from the library and got hooked on them.

THE WINTER FESTIVAL REVOLUTION: The secret police made use of the security around Maslenitsa (a winter festival) to launch a coup with the army's endorsement. The army's main players were restrained, allowing the Japanese government to spectacularly occupy Karafuto and put an end to the Northern Japanese government. This is probably known as the "Maslenitsa Revolution" abroad.

VASILISA: Her official title is "Vasilisa the Beautiful." Though a separate story, there is also a Russian fairy tale called "The Sea Tsar and Vasilisa the Wise."

SHISUKA: An area in Karafuto. When joining the Communist Party in this universe, you become one of the upper crust and therefore your family name is changed to the area you were born. There were others than the Shisuka family who betrayed the party and guided Karafuto towards successful reunification with Japan. They were given places as dietmen and nobility to thank them for their deeds.

MODERN
Villainess
IT'S NOT EASY BUILDING
A CORPORATE EMPIRE
BEFORE THE CRASH

A MEETING WAS OCCURRING in the meeting room of Keika Bank's head office, concerning the bailout plan for Teisei Department Stores. I was present at the meeting but wouldn't get any direct input. That might have been hard to believe though, since it was a gathering of executives, i.e., the board of directors. But I wasn't involved in the meeting directly and was instead observing through a TV monitor. Though also an executive, Tachibana wasn't taking part in the meeting either; he was with me. Ichijou, who was a surprise member of the board given his age, wore an earphone that connected to a microphone I had with me.

"I will now explain the restructuring plan for the Teisei Department Stores Group."

The Teisei Department Store Group consisted mainly of department stores, supermarkets, and convenient stores, but also owned hotels, fashion malls, and beef bowl restaurants. Its bad debts had been handed over to the Resolution and Collection Corporation, so as far as any outsiders were concerned, the group's companies were now clean. The problem now was its profitability. Without the option of sending in anyone to help restructure individual companies, the first idea floated was splitting the group up and selling off the pieces.

"Keika Hotels have expressed interest in purchasing the hotels, and several firms have expressed interest in our convenience stores. There are a lot of companies eager for our supermarkets too. However, only Teisei Rail has shown any interest in our department stores."

I knew that convenience stores were to become the core of goods sales from now on, with supermarkets and department stores transforming into non-profitable industries.

The reason Teisei Rail was sluggish was partly because of its bad debts—and because it had put everything it had into the Nagano Olympics. Apart from the hotels, selling off the rest of the group's businesses wasn't a bad idea. I murmured something into Ichijou's ear, and he spoke up.

"Wait a moment. Through our links with Hokkaido Kaitaku Bank, we can obtain fresh goods from Hokkaido. Circulating them around our companies could set us apart from other conglomerates."

We could offer goods from Hokkaido to our urban customers through our different types of stores. Not only would that help boost Hokkaido's economy, it also would help the former Hokkaido Kaitaku Bank, which was struggling with debt.

"That is certainly worth considering, but the problem is feasibility. Managing the Teisei Department Stores Group is a very delicate affair, and there are some unpredictable internal figures at present. I'm sure we can all agree that dealing with the bad debts was a good thing, but we cannot ignore the possibility of the stores falling into the red."

A good example of that was the supermarket group, Sachii. While highly praised, internal discord, power struggles, and financial management failures plunged the company and its books into a darkness that even I wouldn't have been able to pull it out of.

"I can understand where you are coming from. That is why I believe the reconstruction of the Teisei Department Stores Group requires the direction of a company that can oversee everything." Ichijou's words were a cue for the secretary to hand out documents to the executives. "Let's involve the group in the restructuring plan of a general trading company."

General trading companies were one of the sectors that had been damaged through the Asian currency crisis. The transformation of bad debts through cross ownership and the Southeast financial crisis destroyed several retail companies, something that caused direct damage to the trading companies. The bigger companies with their unrealized profits were fine, but many smaller companies were treading the line of financial difficulty.

"The Matsuno Trading Corporation, after being bailed out by the Moonlight Fund, is no longer facing financial problems. We ought to allow them to manage the Teisei Department Stores Group."

Trading companies liked to talk big about their network of everything from "ramen to missiles." We had had manufacturers in Hokkaido, our Keika Bank to tally up gains and losses, and our Teisei Department Stores with a direct connection to our customers. It was our trading company that held the connections between them: the blood vessels and nervous system, so to speak.

"Yes, I understand the Moonlight Fund was fundamental in Matsuno Trading Corporation's bailout. However, are you sure you aren't just trying to foist the corporation onto us because you can't deal with it anymore?"

Ichijou ignored the executive's envious tone. The Moonlight Fund's returns were more than enough to dispel his suspicion.

"I cannot deny that some people may see things that way. However, if we allow DK Bank to carry out this bailout, there should be no problem."

Ichijou's suggestion silenced half of the executives: those who were formerly from the Ministry of Finance. With the Ministry's scandal and DK Bank's corporation bouncer situation, companies that had DK Bank as their main bank were really struggling, with many of them desperately seeking refuge from other financial institutions. Unlike other institutions, Keika Bank had started actively reaching out to the more promising companies to rescue them.

Ichijou continued his assertions. "Bailouts involving DK Bank become a matter for the Ministry of Finance as well. Although I'm sure you all already knew that."

The outcome for matters like this depended mainly on groundwork. The former minister of finance, Dietman

Izumikawa Tatsunosuke, had promised his cooperation with this, and we had also asked for the assistance of the flailing Ministry's budget analysist, Gotou-san. Keika Bank was under the Ministry's control, and with those two on board, it could hardly refuse.

"But can the Matsuno Trading Corporation really handle the *entirety* of the Teisei Department Stores Group?"

The executives were still resisting, so I gave Ichijou permission to use our trump card. DK Bank's rot was what pushed these businesses into a management crisis. They *would* let this happen, for the sake of the resource businesses too.

"I understand your concerns. In that case, let's have the Matsuno Trading Corporation undergo a merger—with the Akamaru Corporation."

The corporation born of this merger would single-handedly support the Moonlight Fund's resource businesses, going on to make a killing in the upcoming commodities bubble due once the dot-com bubble had burst. Also, our general trading companies' networks would expand, meaning the Teisei Department Stores Group would be able to reliably provide fresh food products from Hokkaido, revitalizing the conglomerate.

That was how the Keika Group came to hold a leading role at the center of Japan's economic reshuffle. However, the mountain of bad debts that Japan was holding on to was still piled high.

"The reorganization of general trading companies is accelerating. The Akamaru Corporation, based in Osaka's Chuo district, has

announced it is becoming a subsidiary of the Moonlight Fund, and will go on to merge with Matsuno Trading Corporation. The Keika Group, which owns the Moonlight Fund, will also be merging its core trading corporation, Keika Corp, with the two businesses in a three-way merger. Markets have welcomed this major news.

Keika Corp will be the surviving company, and the merge is planned for fall of this year. It is aiming for an increase in marginal profits from the merger, and while Keika Corp would usually lend its name to the resulting company, instead the new name will take a character from the Akamaru Corporation and the Matsuno Trading Corporation to become the Akamatsu Corporation. The new company's managing director will be Matsuno Trading Corporation's current managing director, and former employee of Keika Corp, Toudou Nagayoshi-shi.

The Akamaru Corporation will follow the same scheme as the MTC, using capital reduction to hold its management accountable and receiving funding from the Moonlight Fund to deal with its bad debts. Additionally, while seeking stable management, the corporation will have all its executives resign.

After the bubble burst, the Akamaru Corporation made little progress on dealing with its bad debts, and there were rumors of management trouble with the Asian Currency Crisis. Meanwhile, MTC cleared its bad debts as a subsidiary of the Moonlight Fund and saw to accelerating its resource dealings. As the Akamaru Corporation was a big name in the power industry, by merging the two, consistent development can now be expected in the energy industry across the entire supply chain.

MTC is planning to build a chemical combine on reclaimed land in Sakata, Yamagata Prefecture..."

"It has come to light that the Teisei Department Stores Group, which is rumored to be struggling with copious amounts of bad debts, is to become a subsidiary of the Akamatsu Corporation, a new company resulting from a merger planned for fall. Insiders have confirmed the rumors, leading to hope that the retail industry can make progress on its bad debts.

The Teisei Department Stores Group is a general retail group that owns companies such as department stores, supermarkets, convenience stores, and hotels. It participated in excessive investment in real estate during the bubble, leading to bad debts in excess of 1.75 trillion yen, and leading to rumors of management difficulties.

As recently came to light, the Teisei Department Stores Group had problems with its main bank in the form of real estate businesses and non-bank businesses accruing bad debts of 1.2 trillion yen. Those debts have been sent on to the Resolution and Collection Corporation for clearance, with an agreement for the Moonlight Fund to pay off the other debts. The Teisei Department Store group is set to become a parent company of the Moonlight Fund's Akamatsu Corporation, with the aim of revitalizing the corporation.

The former Akamaru Corporation was heavily involved in handling and processing grains, and it is expected to undergo a reorganization, starting with its food dealings..."

Avoiding the collapse of Hokkaido Kaitaku Bank changed

the fate of a number of companies. One of those companies was now on the verge of spreading its wings and soaring once again.

"Please go ahead and cut the ribbon!"

It was a ceremony at the New Chitose Airport. I cut the ribbon in front of me with a smile. The local broadcast station's yellow mascot beside me whooshed in to take the scissors from me and—

Wait, those hands can hold scissors?!

This magnificent ceremony was to commemorate the introduction of a route from New Chitose to Haneda by AIRHO, a low-cost airline. Guests came from Hokkaido's financial circles.

It was a route that boasted impressive profits, even by worldwide standards. Japan's airline companies held an oligopoly over the industry, keeping prices high. Dissatisfied, Hokkaido sought to set up its own low-cost carrier. The government was eager to use it as a showpiece for its new deregulation plans, and it had support within the prefecture too, so for the most part, things proceeded well. However, there were financial problems: because banks were struggling to deal with bad debts, there were very few places that would lend funds for the new start-up.

And despite being a start-up, airline companies in particular needed *huge* amounts of investment to be successful, for the simple reason that planes were incredibly expensive. Even the cheapest aircraft easily cost 10 billion yen. The company intended to start off by leasing its aircraft, but the big companies lowered their prices to fight back against it, and the smaller AIRHO was struggling to keep up, now being pushed toward bankruptcy.

AIRHO applied for a loan from Keika Bank, and I decided to make use of Ichijou and Toudou to do some meddling.

"That does not sound like a bad idea to me, but if AIRHO lowers its prices, the bigger companies will simply do the same. And when it becomes a test of strength, AIRCO is sure to lose."

"Does that mean you wish for us to refuse the loan?" Ichijou asked.

I shook my head and took another sip of my grape juice. "I don't want to crush Hokkaido's hope for a new industry. The Akamaru Corporation has connections in the aircraft industry, doesn't it? I'm sure several orders for aircraft were cancelled because of the Asia currency crisis, so go and purchase a few of the same type. If things go well, the airline can buy them from us, and if not, I'm sure the Akamaru Corporation will be able to sell them elsewhere without any problems."

Those aircraft no longer had anywhere to go, meaning we could buy them cheaply. If the Akamaru Corporation bought them and leased them out to AIRHO, then we would be in control of the flow of money.

"The point is, it's okay for prices to go down. And if that happens, it'll be better for AIRHO to come under a parent company than to try and stand on its own. I'm sure one of the bigger companies would buy it at a high price. Go and propose some code-shares to the different aviation companies."

Code-sharing meant that AIRHO could get a look in on the bigger companies' market, and those companies could also use the airport slots at Haneda that were currently fully booked. It would make things much easier for AIRHO to be able to match its selling system and check-in procedures with big companies.

"We'll enter the cargo market too. The appeal will be being able to sell Hokkaido produce wholesale quickly in Tokyo. We can't forget about the tourism companies either. Have them come up with a plan that offers a small discount to AIRHO customers at Hokkaido resorts."

For AIRHO, which had its hub in New Chitose, it would need to offer a flight to Haneda first thing in the morning. Few people flew at that time, meaning there would often be plenty of space in the hold. Hokkaido-based production companies would be able to designate destinations for the perishable goods they sent for the Teisei Department Stores Group's stores, meaning they had nothing to worry about.

While company restructuring for individual aspects was tricky, sometimes things were easier when you stepped back and redrew the entire picture.

"My lady, I have just finished a phone call with the Akamaru Corporation. There are apparently four cutting-edge American aircraft available for purchase. However, one of them is..."

We were in the hangar at New Chitose Airport, an area that the public weren't allowed to enter. I was with Tachibana and Toudou, and we were there to see AIRHO's brand-new aircraft.

"A private jet, hm?" I looked up at them.

AIRHO had started code-sharing as part of a business partnership with the huge Imperial Airways, something that allowed it to charge 30 percent less on flights from New Chitose Airport to Haneda. Imperial Airways was gaining experience in working with low-cost carriers, and AIRHO had gained an ally in a much bigger airline company. Imperial Airways were taking care of the sales and maintenance too, and it was so successful that all AIRHO routes were now fully booked with waiting lists, thanks to the new code-share agreement.

Toudou had overseen negotiating the purchase of these planes.

"Yes. According to the contact from Akamaru, this aircraft was originally made to order for the use of Southeast Asian millionaires. Things fell through when the order was cancelled because of the Asian currency crisis. The four aircraft together were originally fifty billion, but we were able to purchase them for thirty-five billion."

We climbed up the trap and stepped into the aircraft. It was so huge, you wouldn't think you were in an airplane.

"Wow. This is nothing like the planes I know."

Tachibana and Toudou smiled wryly. Toudou gestured for me to go ahead, where I found the lounge in the middle, and a bed at the rear of the aircraft.

"This aircraft can go from here directly to the east coast without refueling."

So you could go to sleep on that bed there and wake up in Europe or America. Celebrities sure knew how to live life large.

"I suppose it's an expensive aircraft to maintain?" I asked.

"Yes. It may even be a little too expensive for you as an individual, my lady," Tachibana said.

"However, I think we should keep it for you. We've had several invitations from individuals in Silicon Valley because of the Moonlight Fund, and this aircraft can also be used to entertain them," Toudou said.

Their opinions were split. That meant it was up to me to cast the deciding vote.

"Let's keep it. Can we use it for cargo?"

"It wouldn't be ready for that yet," Tachibana said.

"Get a license to transport cargo from New Chitose to Narita."

"You don't think it's a waste to use it for regular cargo?" This time, it was Toudou who sounded concerned.

I leaped onto the bed like a child, enjoying the soft, luxurious sheets. "We'll take cargo in the other planes. Wouldn't it be a pain if we had to come all the way up to New Chitose Airport every time we wanted to use this? Haneda's slots are full, so the only place we can take a private jet like this is Narita. If we reserve those Narita airport slots for cargo and rent this thing out, hopefully we can regain some of our expenses."

I spoke without much hope, but I turned out to be wrong. Because of the surviving zaibatsu and noble classes, there was demand for chartering the plane, and we were fully booked within no time at all. Celebrities would fly in their helicopters over to Narita, and then take a leisurely journey in our flying hotel to head onward to the west.

"The Akamatsu Corporation, which is set to come together under the Keika Group this fall, is upping its business activities

in Hokkaido. Due to Keika Bank's bailout of Hokkaido Kaitaku Bank, the Keika Group now owns a sizable amount of shares in Hokkaido, and part of the reason for Akamatsu's acquisition of Teisei Department Stores is to establish a business selling fresh produce from Hokkaido in the retail group's stores. There has always been plenty of business opportunity for fresh produce from Hokkaido within Tokyo, but the transport and investment has always caused hesitation. To combat this, Keika Bank is offering low-interest loans to the first takers and will sell their produce through subsidiaries of the Teisei Department Stores Group. The Akamatsu Corporation will take care of the logistics side of the business.

Some workers have criticized the Keika Group for 'buying out' Hokkaido, but those in Hokkaido itself have said that no one should criticize the group, which bailed out Hokkaido Kaitaku Bank when no one else would come to its aid..."

The Sakata combine was to be the most important project for the soon-to-merge Akamatsu Corporation's resource management department. In fact, it was more than that; it wouldn't be an exaggeration to say that the Akamatsu Corporation came into being in order to further the combine project. That was why the department would be under President Toudou's direct control.

"I'll cut right to the chase. As a domestic project, this is doomed to fail," Toudou told me firmly. A map on the table showed the far east, its resources, and those resources' delivery routes. "The price of resources, including oil and natural gas, have slumped from a lack of demand caused by the Asian currency crisis. We may have government support, but it will be difficult to recoup our costs even if we generate electricity."

The only people here were Toudou, Ichijou, Tachibana, and me—we minimized our numbersfor purposes of confidentiality.

"The Moonlight Fund's unrealized dollar profits from the fast-growing American dot-com bubble have gone up massively. Even if all of our funds from the creation of the Akamatsu Corporation and the Teisei Department Stores bailout goes on this, we still have plenty in US dollars." A report of the Fund's unrealized profits in his hand, Ichijou gave a more optimistic view.

Dollars was the key word. To deal with bad debts, we needed Japanese yen, which meant converting the currency of those dollars. In our negotiations with other banks over our bad debts, they'd always accepted us repaying in dollars at their New York branches, meaning we could pass the exchange rate risk over to them. The large banks were happy to comply; bad debts were as worthless as a blank piece of paper, so they jumped at the chance to take the risk if it meant getting practically the full amount of debt repaid. The fact that we had paid close to a trillion yen of debts and yet the Moonlight Fund still had huge amounts of money left from our IT investments just went to show how huge the dot-com bubble was.

Until now, and because of the urgency of the bad debt situation, Minister Izumikawa had taken a lenient view of our repayment method. However, since his resignation, both parties had started seeing it as problematic.

That left us with the question of how to bring our dollars over to Japan. The answer was the Akamatsu Corporation, and its resource management department overseen directly by the company's managing director.

"How will we be converting our dollars to yen?" I asked eagerly.

Toudou's smile was just as eager as he responded to my question. "This won't work for natural gas, but we have a method when it comes to oil. We simply store it in tanks and sell it when the price is high. Karafuto aside, Japan's current oil self-sufficiency rate is hovering around one percent. The price may be falling, but it's never going to reach zero. If we find ourselves in sudden need of yen, we can convert the oil into money and just take the loss."

In other words, we were using oil tanks like liquid-carrying piggy banks. Japan was reliant on the Middle East for most of its oil, and it took around six months for those oil tankers to make it to our country. All we had to do was buy up as much of that crude oil as we could while it was cheap, store it, and then sell it at a time that suited us. It was a solid plan.

"How much oil are we talking about?" I asked.

"Mutsu-Ogawara's national oil stockpiling base can hold 5.7 million kiloliters, Akita's can hold 4.5 million, and Niigata's joint stockpiling base can hold 1.2 million . We'll be capable of something between Akita and Niigata; I'm guessing you'll be after 3 million kiloliters or so?" The smile on Toudou's face widened, like he really was enjoying this. "Now comes our real problem. Oil stockpiling is part of a national strategy, so we should be prepared for the government to stick its nose in our business, but we'll want to avoid any intervention. Have you got any idea how we might do that, my lady?"

I had some vague ideas, but I kept my mouth shut. One of those was the former minister of finance, Izumikawa, and the other was Secretary-General Katou, whose electoral base was in Sakata. Both names pointed to the importance of one thing: the summer's House of Councilors election.

"How are things looking?"

"Not fantastic, I'm afraid. Realistically speaking, we're looking at a 70 percent chance that Izumikawa-shi will lose; 60 percent if we're lucky."

I asked Tachibana to analyze Yuujirou-kun's brother, Izumikawa Taichirou-shi's chances in the upcoming House of Councilors election. The results weren't great. And without the sugarcoating things: they were *bad*. Dire even.

"He seems to have been disadvantaged by his father's resignation due to the Ministry of Finance scandal, after already being in a poor position from his being a newcomer."

"What's wrong with being a newcomer?" I asked, studying the several reports on the table.

Tachibana picked one of the pages up and handed it to me. "The district Izumikawa-shi will run in is to vote for two Councilors, and the votes are split. The candidates from the ruling party are poised to take more than twice as many votes than the candidates from the opposition, but we cannot assume that those votes will be split evenly."

The problem was vote splitting. If Izumikawa-shi and his fellow candidate each received half the votes for the ruling party, in theory they would *both* win the election.

"The increase in swing voters is not doing us any favors in this situation. A large portion of them seem set to vote for the opposition. There are several of them in the large cities now, including the prefectural capitals, and while their presence doesn't necessarily mean votes for the opposition will increase, they are certainly not set to decrease."

It was those independent voters propping up the opposition in the cities of the constituencies that heavily favored the ruling party. But I knew these voters wouldn't be a threat until at least 2009, so they could be safely ignored for now. In the region we were dealing with, support was overwhelming strong for the ruling party.

"Duty and humanity are what counts when it comes to election. There are several people who are indebted to Dietman Izumikawa, head of his faction and favored to run for prime minister. Unfortunately, the scandal's effects have overridden that and given them reason to turn their backs on him. Izumikawa-shi has likely lost a lot of support to his fellow running party member."

"This is why factional disputes are so annoying..." I lamented.

The opposition didn't get much of a look into the Japanese government because factional disputes among the Fellowship of Constitutional Government fulfilled the same role as an entire regime change. Even if you had two members from the party in the same electoral district, it was almost guaranteed that they would belong to different factions within the party itself. They were allies on the surface, but when it came to the vote itself, they would try to trip each other up, which was amusing to watch to say the least. Although the election reforms in the nineties were supposed to do away with such internal politics...

Regardless, all of this led to a lot of clashing involving the central figures of the party and leading to fierce quarrels.

"What are the central members of the party saying?"

One of those central figures leading these elections was Secretary-General Katou Kazuhiro, who had launched a vicious attack to poach Dietman Izumikawa's faction from him. Tachibana answered my question matter-of-factly as though he had already looked into what the secretary-general was doing.

"He said that recognizing Izumikawa-shi was 'difficult,' and that he would put further thought into it after the election."

Talk about a lack of enthusiasm.

Even the center of the party had concluded that Izumikawa Taichirou-shi was likely to lose, which was bad news for me. If he lost, he might take it out on me and perceive me as an ally of Secretary-General Katou's. Given the future I knew, I wanted to lower the risk of being on bad terms with Yuujirou-kun as much as I could.

"Is there anything we can do to get him elected?"

Tachibana's gaze was a little stern as he asked, "Is this something you wish to do for Izumikawa Yuujirou-sama?"

"I suppose. I've made friends with him; I don't want that to be destroyed because of all these adult problems." I followed up with a reason Tachibana couldn't deny: something Yuujirou-kun should take pride in. "When I was kidnapped, he and the other two boys put themselves at risk by speaking to the criminals. I haven't returned the favor to him yet."

Tachibana sighed.

Duty and humility: he'd said it himself that they mattered in elections, and now I was showing him how those things fed into my decision.

"Getting him elected to an electoral district will be difficult. Our best bet would be through the proportional representation vote, in which case his position in the candidate list will be vital."

So we weren't completely out of options. Plus, I had my connections to both Dietman Izumikawa and Secretary-General Katou.

"Let's go for it. This is what we'll use our money and connections for."

For Secretary-General Katou, we had Sakata's oil reserves, and the total support of the Keika Group as a bargaining chip.

"What about Dietman Izumikawa?"

I owed Yuujirou-kun, but that same kidnapping incident was more likely to be a source of resentment for his father since it happened at his party. I needed to convince Tachibana using a different kind of logic here.

"Hokkaido."

Tachibana cocked his head.

"The Keika Group now has a foothold in Hokkaido financial circles after bailing out Hokkaido Kaitaku Bank. The economy up there is all about public works projects, and our Keika Group will need a representative in those circles."

Public works projects required consideration when it came to getting money from Tokyo to the region in question. The existence of someone in a high position with connections to the capital could make all the difference in attracting funding.

"You mean, use Izumikawa-shi to get his father's assistance?"

"He may have resigned, but Izumikawa-shi is still a major player who made it to minister of finance. I don't think the Keika Group could ask for a better representative!" I smiled.

Tachibana let out a resigned sigh. "Elections are about *money* too. You ought to make sure you're ready to make a sizable donation."

"Oh? Don't tell me this is going to cost more than all the money we threw away creating Keika Bank..."

Elections cost money—but the numbers were nothing compared to the massive figures we'd earned from playing the markets.

Later reports from Tachibana showed we spent around 10 billion yen on the election—a mere *fraction* of what the Moonlight Fund currently had in its possession.

With his father caught up in the scandal, Yuujirou-kun had been doing his best to keep to himself. But a few days later, he whispered something to me as I passed him. It was the day after the news broke that Izumikawa Taichirou-shi was going to step back as a regional candidate and focus on getting elected via proportional representation.

"Thank you, Keikain-san."

I doubted he wanted me to stop and turn around, so I did the polite thing and let him go. I tried to pretend I hadn't heard anything when Eiichi-kun came up to me.

"Did he say something to you, Runa?"

"I'm not sure. Are you chasing after him, Eiichi-kun?"

"Yeah. He's trying to be all thoughtful and stay away from everyone, but I don't like that kinda 'thoughtfulness.' So I figured I'd follow him around."

"Good luck. I'm rooting for you!"

"Thanks! If I catch him, let's invite Mitsuya and all go to Avanti."

And with that, Eiichi-kun was gone. Watching him leave, I sent a quiet response to Yuujirou-kun through the empty air.

"You're welcome."

Japan's corporate groups comprised spineless syndicates held together by cross ownership of stocks. A zaibatsu's companies could be directed via a central or holdings company, but nowadays, businesses belonging to smaller and medium-sized zaibatsu were trying to grow more quietly in order to protect themselves, in case of dissolution.

I was in my living room going over some documents that had been prepared for me.

"The Choufuu Council, hm? That's quite the name."

Starting as a medium-sized zaibatsu with Keika Pharmaceuticals at its center, the Keika Group was now trying to grow into a stronger corporate group incorporating the Far Eastern Group, Teisei Department Stores, the Akamatsu Corporation, and so on. The problem with that was how to control the other business via the central business itself. The solution? A group leadership system constructed from a presidents' council.

Presidents' councils were all about vapidness, so naturally, many of them were given elegant names. The Choufuu Council we were creating had its name originate from *kachoufuugetsu*, or the beauties of nature, a word composed of the characters for flower, bird, wind, and moon. The name "Keika" already had the meanings of moon and flower within it, leaving us with bird and wind, or Choufuu.

"We're so big now that we can't just use Keika Pharmaceuticals to run everything," I mused. "So...which of our companies will be included in this council?"

"Keika Pharmaceuticals, Keika Chemicals, Keika Maritime Insurance, Keika Life Insurance, Keika Storage, Keika Hotels, Teisei Department Stores, and the Akamatsu Corporation, when it is formed in the fall," Tachibana replied. "Along with the formation of the presidents' council, there are plans to start cross ownership of shares."

When it came to managing a group, cross ownership of shares wasn't a bad idea, but the Keika Group had expanded so rapidly that things were more complicated. Keika Hotels, formerly Far Eastern Hotels, picked up the former Hokkaido Kaitaku Bank's resorts, and was planning to merge them with Teisei Department Stores' Triple Ocean Hotels, pushing down Keika

Pharmaceuticals' and Keika Chemicals' share of equity. In cutting out their bad debts, Teisei Department Stores and the soon-to-be Akamatsu Corporation suffered a loss, and took responsibility for that through capital reduction, gaining their funding via the Moonlight Fund. The problem companies here were Keika Bank, which was all but nationalized, and its child company, Keika Securities.

Since the two companies received special loans from the Bank of Japan to deal with their bad debts, the Ministry of Finance had a *huge* influence over them. I had been thinking of using the Keika Group to take back our rights of management over them now that the Ministry of Finance was essentially brain-dead from the recent scandal. But I also had a bit of an ulterior motive. The two companies were done dealing with their bad debts and if they were lifted from their quasi-nationalization and relisted on the market, we could show that to the financial world. They were also expected to be prime examples of the successes of the Ministry's financial big bang: namely, its deregulation. Bank holding companies were the centerpiece of the new plans, and the two companies were to be used as the trump card to sound out the industry overhaul that would make it possible to control banking, brokerage, and insurance within a single company.

The Keika Group had insurance firms in the form of Keika Maritime Insurance and Keika Life Insurance: Teisei Department Stores had mid-sized life insurance, damage insurance, and brokerage firms. The Ministry of Finance's initial plan was to merge these companies, as well as Keika Bank and Keika Securities to create Keika Holdings. Yet everything went south after the Ministry's scandal, so now I was considering shouldering the task myself—something the now-immobile Ministry jumped at.

All the legal preparations were in place, and now they would put Keika Bank and Keika Securities up for auction. We would just need to win that auction.

"So the idea is to use the Moonlight Fund to buy shares in them, in order to complete our cross ownership?"

"That's correct." Tachibana nodded.

Though we spent close to a trillion yen out of the dot-com earnings from my Moonlight Fund, we still had hundreds of billions worth of assets left. By using those assets as security, we could borrow capital from Keika Bank to buy shares in the bank and complete our cross-ownership plan. Since the Moonlight Fund was American based, it was treated as a different entity from Keika Bank, which was the key to our plan.

"Japan's current recession all started because zaibatsu and their flighty managers muddied the waters by starting to build these groups! We can't let them get away with their games if we ever want Japan to recover! We need to take Japan's economy out of the grip of the zaibatsu and revitalize it via structural reform!!!"

There was an economics program on the TV, and a dietman from the opposition was speaking. His criticism was focused on Keika Bank, which looked as though it had used its special loan from the Bank of Japan to fatten itself up while the economy waned. I turned the TV off and inclined my head.

"What was that all about?"

"I believe it stems from jealousy," Tachibana replied curtly.

The criticism came just when we were about to start restructuring our group. This recent bout of criticism on these shows and in weekly publications called for the dissolution of the zaibatsu and an end to cross ownership within a group.

"Somebody's instigating this," I declared, though I already knew as much from my previous life. "A vulture fund. That would be a sweet, juicy plum to bite into."

Funds that bought up failed businesses, sold off their assets, rebuilt them, and then made profits by relisting those companies or selling them off were known as "vulture funds" in Japan. It was a great time for those funds to buy now, what with Japan's businesses struggling with their bad debts. Unlike my previous life, financial institutions were holding out better, making them more difficult to poach. But the Ministry of Finance scandal had left Keika Bank and Keika Securities vulnerable to being picked over.

"Just to check, what are Keika Bank and Keika Securities' share prices and stockholders looking like right now?" I asked.

"Keika Bank has currently been delisted due to its string of mergers and capital reductions. The Ministry of Finance holds most of its shares, which was likely their objective. Keika Securities exists solely as a child company of Keika Bank, so winning the bid for Keika Bank means winning Keika Securities as well."

Special loans from the Bank of Japan came with no collateral and no restrictions, but they were still repayable. Because of my instructions to Ichijou to invest in the dot-com bubble once the financial crisis had calmed down, we had made plenty of money, meaning we had achieved the total repayment of those special loans. The best thing about that total repayment was that shares in Keika Bank could now be sold off.

Before the Bank went for auction, the Moonlight Fund would distribute its majority shares among every company of the Keika Group, and then sell off the rest after the Bank was listed again, making back the money we spent winning the auction.

The plan was to jump in and snatch Keika Bank back. Fortunately, getting Keika Bank meant getting Keika Securities too, and since it was the group's central bank, that meant Teisei Department Stores and the Akamatsu Corporation would be able to access it as well. Then we could sell it off or restructure it or whatever—but either way we'd be getting our hands on a lot of treasure.

"An auction, hmm..."

Wanting to earn themselves support before the upcoming election, the ruling party had been discussing the Keika Bank "problem" as a political issue. Ordinarily they would have ignored it, allowing us to deal with our share-acquisition problem without trouble, but now it was being auctioned off in the name of "fairness."

I narrowed my eyes, deep in thought. There was a knock on the door, and I spotted Aki-san—my maid—in the corner of my eye. She went to whisper something to Tachibana.

"My lady, you have a visitor."

"I didn't have plans to see anybody today. Who is this tactless visitor?" I narrowed my eyes.

Tachibana passed me the business card that Aki-san had given him. The name on it was trailing behind a long, elegant title.

"Pacific Global Investment Fund. Far East fund manager. She said her name was Angela Sullivan-shi."

"Would you like some *bubuzuke*?" I asked.

"Oh, yes, please. I love *bubuzuke*!"

Her Japanese was fluent, but her cultural knowledge was lacking, and it had me in a quandary. Offering a visitor *bubuzuke*—a dish of rice and tea—was supposed to indicate that they weren't exactly welcome—in Kyoto culture, at least. That had clearly gone right over this woman's head. There was a reason I didn't like dealing with foreigners...

Completely oblivious, Angela got right to the point.

"The Moonlight Fund. You're the real brains of the operation, right, Little Queen?"

I felt like I was being fingered for a crime. Their vulture fund had a mountain of assets at its disposal, and an *absurd* number of connections. I fully expected to be found out eventually, but this was the first time anyone had ever accused me so brazenly.

"Nobody normal is going to believe somebody who says they run a fund containing hundreds of billions of yen worth of assets belonging to a *grade-schooler*."

"Our intel doesn't lie. Most important investment matters are decided at the Keika Bank's head office, and the communication between that office and this estate is on the increase. It doesn't take a genius to figure out who the boss is."

The United States had a surveillance system known as ECHELON. The true state of that system was shrouded in darkness, but there was a chance they had our bidding information for the auction of Keika Bank.

In which case, this woman was openly *threatening* me.

"In that case, could I ask for your *other* business card? I know you have one. It should have an eagle on it."

Angela was hinting that she was involved in ECHELON, so it would be weird if she *didn't* have said business card on her. Realizing I knew who she was, Angela flashed me a confident smile before handing me her second business card, just like I'd asked.

"So... you're a data analyst working at the Japan-America Embassy. That sounds like a difficult job. It's a surprise that the CIA is bothering to spy on the economy of one its allies."

"The business world is not all sunshine and rainbows to the extent that we can let our guard down just because the East has fallen, Your Little Majesty."

So the CIA had been watching me ever since my parents colluded with the East. All I knew from the game was that the villainess would fall to ruin, but by living out her life, I had learned so much more. Keikain Runa existed in a massive minefield, and right now I was facing the biggest mine of all. Perhaps this was how she ended up as a former eastern spy, who used the protagonist to get involved in a takeover of Teia Motor Co. After Angela, maybe someone from Russia or a different country would make contact with me.

"Let's get back to the point. You're here to tell me not to bid for Keika Bank, yes?"

"Ah, excellent, you've saved me an explanation."

The winning bid for Keika Bank was estimated to be around 800 billion yen. This wasn't the sort of thrilling game where the bidding could be pushed up to a trillion yen: there weren't enough players for that. America's aim was likely to use the acquisition of Keika Bank as leverage to oil up the Japanese economy, which had become stiff thanks to its zaibatsu.

"There's no advantage for me to pull out of the bid," I said.

"Yes, you're right about that. But you will be *dis*advantaged if you win because we'll continue to keep a keen eye on you." Angela beamed at me, which I could only respond to with a wry smile. If that wasn't a threat, what was?

"I'm not sure that's something you should be saying to someone so close to the government of an allied country."

"Please accept my apologies. Money evens the playing field."

Her role was to lay down the initial threat. The plan was probably to play a strong hand from the start, and then win my concession.

"There's a *lot* of money involved in this business. I imagine you must have enough money to win the bidding yourself if you're asking me to withdraw?"

"Of course. We have several plans in place. And please, whatever we do, I truly hope you'll forgive us."

The Moonlight Fund was based in America: most of its wealth was in American tech shares, which we'd needed to put up as collateral in order to borrow money. But we couldn't borrow money from the Keika Bank using those stocks as collateral like we had before in order to win the auction—Keika Bank itself was supposed to stay entirely neutral in the whole affair. Instead, we were using a syndicated loan from domestic banks linked to the Imperial Iwazaki Bank. It was the Ministry that urged those banks to lend to us, of course. Meanwhile, this vulture fund got its money from the markets. It was probably worth considering that one of the domestic banks was ready and willing to betray us, attracted by the promise of profit from the dissolution of Keika Bank.

Keika Bank had Keika Securities, one of Japan's four major brokerage firms, as a child company. I'd bet every large bank in the country had its eye on Keika Bank before the big bang of financial regulation was due to come in.

"I see what you're saying. Even I don't want any scary people watching me. Please tell your bosses that I'm prepared to think things through. Aki-san, please see our guest out."

"Thank you," Angela said, "and goodbye."

I waited until Angela was completely out of sight, her cold *bubuzuke* left untouched on the table, before sneering.

"I wonder if you'll even be able to participate in the auction at all."

"The votes that have been tallied thus far in this House of Councilors election suggest that the ruling Fellowship of

Constitutional Government is unlikely to reach a majority, and will lose the election. Here are the current results by region..."

Once they were out of the Diet, a dietman was an everyday citizen, just like everybody else. And through that process, their true supporters became clear. It was about who was with them in their office before the results were finalized. That was how almost all dietmen selected their successors and who to cut off.

"We're here to play!"

"Runa! Stop pulling on my hand!"

"Excuse us..."

The election results were just about to be announced when our inappropriately cheerful voices caused a stir among the supporters in Izumikawa Taichirou-shi's office. Ignoring them, Yuujirou-kun came rushing up to us.

"You didn't need to come all this way."

"What's wrong with supporting a friend who's helped you out in the past?" Eiichi-kun snapped defensively.

Mitsuya-kun stared at the one-eyed daruma in the room before asking, in a quiet voice, "How's the situation?"

"Not good, but there's still a chance of victory. Things would be much less certain if my brother were still running for his district."

It was always going to be tough for the ruling party to win after bearing the brunt of the Asian financial crisis and the consumption tax hike, but the mistakes made during the Ministry of Finance scandal had an even worse effect, causing the party unexpected losses in quite a few districts.

As a result, the party's cabinet would be forced to resign with a new cabinet formed after the party leader elections. Until normal circumstances, former Minister Izumikawa should have been the top pick for the next party leader.

"Thank you for coming. I won't forget that you did."

Candidate Izumikawa Taichirou was led to us by his secretary. He'd looked so stern before, but now he seemed much more friendly, albeit quite exhausted. When aiming for election via proportional representation, you had two options: fly around the entire country or build up ironclad support in your own district. Candidate Izumikawa hadn't just campaigned in his home area of Kanto: because of me, he had gone around Hokkaido too, which must have been exhausting. It was no surprise; I'd used Tachibana and Ichijou to build him the funding and support base in the region. That support came from Hokkaido's financial circles, not least those involved with Hokkaido Kaitaku Bank.

The Izumikawa family knew how easy it was to run in an election when reputation was the only thing they had to worry about for themselves. They even understood that I was hoping for help with the selling off of Keika Bank in exchange.

"We're just here to support our friend," I said, exchanging a firm handshake with Taichirou-shi as cameras flashed around us. If he won this election, I'd probably end up on the second page of the regional newspaper.

"Father asked to meet you once the results were out. I'm sorry for the trouble, but please do see him." With that final whisper, Taichirou-shi disappeared back into the sea of voters.

It would be past midnight before that circle of supporters would erupt into cheers and applause.

"This year's House of Councilors election has resulted in defeat for the ruling party. We have word from party headquarters that the Prime Minister has just announced his resignation to take responsibility—excuse me for stopping here, but we now have the final space from the Proportional Representation Block confirmed. The winner is Izumikawa Taichirou-shi of the Fellowship of Constitutional Government!"

"Sorry to keep you waiting, Little Queen."

"Honestly, why does everybody insist on calling me that? Although I can't say I dislike it..."

While the rest of the office was rapturous with celebration, I was meeting with Dietman Izumikawa Tatsunosuke in a room further down the hallway. Neither of us were smiling. The dietman's gaze was calculating, as was mine as I stared coolly back at him.

"You assisted my son as much as you did because of Keika Bank, yes?"

"Not exactly."

Dietman Izumikawa looked taken aback. I paid no attention to his reaction, instead sipping on the grape juice he'd had prepared for me.

"If I had to give a reason, it would be Yuujirou-kun. I know it isn't really my place to say anything, but don't you think *you* could have done a little more?"

"...Yes, you're right. Without my position, I'm just a man, so I had no choice but to cling to it. Such is the curse of my occupation."

The Izumikawa family had four children—two male and two female. The daughters caused problems. In order of age, the children went boy, girl, girl, boy, with Yuujirou-kun the youngest child of the four. He was the only child of the diet-man's second wife, which just served to make things even more complicated.

To be more specific, the problem was caused by one girl's husband and the other's fiancé, an influential prefectural assembly member and city councilor respectively. They knew Taichirou-shi lacked popularity and were already vying for his spot as successor. If he'd lost this election, the family would probably start a vicious inter-familial war, just like they did in the game.

"You still have a lot to be proud of," I said. "So how about it? Care for another fifteen minutes in the limelight?"

"You were after *me*? Now that's a surprise!"

Though the story may have been different since Taichirou-shi won, Dietman Izumikawa was originally destined to run in the party leadership contest in one last desperate attempt to hang on, only to lose and leave the political sphere behind him. The presence or absence of Dietman Izumikawa and his authority over financial institutions would have a dramatic effect on the stability of Japan's economy from now.

Suddenly, Dietman Izumikawa's phone rang.

"Excuse me for a moment." He pressed the speaker button, allowing me to hear the call. "Hello? It's me."

"Izumikawa-kun. Congratulations on your son's victory."

It was the voice of one of Dietman Izumikawa's rivals.

"It's rather embarrassing to be congratulated by you, Minister Fuchigami Keiichi."

The minister for foreign affairs. In the world I knew, he became the next prime minister. He was here with a deal.

"How about it? With our loss, there's no room for infighting. Why not team up with me? I'll make it worth your while."

This was a moment that could change the course of history.

Without knowing whether it was a good idea or not, I grabbed a notepad and pen from the table, ripped off a page, and then showed Dietman Izumikawa what I'd written on it. He looked at me, looked at the note, and then looked at me again—this time with a glare. I glared back at him. The silence only spanned a few seconds, but it felt like an eternity.

"I want vice president or deputy prime minister."

"Very well. I can arrange that for you. Prepare me a list of potential ministers from your faction."

I breathed a sigh of relief at the minister's response.

The next thing he said came out of the blue and struck a devastating blow.

"Make sure you give the Little Queen, who encouraged you to work with me, proper thanks."

"I will. By the way, she said she likes that nickname. Goodbye."

I was floored. How did he know I was here? Dietman Izumikawa smiled for the first time since entering the room.

"He has good ears. Apparently, he can pick up even the smallest noises from the other end of phone lines. The writing and tearing of the paper told him I had someone else with me, and the sigh was probably what told him it was you. Didn't you notice that the TV cameras caught you shaking hands with my son earlier? We have workers who set up TV feeds into every office at the party headquarters. Anyone eagle-eyed enough will pick up on that sort of thing."

"My, isn't the world of politics terrifying."

"If you ask me, he reminds me of your grandfather. There was something unsettling about him too."

"How rude! I may be young, but I am still a *lady*!"

We smiled at each other. We quickly rearranged our features when there was a knock on the door and the secretary walked in.

"Pardon me. The media would like a photograph of Dietman Taichirou being presented with flowers."

"You heard her." Dietman Izumikawa turned to me. "Would you like to do the honors?"

"You are asking a lot of me..." I sighed.

Fuchigami Keiichi formed his cabinet, and Izumikawa Tatsunosuke lent his support as the party's vice president. His and his faction's work in doing so was popular, and it affirmed to everybody, both within and without the party, that he was back to his former glory. One of the cabinet's first problems to tackle was the Russian financial crisis and the selling off of Keika Bank. History would record that they managed both while limiting damage to the wider Japanese economy.

"Your brother hit me. He also warned me not to step foot in your estate again."

"Which is why I've come to you directly. Nakamaro-oniisama would be sure to scold me if he found out."

I had brought Tachibana with me to a café in Kasumigaseki to meet Inspector Maefuji Shouichi of the National Police Agency's Public Safety Bureau. We sat at the far end of the establishment.

"Can I ask why you're digging up a settled matter after all this time? Not to mention you're involving Vice President Izumikawa and the foreign—no, prime minister. With those two involved, I'm afraid I cannot speak with you without a good reason." The inspector looked nonplussed, and his eyes weren't smiling.

This was indeed a dangerous conversation.

I sipped my grape juice through my straw before moving on to the main topic.

"That attempt to kidnap me was enacted by the Russian mafia. But there's more to it than that, isn't there?"

"I think that's a dangerous topic to be discussing in a place like this."

"Really? But I trust in your abilities, Inspector."

He was the one who picked this café. It was likely that the staff, and even the customers, were affiliated with the Public Safety Bureau. That was how serious this discussion was.

"The situation has changed. The mastermind who planned the whole thing went too far."

My efforts in merging trading companies, also known as Japan's underground intelligence agencies, was proving effective even here. The man I had chosen as Akamatsu Corporation's president, Toudou, was a professional who had honed his career in the oil fields. The personal connections I had access to through each trading company were enough for me to suspect that things had completely changed behind the scenes.

"The Asian currency crisis held back Japan's recovery while pushing American hedge fund profits through the roof. That's exactly how they planned it. But they couldn't control the chain reaction sparked by the crisis, and they never expected the Hashizume cabinet to implode. Rather, they *wanted* it to, just not with the timing that it did."

"I'm not exactly sure what you're trying to tell me." Inspector Maefuji was playing dumb.

"There will be a financial crisis in Russia," I told him decisively, "and America will be caught up in it."

"What...?"

Tachibana passed a report to Inspector Maefuji. My knowledge of events was corroborated by Ichijou, and his work in the financial sector, and Toudou, who was on the frontline of making deals in oil.

"Is this true?" Inspector Maefuji asked.

"I wouldn't be sharing a drink with you if it *wasn't*."

The Asian currency crisis had pushed several countries' economies into danger, and though Japan helped them to pull through, now that it had gone through a cabinet change, it was diplomatically dead. As a result, anxiety was running rampant through the markets, with debt from emerging nations being dumped, pushing them further into crisis and creating a vicious cycle. American hedge funds were relying on Russian bonds—which they thought were stable—but the damage was about to spread to those too. In short, the reason a CIA agent and hedge fund manager like Angela contacted me, was likely because she was after my money to repair the damage caused by the crisis.

"What did you want to ask me then?" Inspector Maefuji said.

"I want to know the name of this hidden mastermind, of course."

"I'm sure you've already guessed without having to hear it from me. Assuming your report is accurate, said mastermind is doomed anyway, so surely there's nothing for you to do?"

It sounded like a casual conversation, but both our smiles were completely superficial.

"As an investigator, your job is to investigate. You don't arrest people directly."

"Now I see. You want me to name the criminal so you can use it against the big wigs as an 'official opinion.'"

"I'm glad you understand."

I was still in elementary school: even if the Keika Group did anything in its capacity as a business, it would still be seen as a party related to the incident. Bringing the name to the police based on information from an inspector would give us a lot more avenues to use.

"It's just what you're thinking, my lady. At the time of the incident, Russia was in the middle of a power struggle. And, based on your report, the current prime minister may not be hanging on much longer. Is that enough?"

"Yes. That's exactly what I wanted to hear, Inspector Maefuji." Faking an innocent smile, I pulled a recording device from my pocket and pressed the stop button. I did it to show him that our conversation was recorded. The main recording device was a wiretap I'd set up, but that was done recording now too.

"Would you like me to prepare you an official document to back what I said? It's classified either way."

"If you like. It'll be the prime minister and his vice president who'll be seeing it."

Inspector Maefuji sighed. "Seems you're back at your elaborate schemes."

I decided to piece together what I now knew was the truth.

What Inspector Maefuji told me back at Kudanshita was no lie: he just concealed the truth beyond a certain point. The Russian mafia was hired by an oligarch—or one of Russia's emerging business conglomerates—which had colluded with powerful figures in the Russian government to make an enormous fortune. The oligarchs were the background of Russia's internal power struggle, and the previous prime minister was only just clinging onto power when he zeroed in on my wealth and Romanov blood. Incidentally, that prime minister was the minister of the gas industry in the Soviet Union and ran a conglomerate which owned a huge natural gas company.

It was my part in the Sakata combine project which had earned me his attention.

"What do you plan to do now?"

"Well, I was almost kidnapped. I think that now it's important that I settle the score, wouldn't you agree?" I replied lightly, passing the recording device to Tachibana.

"You'll want to keep your head down, or that terrifying American lady will scold you."

Of course, Inspector Maefuji knew that Angela Sullivan had been in to see me. It didn't particularly bother me.

"Don't worry about her; America and Japan are allies. Unless you don't trust me."

At any rate, based on the report from the company that was going to kidnap me, the probably of Russia collapsing and defaulting on its debt was, according to their hedge fund's calculations, three in a million. If I claimed otherwise, it would only be taken as the nonsense words of an elementary-schooler, or an attempt at misinformation to interfere with the auction of Keika Bank. It was already too late for anyone to cut their losses—trying to do so now would be suicide. If I warned them now and they believed me, that would be where it stopped, but I didn't want to join them, so I had no choice but to defer my judgement of the situation until later. I would continue on the path of ruin, just like I always had, and just like I always would, out of reach of any helping hands.

Keika Bank's auction was scheduled for September 20th. As a result of the Russian financial crisis, the world's economies were in an uproar. The Moonlight Fund was the only company to show up at the Ministry of Finance and take part in the auction that day. America was too busy trying to bail out its large-scale hedge fund.

"The nationalized Keika Bank has been sold off at auction to the Moonlight Fund for 800 billion yen. It was the only company to place a bid. Keika Bank is composed of its main part, Far Eastern Bank, a former second regional bank, and the metropolitan banks, Hokkaido Kaitaku Bank, the Long-Period Credit Bank of Japan, and Nihon Credit Bank, with which it merged it order to deal with those banks' bad debts. It took its name from the Keika Group, the owner of the Moonlight Fund, which is the bank's funding company.

The Bank also owns Keika Securities, a company resulting from a merger of the second-tier brokerage firm Sankai Securities, and a large brokerage firm, Ichiyama Securities, both of which were also struggling under bad debts. The Keika Group also owns Far Eastern Life Insurance, Keika Maritime Insurance, and the companies belonging to the former Teisei Department Stores Group, such as life- and damage-insurance brokers.

The government is planning to use Keika Bank, which has dealt with its bad debts, as a model example for its financial Big Bang, and will put forward a law on bank holding companies in the Diet this fall, with the aim of having it implemented..."

"On his trip to Russia, Prime Minister Fuchigami Keiichi signed the 'Moscow Declaration on Establishing a Creative Partnership

between Japan and the Russian Federation.' He has promised a great deal of economic support for the government and people of Russia, showing both at home and abroad that Japan is fully supportive of the Russian economy, which is currently trying to fight its way out of economic crisis.

The syndicated loan, which has the Keika Group's Moonlight Fund as the main lender, has drawn particular attention. It is a massive loan worth 10 billion dollars, loaned through the purchase of Russian debt with an option to repay the debt in crude oil, and sends a powerful message that Japan is supporting Russian's struggling economy..."

"Prime Minister Fuchigami's visit to Russia is causing repercussions within the international crude oil market, with some casting doubt on the country's ability to pay back the syndicated loan mainly funded by Moonlight Fund.

According to oil market experts, the loan is well-thought-out. The Russian government does not need to raise funds in order to pay it back, and it is likely planning to repay the entire loan in crude oil. Japan can then sell off the oil to Europe, with Europe being the only place with an oil pipeline to Russia. Japan can then use the money raised by selling the oil to Europe to buy its own oil from the Middle East and have it brought to Japan. To avoid any delays in either process, futures contracts have been put in place..."

"There are rumors within Russia that Japan is participating in the country's political instability. Russian's political world endured

instability during 1998, with its cabinet changing several times. After the former prime minister's resignation in the financial crisis, there are rumors that Japan was involved in his withdrawal in the race for his successor, despite his popularity as a powerful leader.

The former minister of the gas industry during the Soviet era has recently been involved in an oligarchy that owns a major gas company. It is thought that his company's failure to contribute to the massive, syndicated loan resulting from Prime Minister Fuchigami's visit is behind these rumors. Those involved in Russo-Japanese foreign affairs are officially denying the rumors.

Since the granting of the loan, Russia has announced the construction of an oil pipeline from its oil fields to Manchuria and Vladivostok in the far east.

The pipelines construction will be a joint project between Japan's Akamatsu Corporation, a general trading company, and Russian resource companies. As of yet, it is unclear whether other companies will be involved..."

The Fellowship of Constitutional Government, Secretary-General's Office.

After suffering a heavy defeat in the House of Councilors election, the party was undergoing a major reshuffle under Prime Minister Fuchigami. The installation of Secretary-General Hayashi was part of that reshuffle. In his new role, he was preparing to inherit his faction.

"Please, Sou-chan. I can't rely on anyone else."

The secretary-general bowed his head to his junior within the party, an odd man who had suffered a major loss in the recent party leader election: one Koizumi Souichirou. The former minister of health, labor, and welfare, he had opposed the reshuffle, leading him to stand for party leader. Not only did he lose, but one of his sworn friends, Secretary General Katou, had used the reshuffle to secure a higher spot within the party, which was nothing short of a betrayal.

The split opposition in the leadership election left Koizumi with no support but the core of his own faction, something that had humiliated him.

"You know, I wasn't even able to unite my own faction."

"I think you were just unlucky. I never saw Izumikawa-san ending up as vice president."

The party leader election, held after the damaging House of Councilors election, was supposed to be a battle between Minister of Finance Izumikawa, who had done great things dealing with Japan's bad debts, and the minister of foreign affairs, Fuchigami. However, once Izumikawa lost his support thanks to the Ministry of Finance scandal, Fuchigami and his desired reshuffle were quickly implemented.

With the successor to Ichizumikawa's faction remaining unclear, Secretary-General Katou had resigned to take responsibility for the House of Councilors election defeat. When Izumikawa-shi became vice president, he managed to join the leadership team without losing face.

"He may not have been doing so well now if his faction split, or if he stood up against the anti-Hashizume faction in the party leadership election. I don't want you to lose your role because of these flimsy underhanded dealings more befitting nobility than any political faction. I don't want your political career to end here."

Prime Minister Fuchigami had stripped the Ministry of Welfare of many of the members Koizumi had put there, as though in retaliation for being unable to do so during the party reshuffle. In order to protect those targeted members, Secretary-General Hayashi had prepared them posts within the faction he'd inherited. He had been a senior member of that Ministry as well.

Deputy Chairman—the second most powerful position in the faction, and yet a lone wolf that couldn't be betrayed. Secretary-General Hayashi's ulterior motive was obvious, and former Minister Koizumi must have known what it all meant. After taking some time to mull things over, Minister Koizumi decided to take on the position.

"Hayashi-san, could you tell me something? I'm sure there was someone behind the scenes who chose *not* to break up the Izumikawa faction. The prime minister must have told you about this string-puller, yes?"

Secretary-General Hayashi began to explain the situation, looking as though he couldn't believe it himself. "Yes. The prime minister phoned Izumikawa-san on results day, and there was someone there who recommended him as vice president. I wonder if you'll believe me when I say it was the Keika girl, that Little Queen. She and Izumikawa-san's youngest go to school together and she was there to show their support."

Everyone in Nagatachou knew who she was. In fact, Former Minister Koizumi knew even more than the secretary-general. As a politician involved with the Ministry of Finance himself, he knew about the Keika rules and how they bailed out the bad debts caused by the Ministry of Finance's dysfunction.

"It's scary to think of what that young lady might do in the future."

"I can easily agree."

It was this conversation that led to Koizumi Souichirou seeing Keikain Runa as a political opponent. It would be around two years later that they would confront each other directly.

GLOSSARY AND NOTES:

ELECTION ANALYSIS: One simple way to go about this is for predictions by newspapers and weekly publications to be collected and/or their favorites to win, to see a basic trend of how the election might go. If it would take too much time or money, data from different recent elections can be used. With House of Councilors elections, constituencies may overlap, so gubernatorial election data is often used instead. There is a relatively strong correlation between a loss in the House of Councilors and a loss in the gubernatorial elections.

LOSS OF SUPPORT: In the district described within the story, voters had two choices to vote for their preferred party. Nevertheless, it's a powerful move for a politician to be able to turn their back on one politician due to a scandal just to turn around and support one from the same party but another faction. If the rejected politician goes on to win anyway, they need to be prepared for retaliation. Factional disputes are a real mess.

PROPORTIONAL REPRESENTATION: A system whereby a party chooses its candidate in advance and registers them into a candidate list, where they will be elected in name order according to how many seats the party wins. Nowadays the candidate list is open, so the dietmen on that list will directly influence the election results.

AIRHO: A start-up low-cost airline in Hokkaido.

THE LOCAL BROADCAST STATION'S MASCOT: ON-chan. Mainly sponsored, of course, by the Keika Group—or rather, Runa.

THE PLANES: They are Boeing 737-700ERs.

CAPITAL REDUCTION: A good way to fill in for your accumulated deficit and avoid tax, but it has its disadvantages too: At this time, total capital reductions of 100% were the default (rendering all shares worthless), meaning the shareholders would be forced to take responsibility. A capital reduction like this is almost always accompanied by an issue of new shares.

VULTURE FUNDS: Originally funds that purchase up bad debts, but because several foreign investment funds came to Japan all at once, it's hard to distinguish them from corporate reconstruction funds and corporate buyout funds. There was a time when the average person would think a foreign investment fund equated to a vulture fund.

BUBUZUKE: A type of ochazuke, which is rice served with tea poured over it. In Kyoto, to offer a guest this means you want them out of your house as soon as possible. I don't know if it was originally true, but it's so well known at this point that it's actually fallen into use.

FINANCIAL BIG BANG: A generic term for the financial deregulation implemented from 1996 to 2001. Bans on bank holding companies were lifted, and they joined the world of brokers and insurance companies. Bank deposit guarantees were changed from covering the total amount to a set amount, etc.

IMPERIAL IWAZAKI BANK: Newly merged in 1996. The main bank for the former Keikain Zaibatsu, including for Keika Pharmaceuticals.

LARGE-SCALE HEDGE FUND BAILOUT: Its bankruptcy and bailout involved government guidance just like that given out by the Ministry of Finance. It received "advice" from several countries. The failure to learn from this disaster is what led to the situation with Lehman Brothers.

IZUMIKAWA TAICHIROU'S STRUGGLES: His campaign trail led him to a ton of rural places in Hokkaido.

VICE PRESIDENT AND DEPUTY PRIME MINISTER: Usually these positions mean nothing, but in Japanese organizational theory, if an influential dietman takes the position, it suddenly becomes a functional role.

MODERN
Villainess

IT'S NOT EASY BUILDING
A CORPORATE EMPIRE
BEFORE THE CRASH

AFTERWORD

THERE ONCE WAS AN IDOL who quit her prolific group to make ramen instead. That ramen became so popular, it sold like hot cakes.

What are you supposed to think about something like *that*?

Thank you so much for buying this book. My name is Tofuro Futsukaichi. I write on the website *Shousetsuka ni Narou* ("Let's Be Novelists") under the name *"Hokubu-Kyuushuu Zaijuu"* ("Resident of Northern Kyushu").

My opening sentences reflect my honest feelings about this book. Just to be on the safe side: this story is a work of fiction, and any resemblance to any real names or events, et cetera, is purely coincidental and not affiliated with real people or organizations in any way.

If you look up a story about a villainess in the real world who is the daughter of a zaibatsu, you'll find many examples, but you'll never find *how* those zaibatsu make their money. It's more a convenient word to show that your villainess is upper class and owns several companies, which isn't a problem in itself.

You get those stories on *Shousetsuka ni Narou* about internal politics, where the young protagonist spends their childhood using their prior knowledge or future knowledge all on building a fortune for themselves. I realized they could be doing that in a modern society setting, but then lost hope when I couldn't find any stories like that. That was when I carelessly swung open the door that would lead me to my fate.

"I'll write it myself then."

That's right. The young lady's story is a story I wrote for myself: a meal I both cooked and ate. I stuffed in as many of my interests as I could, made it content-rich just how I like it, but to avoid the story becoming dense, I tried to keep things fast-paced, short, and light. When I started writing, I set out to write the whole thing and leave the editing to the end.

I never expected it to be published and in your hands like this before I'd even written the story to its conclusion. When this novel made the "Hokkaido Takushoku Bank" trend on Twitter, I took it as a sign of the times.

As we move from the Heisei era to the Reiwa era, and yesterday turns into a whole era itself, nothing would make me happier as an author than to be able to look back on that era together with Keikain Runa.

I'd like to give my thanks in this final paragraph.

First to the website *Shousetsuka ni Narou*, the place where I told Keikain Runa's story. I really did become an author.

To the representative from Overlap, who contacted me to get the book published, and to KEI-san for your wonderful illustrations. I cannot thank you two enough.

Thank you, from the bottom of my heart, to everyone who helped this book to be published.

Finally, I would like to sincerely thank all the readers who bought this book. Thank you so much.

That's all from me. I'll pray that we can meet each other again in the next volume.